ALSO BY CHARLOTTE HUANG

For the Record

CHARLOTTE HUANG

GOING GEEK

DELACORTE PRESS

Text copyright © 2016 by Charlotte Huang
Jacket front photograph copyright © 2016 by Shutterstock
Jacket back photograph copyright © 2016 by Getty Images/Klaus Vedfelt

Delacorte Press is a registered trademark and the colophon is a trademark of Penguin Random House LLC.

randomhouseteens.com

Educators and librarians, for a variety of teaching tools, visit us at RHTeachersLibrarians.com

Library of Congress Cataloging-in-Publication Data
Names: Huang, Charlotte, author.
Title: Going Geek / Charlotte Huang.
Description: First edition. | New York : Delacorte Press, [2016]
Summary: "Skylar Hoffman's senior year at her preppy East Coast boarding school should have been perfect: amazing boyfriend, the coolest friends, the most desirable dorm. But it's far from it."— Provided by publisher.
Identifiers: LCCN 2015034406 | ISBN 978-0-553-53943-1 (hc) | ISBN 978-0-553-53945-5 (ebook)
Subjects: | CYAC: Social Issues—Peer Pressure. | Social Issues—Self-Esteem & Self-Reliance—Fiction. | Social Issues—New Experience —Fiction.
Classification: LCC PZ7.1.H74 Go 2016 | DDC [Fic]—dc23

The text of this book is set in 11-point Garamond.
Interior design by Trish Parcell

Printed in the United States of America
10 9 8 7 6 5 4 3 2 1
First Edition

For Jackson and Elliott
First!

CHAPTER ONE

Most people probably don't spend a perfect California beach day dreaming about going back to school, but that's exactly what I'm doing as I tilt my face toward the late-afternoon sun. I inhale salty ocean air and dig my toes into the sand, giving them a massage.

My bliss lasts for exactly thirty seconds before Doug, my boss at the exclusive Hayward Beach Club, busts me. "Excuse me, Skylar? The Pattersons need drink refills." He grimaces at my bare feet before disappearing into the kitchen. I slip back into my wedge flip-flops (cute, but a poor choice for serving food in the sand all day) and walk back to the wait station.

"I got it," my coworker Elijah mutters. He grabs a pitcher of soda and heads to the Pattersons' chaises.

"Is that diet?" One of the very blond Patterson girls (Stacy? Macy?) frowns at Elijah. He peers into the pitcher like he might be able to tell by looking hard enough. Though she's probably all of twelve years old, the girl dismisses him with a haughty wave. "Just get a fresh one."

When he returns, humiliation rises off him like steam. I take the pitcher out of his hand and walk back to the Pattersons with it. "Diet?" I ask.

The girl offers a curt nod, which I take as my permission to pour. Elijah watches me with a smirk.

I sashay back behind the counter. "See, E? You just have to sell it."

A cooling breeze blows in off the ocean, causing the ruffled edges of the oversized red umbrellas to flutter.

Elijah grins. "Yeah? How do you know so much about rich people?"

I shrug. "Just observant, I guess. Anyway, Miss Patterson will thank me someday. Too many chemicals in diet."

"Don't let Doug catch you doing that," he says, laughing. But I know Doug wouldn't say a thing to me, for the same reason he hired me when I had absolutely no experience waiting tables: until last summer I was a member here.

I wave a cheery goodbye to the valet attendants in the parking lot and peel out onto the PCH before they can catch me. Elijah grips his door handle. "Rafael didn't even see us," he says, referring to the lot manager.

"I told you. I've been sneaking in every day." It helps that my mom's white Mercedes blends in with the member cars. And maybe Rafael looks the other way.

Since my mom barely goes to her office anymore, I've been able to use her car all summer. This is a serious perk, because it makes my excruciating daily commute much cushier. She had to cancel satellite radio a few months ago, but I just connect my phone, crank my favorite playlist, and hardly notice the bumper-to-bumper traffic.

Elijah hops out at the public lot where most of the employees park. "Thanks for saving me the trek!" he yells as I maneuver back onto the freeway.

As always, I'm desperate for a shower by the time I get home. I rush in, not bothering to raise the knocked-over FOR SALE sign that's been posted on our lawn since the beginning of summer. Nobody came to the open house last weekend, and my parents probably don't need the constant reminder.

My mom sits on the couch in our great room reading scripts, like she does every night. Her consistency only adds to the air of futility around here. "Where's Dad?" I ask.

"In his office," she says. In other words, the spare bedroom where he conducts his graphic design business.

"Jordana's coming over to help me pack, so I can't eat too late."

"Glad you finally made plans with her," my mom says.

I swing through the kitchen to grab an apple from a wooden bowl on the counter. "Kind of hard to have a social life when I've been taking any shift Doug will give me."

It's mean, but I know that'll keep her off my back. She stares at me, then picks up another script.

After my shower I return to the kitchen to help get dinner together, which means I unwrap the store-bought rotisserie chicken while my mom arranges premade grilled veggies on a ceramic platter. No one in the house actually cooks, so this is our routine.

"We're a house full of working stiffs, yet we can't afford delivery," my dad says.

"Ha ha," I say. My mom just glares at him. He ducks his head and takes his plate to the banquette, narrowly avoiding yet another fight. It actually makes me miss the nauseating googly eyes they used to make at each other.

I don't care about having to work. Tuition at Winthrop Academy, my boarding school outside Boston, isn't cheap, and I'd do anything short of selling my organs on the black market to make sure I get to go back. As far as I'm concerned, senior year can't start soon enough.

"I talked to Ama today," my mom says. "She said she'd try to go up for Parents' Weekend."

I stifle a groan. As much as I adore my grandmother, I imagine her visit would entail the following: yelling at my teachers about why my grades aren't better, repeatedly reminding me how much this "fancy private school" costs my parents, insisting I take her to the only Chinese restaurant in Winthrop, then pronouncing the food inedible. At least, that's what happened the last time she visited. "Don't make Ama come. She's too old to do all that walking. Besides, Parents' Weekend is really for first-years."

My parents glance at each other. My dad clears his throat. "We just feel—"

"I know. You feel bad you can't afford to fly out. But seriously, it's okay. It's my last year, I know the drill."

The list of things my parents feel guilty about is never-ending. They're going to give themselves ulcers. It covers everything from our not visiting enough colleges over the summer to their not being able to give me money for new school clothes—even though I told them it hardly matters, with my talent for scouting sample sales. They mean well, but making up things to worry about has added significantly to their stress level.

I'm not done eating when the doorbell rings, so my mother answers it while I fix an extra plate. I love Jordana, and I'm excited to see her, but even though she's my oldest friend, the sad fact is we have less in common every year. Hanging out with her just makes me more homesick for Winthrop.

"JoJo! So glad you're joining us for dinner." My mom thinks Jordana's still nine.

"Thanks, but I just ate." Nonetheless, Jordana sits and nibbles at some food. She knows that while my mom may not be big on cooking, she's big on feeding people. "So. What's the latest?"

We don't even have to ask what she's referring to.

"No news," my mom says. Jordana's face legitimately falls; she's not even trying to brownnose. They start talking about the trials and tribulations of Hollywood, and I automatically tune out.

My mother produced *Over It*, which is the highest-grossing teen movie of the last decade. Everyone my age is obsessed with it. When the sequel kept falling through because the studio "didn't get" the screenwriter and director's vision, my mom left to form her own company in order to finish the job. That was four years ago. Still no sequel. That doesn't stop her from being consumed by it, though, and predictably, my friends are an attentive audience.

She looks for other projects, but her heart is never in them the way it is with *Over It*. So right now we're living off *Over It* residuals, which get smaller every day, and my dad's graphic design work, which was never that busy to begin with. And now my Hayward Club paycheck, I guess. Since it's a private club, I don't even get tips, which is a total bummer.

Jordana and I go upstairs, and she sprawls out on my bed. We go months without seeing each other, but since she practically grew up in this house, formalities don't exist. "I didn't think I'd get to see you before you left," she says, taking a long look around. I'm sure everything's familiar; my bedroom's a shrine to my eighth-grade self. Pictures of us with our middle school friends are still pinned to the bulletin board, my bookshelves are stuffed with novels that are way below my current reading level, and my dresser is lined with shiny gold soccer trophies. I've tried to throw the trophies away many times. They're all feel-goods—tokens for participation, not evidence of any ability or even a winning team—but my dad always rescues them from the trash anyway.

I toss a pile of clean laundry onto the bed, and we both start folding. This is our ritual. The only difference is that we don't sob through it like we did the first few times I left.

"Everyone asked about you all summer," Jordana says.

I raise my eyebrows. Sadly, I don't know many of Jordana's friends anymore. I still remember names, but I stopped trying to keep in touch with everyone after winter break my first year.

Telling stories about people they didn't know got old on both sides.

"Don't worry. I didn't say anything," Jordana says. "Although, can I ask, why's waitressing such a big secret?"

"It's not. I just don't want to deal with the onslaught of questions about the movie that would definitely follow." This is what complicates the issue. Being open about waitressing also means addressing my mom's ongoing failure, which is not something either of us is prepared to do. I move the stack of folded T-shirts onto the floor.

Jordana picks up a framed photo of me with my friends from my dorm. "Wow, look at Whitney. She's changed so much since freshman year."

We call it "first year," but I don't correct her. Hearing Jordana talk about my best friend at school is weird, since they've never met, but Jordana has been seeing pictures of her on Instagram forever.

I take the photo out of her hand, barely able to remember what Whit looked like back then. She was always beautiful and had the same take-charge swagger, tastefully packaged in prim Bergdorf Goodman outfits. She befriended me right away and later admitted it was because my LA style set me apart at Winthrop. Then, when everyone found out that Lisa Chen, producer of *Over It,* was my mother, well, that sealed the deal. We've been inseparable ever since.

"Tell me about your summer," I say. "Did you love teaching?" Jordana interned at our former preschool because she's thinking about studying child psychology in college.

"Not exactly. Nora's senile," she says, referring to the principal.

"Well, then, did you go out a lot, at least?"

She props herself up against my pillows. "Every night. But I've been hanging out with the same people for twelve years. I wouldn't be opposed to some kind of massive shake-up."

I laugh. "Any kind in particular?"

"Hmm. Maybe some gorgeous stranger could transfer in. Or aliens could abduct me and turbo-boost my brain so that I skip senior year and go straight to college."

"Just one more year," I say.

"Easy for you to say." She throws a balled-up pair of socks at my head. "You love school. And you have Leo. Tell me there's *something* wrong with that boy."

I think about it. "Not a thing," I admit. Jordana looks even more deflated than before. "But just like your 'meh' year, my great year will have an end. Nothing lasts forever."

"Not even you and Leo?" she asks with a grin.

"Well, maybe me and Leo."

On cue, my phone chimes, and I pick it up, excited to read some sappy-but-adorable text from my boyfriend. Instead, it's an email from the Winthrop Housing Administration.

I tap on it immediately. "If they think they're giving me a roommate, they're insane." Getting a single your senior year is practically a god-given right.

Dear Miss Hoffman:

Due to an error in the housing office, some students have been reassigned to different dormitories. We regret the inconvenience this may cause. Your faculty advisor will have your new placement when you arrive on campus. Please come prepared to remove your belongings from your previous dormitory and transfer them to your new home.

Sincerely,

Winthrop Housing Administration

I click my phone off and clutch it to my chest, staring into space. Around the edges of the phone, my fingertips grip and release my T-shirt.

Jordana sits up straight. "Will you please blink? Are you having a heart attack?"

"Pretty much," I whisper.

"But, I mean, how big is the campus?" she asks after I tell her. "It's not like you'll be miles away."

"I could be a mile away, I could be next door. But that's not the point. It's my *home*. I've lived in Lincoln since day one. All my friends are there. We do everything together—study, watch TV, share beauty products. I barely know any girls from other dorms."

"Really?" Jordana wrinkles her nose. "How's that possible?"

I glare at her. "Because. Anyone worth knowing lives in Lincoln!"

She holds up her hands in surrender. "Okay, but can't you still do those things together?"

I sigh. "It's not the same. There's something special about living next door to your best friends or down the hall from them. Someone's door is always open. We don't have to go through the chore of scheduling and picking a meeting place."

"Learn to make plans like the rest of the world." Her tone is flat, but I hear the accusation there. "Anyway, maybe the worst is that you'll graduate with two sets of friends."

Jordana has no idea what she's talking about, and I'm about to tell her as much when my mom pokes her head in. "How's the packing going? It feels like you never unpacked, so you must be almost done."

"Mom, good, you're here. I need you to leave a strongly worded voice mail." I get my game face on.

Her brow furrows. "Really? And where shall I leave this strongly worded voice mail?"

"At the school housing office. They're trying to tell me that I'm not in Lincoln this year!" Just saying it aloud makes me want to burst into tears.

My mom's expression turns from quizzical to anxious. "Well, honey, I'm sure they wouldn't have done it unless there was a very good reason."

"No. Uh-uh. I don't need reasonable, keeper-of-the-peace Mom. I need badass producer Mom. Get-shit-done Mom."

"Language." She glances meaningfully toward Jordana, who's busy plucking at my bedspread, pretending she's not here. "I'm sure it has to do with the change in circumstances."

What she's trying not to say in front of Jordana is that maybe Winthrop Housing shafted me because I'm now on financial aid. She feels like they're doing us a favor and is therefore hesitant to rock the boat.

"I don't care," I say. "I'm not going to be treated like some back-of-the-bus, second-class citizen no matter what the circumstances are. Honestly, I can't even believe you'd suggest that. You know, now that I think about it, they wouldn't do this to a senior. I'm sure they meant to shuffle around some first-years or sophomores."

My mom's eyes widen. "I'm not saying it's right, but it might be the reason. I don't know if it'll do any good, but I'll leave a message in the morning."

"No, can you do it now? I want it to be the first thing they hear when they get to work in the morning."

"Fine, Skylar." She gives me that look she gets when she's mad but too worn out to fight me.

When the door closes, Jordana flops over. "Are you always so hard on her?"

"What? It'll be good for her to get in there and ruffle some feathers."

But when I get downstairs the next morning, my mom is on the phone with housing, and I can tell by the tone of her "mmm-hmm's" that the only feathers getting ruffled are hers. Guess I'll have to put this fire out on my own when I get to school.

CHAPTER TWO

A few days later my airport shuttle van turns onto the main road that runs through Winthrop, which is creatively named Main Street. When Winthrop Academy comes into view, my sigh of relief is so loud that my fellow passengers turn and the driver glances at me in the mirror. Oh, how I miss the days of car services and taxis.

Winthrop looks like an Ivy League college, all redbrick buildings, stretches of pristine green lawn, and huge, centuries-old trees. In the tradition of East Coast prep schools, it's elegant, staid, and just the teensiest bit pompous. I love it so much.

My plan is to go straight to my advisor's office. If anyone can bust heads in housing, it's Ms. Randall. I get out of the van, and the driver helps me haul my suitcases onto the sidewalk. I scurry away, putting as much distance between the van and me as possible.

As he pulls away I truck down the central path through the academic quad wearing a super cute straw fedora and black leather shorts with a slouchy tee, towing two designer suitcases behind me. Scores of people pass—each one more preppy and drab than the last. Sorry, but I could never date a guy who felt the need to wear anything with whales on it.

They all step off the path to avoid getting run over by me. I always feel very conspicuous on this campus, but it's important to have a brand, and mine is definitely LA Fabulous. It's kind of hilarious.

A warm, calloused hand closes over mine and takes one of the suitcase handles from me. Leo. I know it's him even before I turn to smile up into his handsome face. "Hey." He gives me a quick peck on the lips. It takes all of my self-restraint not to launch myself at him. My hat gets knocked to the ground when I hug him, but I don't care. I feel him smile against my hair as I refuse to let him go. We haven't seen each other in nearly three months, but boarding school can feel like a fishbowl, so we're forced to be chaste in public. That's Leo's idea, not mine. I don't care, but Leo doesn't like to make people uncomfortable. It's not like we have a choice; we're constantly surrounded by people who know us—after school, weekends, breakfast, doesn't matter. So if they have to deal with a little PDA once in a while, so be it.

Leo has some distance because he's a day student. He might spend most of every day and night on campus—even a good part of the weekend—but at the end of every night, he gets to brush his teeth without an audience.

"Did you come just to see me? Classes don't start for two more days." I scoop my fedora off the ground and loop my arm around his as we resume walking. Leo's now wheeling both suitcases like the sweetheart that he is.

He chuckles. "Yes. I wanted to see you, but I'm also a Winthrop Key, remember?" he asks, referring to the new-student orientation committee.

"Of course. You're such a do-gooder." I grin.

Leo kisses my cheek. "You should try it sometime." He ducks out of my reach, laughing as I swat at him. "So you ready for Ms. Randall?"

"Ready as I'll ever be."

Poor Leo endured about a dozen phone calls during which I schemed ways to get reassigned to Lincoln. He was definitely concerned, but unfortunately, since he has obviously never dealt with housing, he didn't have much to say, other than that I should talk to Ms. Randall. I've been trying to minimize my panic, because I don't want to stress him out when he's so busy with school and soccer.

We approach a wide building with steps that span the front and four sets of glass-paned double doors. I reach for my suitcases. "Let me bring these in. Maybe she'll take pity on me if I seem really pathetic."

He looks both doubtful and worried. "I don't see her going for that. Better to go in strong."

"Okay, yeah, you're right." I try to discreetly wipe my hands on my shirt. Leo gives me a quick hug and turns back down the central path that cuts through campus. I watch him go.

His easy, athletic gait, strong calf muscles, and broad shoulders sweeten the view.

With a groan, I pull my luggage into Parsons Hall, Winthrop's administrative building. I take the elevator up but leave my things in the hallway before knocking on an old wooden door with a nameplate that reads KIM RANDALL, then HEAD OF COLLEGE COUNSELING underneath. My faculty advisor is also my college counselor. Double whammy.

"Yes." It's a deceptively soft voice that somehow manages to penetrate through the closed door.

I push it open. "Hi, Ms. Randall."

She's really not a scary-looking woman. She has rich brown skin, shrewd eyes, and light, springy curls, cut in a way that gives her head an almost heart shape. Despite her pleasant voice and appearance, nobody who's met her more than once would underestimate her ability and fondness for cutting people to the quick. "Ms. Hoffman. Welcome back. Was your summer productive?"

"Yeah. I read scripts for my mom while working on my tan by the pool. It wasn't a terrible way to spend the summer." This is what I've been telling everyone. Waitressing would destroy my cred with this crowd.

Ms. Randall eyes me, unimpressed. "I see. Do we have an appointment so early in the year?" She slides her rolling chair back slightly from her desk and peers at me over the top of her reading glasses.

"Kinda sorta," I begin.

"Try to be more precise, please."

I take a breath and start over. "I received an email about housing—"

"Ah, yes. Thank goodness. I am not ready to discuss colleges with *you* yet."

Ouch. But I smile, like I think she's joking, even though I'm already dreading our first college counseling meeting. I didn't do half the things she wanted me to do over the summer. Oh well. First things first.

While she scrolls through her inbox, I resist fidgeting. She scared the habit out of me when I was a first-year.

"Yes, due to a technical error, too many students were placed in Lincoln. The problem was discovered only last week, and, as a result, Housing had to move people without any input. You've been reassigned to Abbot House, where you'll share a room with Opal Kingston."

The floor drops out from under me. "What?" My voice comes out shaky. There are twenty girls' dorms at Winthrop, and I get stuck with Abbot House?

Ms. Randall gives me a cool stare. She's waiting for me to collect myself, to say something more eloquent, but that's not likely to happen. "Your keys should be downstairs in your mailbox. Is there anything else I can help you with?"

"Yes. Help me find a way to stay in Lincoln. That's where my life is. After three years of being at the center of everything, Abbot would be way too removed, not to mention bleak and depressing." I'm aware that I'm babbling, but nobody with a brain would've made this recommendation.

She's still looking at me, completely dispassionate. "Maybe a change of scenery will do you good. I'm not entirely sure three years of being 'at the center of everything' has brought out the best in you."

I have no idea what she's talking about. Since she's not exactly approachable, it's not like I've been running to her office every five seconds. Where does she get off acting like she knows me? "Is there anyone else I can talk to about this?"

"I'm afraid not."

I press my lips together, deciding whether I should say what I'm about to say. "Is this about money?"

Ms. Randall snorts. It's such a condescending sound that my cheeks flush with both anger and embarrassment. "Winthrop Academy has an extremely healthy endowment. One reason I took this job is because that allows us to offer meaningful financial aid. Providing assistance for one more student isn't going to break this place."

My glance darts to the door, and I'm relieved to see that it's closed tightly. "I can't believe they'd do this to a senior. Why wouldn't they move a first-year instead?"

"If a first-year was moved to accommodate you, you'd have to room with another first-year. That wouldn't work, since first-years and seniors have different restrictions. Besides, it wouldn't be fair to either of you."

I'd almost be willing to suck it up if it meant staying in Lincoln. "It's my home. I can't believe they can just uproot me like this."

"You're still here. Abbot is a fifteen-minute walk from Lincoln. You're going to be fine." She lets that lie sink in.

"How many other seniors got moved?"

"I'm not at liberty to give out other students' information. Now, Ms. Hoffman, I like to end meetings with my seniors on a single word. You should mull this over until the next time we meet. Your word is: *embrace*."

Dismissed, I trudge to the door and let myself out.

Embrace, my ass.

Down in the basement I go to my mailbox, number 267, which is perfectly situated at chest level, in the center of a wall full of silver-doored mailboxes. I fish the keys out, along with my class schedule, invitations to a bunch of dumb socials, and about a thousand flyers in every color of the rainbow, encouraging me to join clubs like Robotics or Ballroom Dance. I mean, seriously. Those go straight into the recycling.

Twenty minutes later, after numerous consultations of my campus map, I finally locate Abbot House. It's such a long, meandering way from the main campus, past the school cemetery, not near any other dorm, and it feels like it's in the middle of the woods. I'm going to have to start carrying bear spray. By the time I get there, I'm actually fighting back tears.

And then there's the way it looks. It's not a grand brick structure like most of the buildings; it's an off-white wooden house—small, rickety, and utterly sad. I have literally never laid eyes on the place even one time in the years I've been at Winthrop. They should have razed it decades ago.

Inside, I go up carpeted stairs to find my room. Of course, there are two beds, two desks, and a window, which serves as a natural divider. Luckily, the room is empty, so I sit down on one of the beds and cry my heart out.

There's a faint knock on the door. I quickly wipe my face with my hands and stand up. A woman with frizzy hair, ashen skin, and a pilly cardigan enters. "Hi there," she practically whispers. "Welcome. I'm Dr. Murdoch, your house counselor. Classics department." Saying those few words seems to have taxed her—she looks like she's about to fall over from exertion.

"Skylar Hoffman. Disgruntled, displaced senior." My biting remark has absolutely no effect on her.

"Wonderful. I think some of the others are already out and about. We're a small group here, only seven girls and me, but we're a family. I'm usually available if you need anything." Great. One of the other selling points about Lincoln was the Blums, house counselors who were so consumed with raising their actual family that they hardly bothered with us. They looked the other way more than once when Leo was over and my door was less ajar than it should have been.

"I still have to get my things from Lincoln," I say. Dr. Murdoch blinks at me, her eyes big and owl-like behind her thick lenses. She's like a cat lady without the cats.

I slip past her, run downstairs, and let the screen door slam behind me, then hike through the forest and back into civilization. The urge to cry has left me, thank god. I wouldn't want anyone to see me in this state of disarray. I keep it together until I walk through the doors of Lincoln.

Processing that this is no longer where I live seems impossible. I grasp at the reality like a little kid trying to catch a balloon that's accidentally slipped off her wrist and is already flying away. Everything about this building feels comfortable and right—more like home than the house I grew up in. Even the smell (bleach with a hint of sawdust) overwhelms me with nostalgia.

Anything important that's ever happened to me has taken place in this dorm. I met my best friend here. My friends cheered me on and took turns bringing me coffee when I left a term paper until the night before it was due. I had my first kiss and my first breakup here.

Before things can take a turn for the truly maudlin, I hear a squeal and spin around just as Whit body-slams me and wraps herself around me. I get a mouthful of her perennially sun-streaked blond hair and a whiff of bergamot and rose, her signature scent. "Tell me the whole thing was just a hideous dream!"

I spit some hair out and rest my chin on her shoulder. "No. You're looking at the newest addition to Abbot House."

Whit's arms fall to her sides, and she pulls away to look at me, her nose wrinkled. "Abbot? You couldn't even get Baldwin?" She's referring to the dorm across the quad from Lincoln. It's a very distant runner-up. My distress swells again. "Never mind," she says. "If you're going to live someplace different, it might as well be really different, right?"

I nod, unsure about her logic. Also, her seemingly easy acceptance of my predicament unnerves me.

"I'll sleep over sometimes so you won't be lonely," she says.

"I have a roommate."

She inhales, sharp and surprised. "This just keeps getting worse. Who is it?"

"Opal Kingston."

"Who's that?"

"I have no idea." Whitney and I privately refer to everyone not living in the main quad as "extras." Even most quad people are only vague acquaintances. People know us. Not the other way around.

"Why didn't you have your mom call?" she asks.

"I did." Saying much more would be hard without publicizing the fact that my mom might not have as much influence as she once had. "Who else had to move?"

"I'm not sure. You still have to eat with us." Whitney grabs my hand and says this with an air of generosity, even though it hadn't occurred to me that I'd be eating anywhere else. "And come to Thursday-night common room hangs."

My eyes well up again. I'm turning into a damn faucet. "It won't be the same. I won't be just padding down the hall in my bare feet and pjs. I'll have to *sign in*."

Whitney looks aghast and gathers me into her arms. "I hadn't thought about it like that." She doesn't let go of me. "This could be our last year together. It's not supposed to be this way."

"It definitely isn't," I say as I hug her back, holding on to hope that this housing thing is just a blip before everything goes back to normal.

CHAPTER THREE

Two hours later, with Leo's help, I have everything moved into Abbot. He texted me right after Whitney left, saving me from another fit of despair.

I'm done. Do you need help?

I smiled as I tapped.

How strong are you exactly?

My roommate still hasn't appeared, so we're getting cozy on my new bed. I'm distracted by the hum of the air-conditioning. There are no voices in the hall, no signs of human life coming from outside the window. Even the bed creaks differently. The door is shut (at least I still get one perk of being a senior), but I can't relax. "This is weird," I whisper.

"Not for me it isn't." Leo nuzzles my neck and pulls me closer.

I laugh. "I mean, she could walk through that door at any moment, and I'd have no idea who she is."

Leo props himself up on his elbow and peers into my face. "You don't know who Opal is?"

"No. Should I?"

He shrugs. "I guess not. We had English 200 together. She's kind of the opposite of you. She wears cotton and doesn't like makeup."

"Are you saying I'm high maintenance?"

"How many boxes did I just carry over from Lincoln?" Leo straightens and bends his arm, pretending to be sore. I put my hand on his chest and shove. "Oh, come on. You know I wouldn't change a thing about you," he says, laughing.

Leo's phone rings. "My mom." He answers. "Hi. I'm helping Skylar move into her new dorm. . . . Yes, I'll invite her. . . . Classes don't start tomorrow, so curfew isn't until eleven-thirty. . . . Okay, don't wait up." He rolls his eyes as he hangs up. "You're invited for dinner next weekend."

"I'm in!" I snuggle back onto his chest. "It's so cute that she misses you."

He sighs. "I was gone all summer. You'd think she'd be used to it." Leo taught soccer at a camp for underprivileged kids in Maine. I didn't even know they had underprivileged kids in Maine. His entire Instagram feed was pictures of him with his players—on the field, splashing around in the freezing ocean, going for ice cream . . . Like I said, he's pretty much perfect.

"She just doesn't want your bad LA girlfriend taking advantage of you." I lift my head and bite his earlobe.

"Yeah, let's stop talking about my mom now."

We're in full-on make-out mode when I hear someone clearing her throat. Loudly. Leo sits up so fast he pushes me off the bed. We both leap to our feet. "Hi! How are you? You must be Opal." I hold out my hand. She shakes it even though she has this spacey, unfocused smile.

"I am indeed." She shifts her gaze to my boyfriend. "Leo Diaz. Welcome to my dorm room."

"Technically he's in my dorm room, but whatever. Semantics." I don't know why I'm bothering with the territorial act. Leo's description of her was generous. A little mascara would go a long way on this chick—her eyelashes are practically transparent, but stand out in the worst possible way against her naturally ruddy skin. Her hair is in two French braids like she's in fourth grade, and she's wearing some unattractive, shapeless caftan in an Indian print with matching pajama pants.

To her credit, Opal smiles and doesn't take the bait. An older couple steps into the room. They're dressed just like Opal. They must belong to a cult. "This is my mom and dad." She turns to them. "This is Leo. He's the star goalie on the varsity soccer team. And my new roommate, Skylar."

"Pleasure to meet you," Mrs. Kingston says.

"I've read a bit about your yoga school," Leo says. "I'd love to check it out one day."

"You do yoga?" Opal asks, sounding way too excited.

Leo shakes his head. "No. But I keep thinking it would be good to keep me from getting injured. Your school's pretty famous, right?"

The Kingstons collectively beam. "We'd love to have you

visit. Next time you're in New York, look us up," Mr. Kingston says. He seems to be extending this invite to both of us, but I know he really means Leo. My boyfriend could charm a doorknob.

"We're going out to dinner. Feel free to, um, carry on," Opal says, a beatific smile on her face. Now it's my turn to beam while Leo goes red with embarrassment.

Once they're gone, Leo turns to me. "See? She's not horrible."

"I'm not making any snap judgments," I say. "Now, where were we?" I pull him back down onto my bed.

Some time later, we come up for air and decide we should probably feed ourselves. We hold hands until we get to the main campus. "When does preseason practice start?" I ask.

"Team's already been here a week. Tomorrow I have more Winthrop Keys stuff to do—meet with my group, give the 'unofficial' tour, and then we have team wars. So I'll be around all day. What do you have going on?"

"Catch up with Whit, maybe go to the Southern California social, buy my books." Leo nods, and there's absolutely no skepticism on his face, but I can't help noting the differences between our two schedules. Leo's applying early to Harvard, and in my unbiased opinion they'd be crazy not to grab him. The thing is, he's not some resume-building drone; he genuinely loves everything he does. I admire him so much, even as I'm just the tiniest bit envious of him.

We walk into the Canteen, a two-story Neoclassical-style building (as they tell you on the tour) consisting of four dining rooms, each with its own distinct feel and named for its geographical location within the building. They all look the same and have the same food; it's more about who hangs out in each of them. Lower Left is arty, and Lower Right is brainy. Not that I've ever eaten in either one of those. Leo and his friends hang out in the jock dining room, Upper Right. My crowd hangs out there too sometimes, because a lot them are also athletes. We're most likely to be in Upper Left, where people who work on the Social Calendar can be found.

The Social Calendar is like Yearbook, Prom Committee, and Cheerleading all rolled up into one and injected with steroids. We have Yearbook and Prom Committee (not Cheerleading), but the Calendar rules the school. This year, at long last, Whitney's president.

"You want to sit with your fraternity brothers?" Leo asks. That's my affectionate nickname for the soccer team guys. I catch a glimpse of Whit and some of my other Lincoln friends heading into Upper Left. I'm about to tell Leo that I'll meet up with him later, but Whit makes a shooing motion, indicating that I should enjoy my time with Leo. So I grab a tray and resign myself to an evening of soccer trash-talking and boy buffoonery.

When we show up at the table, the guys give me a once-over. Suddenly my leather shorts seem really small. But I brush it off and sit down.

"Hey, Skylar. Ready to see our boy break the record for killer saves this fall?"

"Hey, Skylar. When's Whitney going to give in and go out with me?"

"Hey, Skylar. Diaz had such a good summer he said he wants five kids. Hope you're fertile."

I nod and smile along through all of it. Over the last year I've learned that the only way past it is through it. They get bored eventually. And the truth is, they love and respect Leo so much that they'd never say anything seriously out of line.

"Guys, take it easy. We have a whole season for you to torture my girlfriend." Leo smiles at me.

"Whatever. You're not the only one who's excited to see her." Remy, one of the midfielders, leans down for a hug on his way to the dessert table.

"So did you discover the next script that will define our generation?" Wyatt, a defender, asks.

Okay, so I haven't even told my friends the real story. Not Leo, not even Whit.

"Not quite," I manage to say. "There's a lot of really bad material floating around out there."

"You have the coolest life," Sid says. He's starting center forward and has the attitude to match. This might be the warmest thing he's ever said to me, and I guess it's true. I did have the coolest life.

"What's the best thing you read?" Remy asks, returning with a bowl of ice cream.

Everyone's paying attention. For some reason, even people outside LA are really fascinated by Hollywood. I scramble for a way off this topic. "I read a super cute rom-com," I say. Groans all around. Bingo.

"What the hell is a rom-com?" Sid asks.

"Romantic comedy." I wrinkle my nose at him, implying that any idiot would know that. "It just needs a scorchingly hot leading man attached to it, one who's dripping with sex appeal but also intelligent."

"Stop. Not interested," Sid says.

"Actually, you'd be perfect, Remy," I say, turning to him. "With those quads?" Leo and the rest of the table snicker as Remy mumbles into his ice cream. "What's going on with you and Zoe?" He started dating a cute sophomore from Baldwin at the end of last year.

"She dumped me. Over the phone, right before we came back."

"She strung you along all summer?" My spoon drops to the table with a clank. "You want me to order a social hit on her?"

"You're the best, Skylar, but no. She's a good girl, it's just not meant to be. Maybe you can hook me up with one of your new dorm mates."

I stare at him, eyebrows raised. "I take it you don't know where I'm living now."

Remy shrugs. "Yeah. Abbot. Whatever, I'm equal opportunity."

"What you are is undiscerning," Sid says. Everyone laughs.

"You should wait until the season's over. Not many girls are as cool as Skylar." Wyatt's referring to the team's hectic schedule, which leaves me flying solo for most of the fall.

The conversation dissolves into soccer talk, so I eat quickly, realizing that I still have a lot of unpacking left. Leo follows me as I take my tray back to the kitchen. "Can we keep hanging out after dinner?" he asks.

"Did you miss me or something?" I grin over my shoulder.

"I just want to spend as much time with you as possible before the craziness starts," he says. I turn to face him, and he brushes a strand of my long black hair behind my shoulder. The way he's looking at me makes my cheeks heat up.

"I'm pretty sure Opal will be back from dinner soon."

"It's not about that. What Wyatt said is true. You are very understanding about the team and my schedule, and I appreciate that. I hope you know that I want to be with you all the time." He takes my tray and places the dirty dishes into a bin along with his.

With an argument like that, how could I refuse? "Do your talents extend to unpacking?"

Leo rests his chin on the top of my head. "I mean, I don't want to brag . . ."

So we walk back to Abbot, linking hands once again as soon as the path turns off the main campus and the foot traffic disappears.

Opal returns to the room soon after we get there, but she seems more than happy to have Leo here as a buffer. As they gab I unpack and survey the contents of my life. Some of the stuff I saved from last year no longer seems worth keeping, so I go out to find a garbage bag.

The kitchenette is on the ground floor and is really nothing more than a sink, fridge, and microwave. I walk in to find a small girl with tawny skin, dark, wavy, shoulder-length hair, and a smile that's way too bright for the late-ish hour. She pulls a bag of popcorn out of the microwave and empties the contents into a bowl. The smell of fake butter overtakes the small space.

"Hey. I'm Raksmey," she says. "Junior." She's practically trembling, she's so wired. Could be sodium overload.

"Skylar," I say, extending my hand. I know it's weird that we shake hands like we're about to enter into a business agreement, but it's a thing here. Supposed to build strong character.

"I know who you are."

"Oh. Are you watching a movie?" I stick my head under the sink and find a roll of garbage bags.

"Nah. I just forgot to go to dinner. So you got booted by the cool kids?"

My head smacks the underside of the counter as I back out from under the sink. "It wasn't just me. There was a reshuffling because of a computer mix-up in housing."

Raksmey laughs. "They always blame the computers. But seriously. It's not like computers were invented yesterday. What really happened? Did you have a falling-out with your queen bee?"

"Sorry to say there was no drama, only administrative ineptitude and terrible luck."

"Okay." Raksmey throws a handful of popcorn in her mouth. She leaves me standing in a cloud of popcorn-scented steam, unsettled, with a fistful of garbage bags.

I go back to my room to find Leo dozing on my bed. Opal is in her pjs (or maybe not, I can't tell) and reading on the floor. "Classes haven't started yet," I say.

"This is the *Yoga Sutras,*" she says.

"Is that a sex thing?" I glance at Leo. Still dozing.

Opal smiles. "No. It's a yoga thing."

I start tossing things, keeping an eye on the clock so Leo can be out by curfew. "It's ironic that LA's, like, land of a thousand yoga schools, yet I've never taken a class."

"But those classes with plinky music, incense in the room, and an instructor who took a five-week training course? That's not real yoga." She doesn't even bother to look up from her book as she belittles the billion-dollar industry that she just described. But since I really don't care about yoga, I let it slide.

Leo rolls onto his side, and I decide it's time to put him out of his misery. I place my hand on his hip and give him a shake. "Hey, why don't you go home? You have a big day tomorrow."

He groans and stretches before opening his eyes just a sliver. "Why'd you let me sleep? This was supposed to be quality time."

"It was. I love watching you sleep."

"You look very peaceful," Opal chimes in from across the room. I ignore her.

"Come on. I'll walk you out."

With another groan Leo lets me pull him to his feet. We stop by the table in the entryway so he can sign out. Dr. Murdoch doesn't appear to be nearby, but the door that connects the dorm to her apartment is open.

On the front step I duck out of the light, pulling Leo with me. What comes next is without a doubt the most action this porch has ever seen. "I'm so glad summer's over," Leo says, his forehead resting against mine.

"What? You had a fantastic summer."

"I did. But I'm ready for a fantastic year. With you."

With that and one last kiss, I trudge back to my room and my gloomy new life. Opal turns as I walk in. "I'm sure you already know this, but Leo has a very special soul, and I hope you treasure it."

Even though she has the same serene, spaced-out look that she's had all night, her words feel pushy and invasive. Maybe it's my guilty conscience over not being completely honest with him. Or maybe my roommate's just annoying.

CHAPTER FOUR

The Willow Tree is one of the first storefronts on Main Street, going into Winthrop's adorable center. They probably put it here as a strategic reminder that whatever fun we're about to have in town, we really should be doing homework. With my class list in hand, I enter the white clapboard cottage.

Inside is all light wood, gleaming windows, and nubby upholstery. Bookshelves with regular books line the walls, while student textbooks stand in tight stacks on a few large tables in the center of the room. I haven't even had my coffee yet, but the place is already bustling.

I stumbled here shortly after waking up, partly to escape the slightly musty, sauna-like smell in my room. Opal was already long gone. Of course I get paired with an early riser.

I grab a tote bag and proceed to fill it with all the books I'll need for the term. My physics book is a tome, and I have a flash of anxiety when I note the price. It's a shame to spend so much money on a subject I'm sure to hate. Though, in all honesty, I don't love any of my classes. I do just well enough in all of them but don't excel at any. Ms. Randall has explained to me, "Being a mediocre generalist is not going to capture the imagination of any college admissions officer." My first official meeting with her is next week. Can't wait.

I exchange nods and smiles with a few people before continuing on to the second floor. Elizabeth, one of my Lincoln friends, stands in front of a display of journals. "You're back!" She comes over to hug me.

"I had to come a day early to deal with the whole moving debacle. You're still in Lincoln?" Her entire family, going back four generations, has gone to Winthrop, and I think her mom lived in Lincoln.

Elizabeth bites her lip and gives me a sympathetic smile. "It's unconscionable, really. I asked my brother, and he said he'd never heard of a senior getting transferred unless they specifically requested it."

"My new roommate is totally odd, and my house counselor is a bit eccentric, but I'm trying to embrace having a new experience." Apparently, Ms. Randall has succeeded in implanting her word into my subconscious.

"Ugh. Sounds grim. Which journal do you think I should get?" She holds up a brown leather-bound one and one with a pretty floral fabric cover.

I try not to show my hurt over the abrupt subject change and inspect the choices. "They're both beautiful. But seventy-five dollars seems like a lot to spend on a journal."

Elizabeth shrugs. "It goes on the account. My parents will assume it's for school." She tucks the leather one into her shopping tote.

"I'm going to be a few more minutes, but I'll catch up with you at the Calendar meeting."

"Okay, fun! Whit said she's going to ream us if we don't bring at least five good ideas."

"I better get on that."

"She already knows you're a slacker. I wouldn't worry too much."

Her offhand comment stings even though I know I've earned it. The Calendar has to approve and facilitate every single on-campus social activity for the entire year. It could be a campus-wide formal or a one-woman improvisational dance/poetry reading. It does not matter. Anything that is put forth for consumption by the greater Winthrop student body must be approved by the Calendar.

I love being on the Calendar, but I mean, it's not like any of our events get written up on Page Six or in *Variety*. And since Leo tends to lie low during soccer season, I don't get involved in the actual events as much as I should. But it's the only extracurricular on my college apps, and Whit made me vice president this year, so I have to be more engaged.

Elizabeth leaves me to finish shopping. I pick out a few of the novels assigned for my Gothic Lit class and then go downstairs. To my dismay, she is still paying. "Six hundred seventy-three dollars and eighty-five cents," the cashier says. "Last name?"

"Ames." Elizabeth signs her name on an electronic pad and scoops up her bags of books. She notices me at the end of the line. It's not long enough to deter her. "I'll wait for you," she says.

When it's my turn to pay, rather than sign my name and have my book expenses fly out into the ether, to be taken care of by dear old Mom and Dad, I produce my debit card. Elizabeth cocks her head, puzzled, but doesn't say anything. The vast majority of Winthrop kids have accounts. I asked my parents if they could keep my account open and I'd reimburse them, but my mom mumbled something about cash flow. My total's almost as much as Elizabeth's. More than a week's pay at Hayward. My breathing goes shallow as I punch in my PIN.

We don't say much on the walk back to campus, and I hate that she can tell something's amiss. But Elizabeth's a Boston Brahmin, which means really old family with really old money. It also means she'd never bring up anything impolite or potentially embarrassing. Instead, we make small talk about college visits and classes and Leo. She's never been enamored of the Hollywood thing like a lot of others are, and I respect her for that.

We stop in front of Lincoln and hesitate at the door. "Do you want to hang out for a while?" Her tone is too cheerful and makes me want to melt into the ground. I can't bear the indignity of it all.

"Sure. I've got time to kill before the SoCal social."

Elizabeth opens the door and holds it for me. We go through another set of double doors, up the stairs, to Whit's room. She didn't answer her phone when I called earlier, and she's not in now. I scribble a note on the whiteboard outside her room, use an overabundance of underlining and exclamation points for emphasis, and text her for good measure before we continue down the hall to Elizabeth's.

It's a perfectly appointed room, the kind that makes you nervous just to be in. Her floral bedspread matches the throw rug, and rather than posters stuck all over the walls, one framed Impressionist print hangs in the center of the largest wall. I sit on her bed, careful not to mess it up, while she arranges her new purchases on the bookshelf.

Olivia Woodward, who grew up in Hong Kong as an expat, stops in. She's Caucasian and went to American schools but is fluent in both Mandarin and Cantonese thanks to her Chinese nanny. We're in the same Mandarin class, but her accent is way better than mine, which amuses her to no end. "Hey, Skylar, you camping out here in protest?" she asks.

"If you're offering up your room . . . ?" I say.

"Girl, you know I'd let you hide out," Olivia says. "Is there any chance of you coming back?"

"Not unless someone volunteers to move out."

"Well. That seems unlikely," Elizabeth says.

"Yup," I agree. Awkward silence. "So how many people transferred in?"

Elizabeth and Olivia exchange a look.

"What's up?" I ask. "Come on, you guys know something. Was there a mass exodus from Baldwin because of Megan Taverna?" Megan is one of those loud, abrasive girls who are feared more than liked.

Olivia clears her throat. "I think there's only one new senior this year." Their shared look is nervous this time.

I'm dumbfounded. "One?" They nod. "So it wasn't a whole

reshuffling? It was just me getting booted?" Raksmey's words come back to me.

"Some sophomores and juniors moved. I don't know if they requested or not," Elizabeth says.

"It makes no sense that you'd be reassigned," Olivia says. "You've lived here the longest. Well, you, Elizabeth, and Whitney."

"I'm sure they pulled a name at random," Elizabeth says.

"Yeah. Probably." I know Ms. Randall says it wasn't the financial aid thing, but I'm starting to doubt her.

Whitney bursts in, flings her bag on the floor, and throws herself on the bed, not caring if she ends up on top of me. "You rang?"

"Where have you been?" I ask.

Then a pretty girl with porcelain skin and green eyes, wearing an expensive-looking navy sheath dress, appears in the door. She's not wearing pearls, but they're implied. I don't fully recognize her, and I'm suddenly aware of how my boho chic ensemble could read as homeless. "Hello," she says, looking only at me.

Whitney jumps up. "Hey, Li, this is Skylar. Remember? From LA? Her mom produced *Over It*?"

I shoot Whitney a questioning look. Not because she mentioned my mom's movie but because she's using an uncertain, tremulous tone I've never heard before.

"You're kidding me," the girl says. "That movie changed my life." She looks at me with slightly more interest than she had a second ago.

"They're working on a sequel!" Olivia chimes in.

I neither confirm nor deny. "Sorry, what was your name?"

Whit nudges me. "This is Lila! My best friend from New York? She's taking a postgraduate year here. Skylar was supposed to come to the Hamptons this summer, but she was too busy interning at her mom's production company and getting ready for the sequel."

"That's so exciting," I say. "Welcome!" I've heard a lot about Lila over the years, and most of it isn't good. That all seems to have been forgotten, however. She reaches into Whitney's bag like it's her own and pulls out a tube of lip balm. I can't exactly feel jealous. If Lila's taking a PG year, things were definitely not picture-perfect at her prep school in New York. "Where will you be living?"

Lila finishes smearing the balm on her lips and tosses it back into Whitney's bag. She looks at me, puzzled. "Here. Whit said this is the only dorm to live in."

The room tilts sideways. "In Lincoln?"

She cocks her head and continues looking at me like she's unsure whether I'm hard of hearing or just stupid. "Of course."

Whitney does seem to understand that this bitch stole my room, and she won't make eye contact with me. I stand up. "Excuse me. I have a meeting. It was nice to meet you, Lila." My self-possession makes an appearance just in time for me to return Lila's long, appraising look.

Outside, I hear someone running behind me. "I know what you're thinking, and I can't stand you being mad at me," Whitney says. I turn to face her. "I thought they'd toss out a junior or something."

"How long have you known that she was coming here?" I ask.

Whit shrugs. "Since the spring. I was shocked when she got in and even more shocked when she said she was coming. She's literally changed her mind at least two dozen times since she got the letter. Of course I told her she had to live here, but I didn't think she'd actually come." She makes pleading eyes at me.

"Did your dad get involved?" Mr. Lambert is on the Winthrop board of trustees.

She looks over her shoulder. "Well . . . yeah. But it wasn't just him. Lila's parents called too, and they know absolutely everyone in the art and finance worlds. I'm sure they had to call in a million favors just to get her in. I had no way of knowing it would affect you."

"Well, even if it wasn't me, it would've been one of our friends. It hardly seems fair to create all this turmoil for someone who's just here for a year."

"There was nothing I could do. Her parents totally peer-pressured my parents. They want me to be a good influence on her, so she has to live in my dorm. Otherwise they were going to let her rot in community college for a year."

I wonder why, exactly, I'm supposed to care about Lila. But it's clear that Whitney does. More than she cares about me.

CHAPTER FIVE

I stalk to the Study, Winthrop's answer to Starbucks, on auto-pilot, grateful to have a destination that will take me away from Whitney's little bombshell. I'm moving so fast that I have to keep hopping off the path to pass people, weaving like a crazy driver on a traffic-filled LA freeway.

Lila's going to be instated into our group whether I like it or not. I see no way to win that battle, so resistance is pointless. But Whitney's not being more upset and apologetic about Lila taking my place in the dorm and our other friends' not bother-ing to mention it to me feel like massive, deliberate betrayals.

By the time I get to the Study, patches of my shirt are stuck to my skin. The Southern California Students Association social is already in progress, so I order a small iced tea and find a seat. Twenty or so people sit on couches and chairs arranged in an approximate semicircle.

As soon as I sit down, I debate skipping it altogether. At the moment I hate everybody, which seems counterproductive to mingling with strangers. Traditionally, I show up at the first gathering of the year to see if there are any people I should know. So far the answer has been a big fat no. Most of the group seems to come from San Diego or Orange County. There's nothing inherently wrong with those places, but they're pretty different from where my parents live.

A boy standing at the front drones on: "We're here for lots of different things, but the number one reason is to give you guys a base. As they say, there's no place like home, and we want you guys to meet other people who understand earthquakes, car chases, and awesome Mexican food." Everyone laughs, but I'm barely listening.

There are quite a few new people, but their shining faces and quick laughs reek of desperation. I think I recognize one girl, but she looks (and acts) like a first-year, so I must be wrong. Maybe it's narrow-minded, but cultivating new friendships at this stage feels like a lot of pointless work.

The group starts introductions, and I stand back up. "You're leaving already?" the boy asks. "We have door prizes."

"I'm okay, thanks." Everyone watches me make my way to the door. Awkward.

"We must smell bad or something," he says to the group. Everyone laughs again. Bunch of sheep.

That evening I get to Upper Left just in time for the first Calendar meeting. Whitney wastes no time getting us off the ground. She really wants her presidency to be her legacy.

"Did you bring ideas?" Elizabeth whispers.

"No," I say in a normal voice.

She takes in my bitter expression. "I'll tell Whit to ease up."

I snort. "Please. I can handle Whit." I thought I'd calmed down, but maybe not.

Of course Lila joins us. I bet Whitney handpicked her schedule too. She's still wearing the same impervious expression as when we met earlier. Like she already knows she's won.

Once we all have food, Whitney clinks a spoon against her water glass. "Let's get started. We all know why we're here, so let's jump to introductions for the new members." She looks to her right, where Lila sits, and motions for her to stand up.

"Hi, everyone! My name's Lila Duncan. I'm new this year, and as Whit knows from my fabulous summer parties in the Hamptons, I am no slouch when it comes to entertaining." I didn't notice in our brief meeting earlier, but she has the most grating voice I've ever heard, like she's trying to force it down a register while simultaneously choking on a ball of cat hair. "I plan to bring my expertise and exemplary taste to the party circuit here at Winthrop."

Everyone applauds. I stare at my lap. Barf.

The next girl stands as Lila sits down. "Hi! I'm Christy Foster, and I'm new this year too, but I'm a first-year. I know a lot about parties and dances, being from LA, but I'm excited to learn the ropes and contribute however I can." I look up when she says the part about LA. Applause starts. "Um, excuse me? Don't I know you?" Christy asks. "Were you at the SoCal social?"

"Oh, yeah, just for a few minutes." She's the girl I thought I recognized. Even her name sounds familiar.

43

"You worked at my beach club this summer! The Hayward Club? You were my family's favorite waitress! I had no idea you went here. Why didn't you ever say anything?"

All the blood leaves my heart and rushes to my extremities, most noticeably my face. My brain goes blank for what feels like several long minutes. Should I lie? Find some way to discredit her? Fake a blackout? In my peripheral vision I notice Lila hiding a smile behind her hand. She nudges Whit. "Sorry, you have me confused with someone else," I croak.

"No! For sure. I was there almost every day at the beginning of summer before I left for surf camp in Costa Rica. Skylar, right? Oh my god, my parents are going to die! They love telling stories about how you never brought them the right order. That was the running joke—an affectionate one, of course."

Finally, finally, she sits back down.

The table is silent. It feels like the entire dining room is silent. Lila clears her throat. "I thought Whit said you were some kind of movie development executive." Her expression is mocking, scornful. "Was she mistaken? It sounded intriguing, I'll give you that."

I avoid letting my eyes land on anyone, but I can feel their stares boring holes into my forehead. Christy seems to know that she said something unfortunate. "It's not impossible to be both," I manage to get out.

"God, Skylar, we all know you're not one to let facts get in the way of a good story, but this takes it to a new level," Whitney says. "What's with the waitressing thing? And more importantly, why have you never mentioned it?"

"You know, we do have friends who work," Lila says. "Hope you didn't cover it up on our account." She doesn't even look at me while she's talking.

And how is she all of a sudden a "we"? She got here all of five seconds ago. But I'm fully aware that if Lila was at all worried about claiming Whitney as her best-friend prize, I've just handed her the winning ticket.

"No, that wasn't the reason." Yes, it was. Maybe some trust fund kids try to keep it real, but not these ones. I sigh. "I just wanted to earn my own money for once. Getting into a whole thing seemed pointless." Clearly this isn't the moment for the full truth.

"Couldn't your mom just pay you?" Whitney asks.

Elizabeth shoots me a nervous look.

I clear my throat, searching for a plausible explanation. Eventually I say, "I guess, but that wouldn't really be earning my own money."

Whitney grimaces. "Fair enough. But did you even work on the sequel to *Over It*?"

I settle for a half-truth. "When I could. I also read some new stuff."

She waves a hand dismissively. "Okay, whatever. But by the way, those shorts you were wearing yesterday? I could totally tell they were pleather." Whitney's smiling, but her voice is shards of smashed glass.

Lila's cackles ricochet around the dining hall.

CHAPTER SIX

Uncertainty about where I stand with my friends plagues me through the night, making sleep impossible. I texted Leo frantically when I left the Canteen, but he was busy dealing with one of his first-years' meltdowns. There are always a handful who are inconsolable and want to go home in the first few days. I want to take them by the hand and then very gently but very firmly shake them; first year is all pass/fail. It only gets worse.

Absolutely no one tried to talk to me after the Calendar meeting or even texted me later, but still, I'm determined to face the day with my head up. So what if they found out? So what if they now suspect we're a little hard up for cash? I'm still the same girl. My mother is still Lisa Chen, and *Over It* still exists, largely because of her.

I actually feel lighter now that I have nothing to hide. Even my physics book can't weigh me down. I practically skip out of Abbot.

"Skylar. Hold up." I turn to see Leo sitting on the porch banister.

"Hey, handsome!" I walk over to give him a kiss, but I get his cheek. There's not even anyone around. "Take me to breakfast on our first day as seniors? I have stuff to tell you."

He looks down at the ground. Now that I take a better look, Leo kind of looks like hell, which is not easy for him to achieve. Almost like he didn't sleep either, and definitely like he didn't shave. I reach my hand out to him. He takes it and slides off the banister but drops it as soon as he's standing. I glance at him with a questioning look. "Let's walk," he says.

It doesn't take a genius to see that something's up. "Is everything okay with the team?" I ask.

"Yeah, fine," he says.

"How about your first-year? Is he okay?"

He gives a brief nod, then stops in the middle of the wooded path. "Skylar."

"What's the matter? They stop serving hot food in fifteen minutes." I try to keep walking, but it's obvious that Leo isn't thinking about waffles right now.

"Why didn't you tell me what you were really doing this summer?"

And there it is. I hear the hurt and bewilderment in Leo's voice and hate myself for putting it there. I close my eyes, take a deep breath, and then turn toward him. "I'm sorry. That's what I was about to tell you. I should have mentioned it sooner, but things at home were just so tense. All I wanted was to come back here and put it behind me."

"But all those times I talked to you and you said you'd spent all day reading in an office or that you went to lunch with your mom while she met with actors who wanted parts. That was all made up?"

I look at the ground. "It's all stuff I've done before, but I didn't do much of it this summer."

Leo rubs the back of his neck. "I don't get it. Why did you lie? Is it that shameful to have to earn a paycheck?"

I have to tread carefully here. Leo's family isn't poor, but his tuition is covered by a soccer scholarship. "I mean, my family hasn't been doing as well, and it's hard to watch, but I was glad to help out. The only thing I cared about was making sure I got back for our senior year." The last part is intended to re-mind Leo of how happy we are to be together for these next ten months. Harvard's not going to be knocking down my door anytime soon, so my goal is to enjoy our time before we have to do some stressful long-distance thing.

But he doesn't reach for my hand or brush my hair off my face or make any of the affectionate gestures that might imply that he understands and forgives me. He stares at me, his ex-pression harder than I've ever seen it, at least off the soccer field. "How could you keep something like this a secret from me, of all people? Did you think I'd care if you weren't rich? Or some movie wasn't happening?"

"You wouldn't understand. Your family's always been the same," I begin. His face—mouth tight, eyes flat—closes down further. "Wait, that's not what I mean." I wish for a do-over where I actually don't say something stupid or insulting.

"Yeah. We've never had a ton of money. Until now I never thought that bothered you."

"It doesn't matter to me one bit. God, Leo." I grab his arm, desperate for him to believe me. "But it's hard to go from being known as one thing and then having to get used to being something else. If anything, I just didn't want to ruin your image of me. Being with someone who sees only the best version of you is really kind of uplifting. And with all the unhappy and annoying stuff happening, I needed some uplifting."

"My image of you is of someone I trust, who trusts me. That's all I care about. I never knew you thought all the Hollywood bullshit mattered to me. I thought we worked because we could be ourselves with each other."

"We can," I say, hoping that my conviction is enough to pull us through this.

"Evidently not."

I rack my brain for a way to explain this to him. "What if you got hurt and couldn't play anymore? Somebody else would take your place as the star of varsity soccer, and you probably wouldn't feel normal for a very long time."

From his serious expression, I can tell he's thought about this before. "Yeah. That would obviously suck. But I wouldn't be able to hide it, and even if I could, that isn't really my style. And I definitely wouldn't be worried that you'd feel any different about me." His eyes narrow. "Would you?"

Could this conversation be going any worse? "Of course not!

That's not what I'm saying at all. But wouldn't it make you even a little scared that your entire identity would change?"

Leo gives me a stern look. "I would miss playing and being with the team. And I'd have to figure out a new scholarship. But I have plenty of other stuff going on, and my real friends would still be there."

"Yeah, well . . . lucky you."

He lets out a long exhale. "I guess what bothers me is that you cared what everyone else thinks more than you cared about being honest with me."

From where he's sitting, I'm sure that's exactly what it looks like. Anything I say will probably make it worse, but I have to try. "You're right. That shouldn't have been more important."

"But it was."

"What can I say? I wasn't thinking about it from your point of view, and I'm sorry." I watch him. He chews the corner of his bottom lip, his gaze unwavering. A heavy feeling of dread settles in the center of my chest.

"I don't know, Sky." He's the only one who's allowed to call me that, but hearing him say it now is disconcerting. "Most of that is made up in other people's heads, which is their business, but I didn't know that it was so in *your* head. You never talk about Hollywood or parties or money when it's just you and me."

"Because that's not us." My voice is barely a whisper.

"But you lied for an entire summer—probably longer—so now I don't know what *is* us." His whole body is a stormy clash of hurt and anger. "Maybe we need some space to figure this out."

"I don't need space. I didn't do this to hurt you, and I still want to be with you."

Leo kicks a rock out of the path. "Okay. Then I need time."

Space and time have never sounded so ominous. I want to ask him to define exactly what that means but sense that pressing him right now would only end badly. Better to let him cool down for a couple of days.

But he looks so upset, and it hits me that I can't be the one to comfort him. Not this time. It's such an unfamiliar, gutting feeling. I have no choice but to keep going to the main campus. At least I manage to get far enough away before the sobs start.

I fly up the Canteen steps and duck into the bathroom. Even though there's no one here, I run into a stall and lock the door behind me. After several minutes of trying to cry quietly into a balled-up wad of toilet paper, I feel reasonably sure that I can pull it together. Or at least fake it. I step out of the stall and stare in the mirror.

My eyes are red-ringed and puffy, and my eyelashes stick together in wet spikes. The healthy bronze glow I acquired from a summer outside seems to have faded overnight. I get out my compact and lip gloss and do the best repair job I can. I perch my sunglasses on top of my head so that they'll be accessible as soon as I step outside.

It's late enough that the dining rooms have thinned out. The thought of eating makes me nauseated, but I could use some coffee. I consider skipping classes, but I know all too well how easy it is to get behind here. That's the last thing I need. Problems on top of problems.

Of course, Whitney's waiting for her toast by the buffet. I went to Upper Left on autopilot but clearly should've chosen one of the other dining rooms.

"You look awful," she says matter-of-factly.

"Thanks," I mutter.

"Couldn't sleep? Guilty conscience?" Whitney smirks as she smears peanut butter on her toast.

No point in delaying the inevitable. "Leo found out. I didn't even get a chance to tell him myself."

She doesn't even look surprised. "Well, that was bound to happen. What did he say?"

"He said we should take a little space for a bit."

Whitney shrugs. "Can't blame him. That was a pretty big omission."

"Wow, Whit, thanks for your sympathy and concern." I turn and walk out, sans caffeine. She calls after me in a wheedling, placating voice, but I don't stop. She can pretend to be all concerned, but we both know that her reaction yesterday helped set the tone.

CHAPTER SEVEN

I sit through a full morning of classes, where I manage to raise my hand for attendance, collect syllabi, and not much else. Since I have a free period right after lunch, I make the trek back to Abbot. Hopefully I'll have the room to myself.

One of the doors on my floor is wide open, so I try to open my door as silently as possible.

"So that was a bummer this morning."

I jump at the sound of the gravelly, braying voice and turn to see a tiny, freckled girl with fiery red hair pulled into a tight ponytail sticking her head out the open door. I'd say there's no way that color is natural, but it complements her fair complexion perfectly, and honestly, she doesn't look like the type to bother with her hair. She's cute, but that voice and her jeans and running shoes—a combination that I've always found particularly frumpy—aren't doing her any favors. "Um, excuse me?" I ask.

"Getting dumped is a seriously sucky way to begin senior year, am I right?" she says.

Between lack of sleep and fighting with Leo, my nerves are frayed, and I'm ready to snap. "That is not what happened. And I'm sorry, have we met?" I glare at her.

"I'm Jess. We were in the same orientation group as first-years." I suppose that I should feel bad enough to pretend I remember her, but Jess waves her hand as if to say she doesn't care. "Save your breath. I like to keep a low profile anyway. So you were saying?"

"I wasn't actually. I'm still processing, and I don't really know you, so maybe I can fill you in some other time." *Like never.*

Inside my room I stare at my phone, hoping that Leo had a change of heart, when the door swings open and hits the wall. It's not Opal (the only person who has the right to open my closed door without knocking) but Raksmey. At least she appears calmer than she did when we first met in the kitchenette.

"We heard about you and Leo. I'm really sorry," Raksmey says, then shifts to the side so that I see a girl standing behind her.

I'm actually not surprised that something as noteworthy as problems between me and Leo has misfired through the gossip-sphere. Every girl on campus has probably been waiting for some sign of trouble. They can keep dreaming, because we're not over.

I sigh, and somehow they take that as an invitation to come in. I'm pretty sure the other girl isn't in my class, but I've definitely seen her around. She stands out, with thick black hair that hangs long and shiny past her shoulders and a style that, while a tad on the uptight side, does show that she has impeccable taste. And money. She's wearing a slim blue oxford shirt tucked into a gray pencil skirt. I'll overlook her flats, since we do live out in the hinterlands. People call her The Princess, and I have no idea if they do it to her face or even if she's an actual princess, but just looking at her makes me wish I had better posture.

"You're Jasmine, right?" I say.

She rolls her eyes. "It's Yasmin. Jasmine's what those fools who made up the princess rumor call me."

Oh. That answers that, then.

"Personally, I think that had more to do with your wardrobe and demeanor than it did with the fact that you're from the Emirates," Raksmey says.

I nod stupidly, and Yasmin squints at me. "Anyway," she says, "we wanted to stop by and see if there's anything you need. We've both lived here since we were first-years, and I love this dorm because we're like a family."

"Seriously, if you need ice cream, sushi—you name it—we'd be happy to take you out, or even bring it to you!" Raksmey's offer is sweet, but I don't think my situation quite warrants these dire breakup recovery tactics.

"That's so nice. But, uh, I can't really eat sushi on this coast, being from California." I realize it sounds snotty the second it's out of my mouth. But to my surprise, Yasmin nods.

"We have a Katsuya back home, so I know what you mean," she says, referring to a famous sushi restaurant chain that started in LA.

"There's a Katsuya in Saudi Arabia?" I ask. Who knew?

Raksmey and Yasmin glance at each other. "She's not from Saudi Arabia. That's not even part of the Emirates," Raksmey says.

"Oh, right, of course." I'm uncomfortably aware that I'm being moronic and should probably just stop talking. This is what I get for trying to be polite when I'm too upset to think straight.

"But Dubai, where I live, has a Katsuya. And yes, Rock-n-Roll Sushi really can't compare." Yasmin smiles, which makes me feel less like a jerk, but I need to cut this visit short before exhaustion makes me say something even dumber. Unfortunately, these girls show no sign of leaving.

"I didn't sleep well last night, so I'm going to try to nap before athletics," I say.

"No problem. We're heading to lunch," Yasmin says.

"If you're up for it, Club Raks is happening tomorrow night," Raksmey says.

I have no idea what she's talking about but smile as I close the door behind them. I'm sure I'll find out about this club business later whether I want to or not.

After dragging myself through mandatory afternoon athletics, I have my senior elective, Images of Women in Film. It was the one class I was actually looking forward to, but now it seems like a cruel, term-long punch line to my humiliation. I enrolled thinking it would be a cakewalk based on my background, but now that everyone thinks I'm a liar, anything I say will be scrutinized. The easy A hardly seems worth it now.

When I get to Hartley Hall, the English and media building, I'm bummed to see Remy and Sid, Leo's teammates, already sitting in the classroom. I'd forgotten they were in this section.

I deliberately choose a seat on the other side of the room but sense Remy staring at me. I meet his eye and offer a wavering half smile. There are only ten students in the class, which means there's no chance I'll be able to avoid them all term.

As Dr. Fan hands out the syllabus and gives an overview of the class, I focus all my energy on looking natural. Judging from the way Remy keeps shooting worried looks in my direction and Sid hasn't acknowledged me, I know they've heard. I wonder how much detail Leo went into. Knowing him, I doubt he said very much.

"Screenings are every other week in this room, but since those classes run longer, we'll meet after dinner. Manage your time accordingly." Dr. Fan peers at me, so I nod.

We spend the next thirty minutes watching clips from old movies. While I haven't seen all of them, I'm definitely familiar with the titles. Dr. Fan pauses occasionally to point out how camera placement or use of music influences the mood of a scene. It's a testament to her teaching that I'm absorbed enough to forget my personal problems.

When class ends and the lights flicker back on, I take a long time to gather my things, giving Remy and Sid time to leave first. I keep my head down, pretending to peruse the syllabus as I walk, so naturally I plow right into Remy, who's stationed outside the door. "Oof. Hey," I say.

Sid looks as uncomfortable as I feel. "That was a pretty cool class," he says.

"Yeah, I'm excited to watch *Broadcast News*—never seen it before," Remy says, trying to smooth over the awkwardness.

"It's one of my mom's favorites," I say, earning an eye roll from Sid.

"I'm going to go ahead," he says, looking only at Remy.

"Cool. Be there in a minute," Remy says.

I watch Sid jog away. "I guess now that Leo's mad at me, there's no reason for him to pretend to be nice to me."

"Don't worry about him. He just likes being contrarian. So, what's going on with you and Diaz?" Remy asks.

I start walking. "We're just giving each other a minute to digest some information." On the one hand, I'm touched that he cares enough to ask, but on the other, talking to him about it feels traitorous. Remy and I are friends, but there's no question that he's Leo's friend first.

"I don't get it, you guys were totally fine the other night. What could've happened between then and today?"

"What did he say?" I ask, dreading the answer.

"Not much. That guy's a vault. He's really bummed, though. Did you mess around over the summer?"

I whack him on the arm. "No! God, are you serious? I'd never do that."

Remy relaxes. "Then what could be so bad?"

"I . . . don't want to get into it, but I didn't tell him something I should've told him, but it didn't involve another person."

"You mean you lied?"

The word makes me squirm. "Not exactly."

"Come on. If it's not cheating and it's not lying, then I'm sure he'll get over it eventually."

"Okay, it was kind of lying."

Remy winces. "Oh."

I groan. At the moment I feel like I have nothing more to lose. Plus, Remy's always been nice to me. "I didn't tell him that I waitressed over the summer. Or that my family's struggling financially."

"I thought you worked for your mom," he says.

"Right. Because that's what I told everyone. I'm honestly just stressed about my family, but Leo thinks I didn't tell him because I'm ashamed that I had to work a regular job."

"Ooh. I can see that being a tough one for him."

Another wave of misery engulfs me.

We arrive at the Canteen, and there's a mortifying moment when I can tell Remy's wondering how to ditch me before we go in. "I'm going to run over to Lincoln and see if anyone's around," I say quickly. "I'll see you later."

"Cool," Remy says. I try to ignore the relief that flashes across his face.

I retreat down the path. Even though I'm not dying to share the gory details, it does feel better to tell my side of the story. Hopefully Whit's had a chance to calm down and is ready to hear me out.

Her door's closed, and a girl I don't know stops me as I'm about to knock on Elizabeth's door. "All the seniors went off campus to eat."

"Really?" I check my phone, but there are no texts or missed calls. By now Whit's definitely told everyone about me and Leo. Guess no one's overly concerned about my shattered heart. "Where did they go?"

She shrugs and gives me a little wave as she joins another first-year girl coming out of her room. They walk downstairs, talking and laughing, so close that their elbows and shoulders knock together.

"Name?" the guy on the phone asks when I'm done ordering a pepperoni pizza with onions and mushrooms. If all my friends bailed on me, at least I can console myself with my favorite Winthrop meal.

"Skylar Hoffman."

"Lincoln, right?"

I guess I've ordered from them a few times over the years. I'm a reverse snob when it comes to pizza and sandwiches— East Coast wins, hands down. "Actually this year I'm in a new dorm. Abbot House."

"The really far one? We charge extra to deliver there."

"Of course you do."

"That okay?" he asks.

Like I have a choice? "Yeah, fine," I say.

"Herb's driving today. You want to add anything to your order?" he asks.

That's the code name for the delivery guy who also supplies half the campus with weed. I'm not much of a smoker, and besides, I can barely afford the pizza. "I'm all good," I say.

Eating alone in my room is absolutely not how I pictured starting this year, but it turns out to be about all I can handle. I sit on the floor, leaning back against my bed, imagining the conversation I'd be having if I were out with everyone right now. Would my lie be the elephant in the room? Or would I get an inquisition about my life? Comforting words about Leo and how none of the rest matters because I'm still the same person? The sad fact is, I'm really not sure.

Desperate for any silver lining, I mull over the idea that I can eat as much pepperoni and onion as I want, because I won't be kissing Leo anytime soon. As soon as I think it, my appetite disappears, and I put down my slice.

Opal comes in and wrinkles her nose at my dinner. "Sorry, does it stink?" I ask, even though she really shouldn't be complaining. Patchouli isn't exactly a socially acceptable scent.

"Well, yeah. But also, I'm vegan." I must be looking at her blankly, because she helpfully explains, "That means I don't consume any animal products."

I give her a dead-eyed stare. "I'm from LA, remember? But does that mean . . . I can't eat it either?"

Opal relaxes. "Of course not. But I'm not used to smelling meat and cheese in such close proximity." She puts her hemp backpack in her closet and sets up on the floor to study. I glance at her desk, which is covered with a floral tapestry that also appears to be hemp. Books and notebooks sit neatly on the surface, leaving no work space.

"Um, you do go to restaurants, don't you?" Just when I thought she couldn't get any stranger.

"Only vegan ones, usually. Sometimes we get special meals

here, but normally I just eat salad. Believe it or not, I'm not the only vegan—"

And suddenly I can't take it. "Just stop right there. If I have to listen to one more word about veganism, I might actually scream."

Her expression seesaws between sympathetic and offended. "Long day?" she finally asks.

"Let me guess, you heard about me and Leo," I say.

"Pretty much everyone has," she agrees.

Fantastic.

CHAPTER EIGHT

My phone finally rings, and I snatch it off the floor so fast that Opal actually looks up from her reading. It's Jordana, which, I'm ashamed to admit, is a tiny bit of a letdown, especially since I'm the one who texted her earlier.

"Hi."

"Uh-oh, that doesn't sound good. What's going on?" Jordana asks.

Following good dorm etiquette, I defer to my studying roommate and step into the hall. "Okay, I have to apologize in advance. I'm going to be *that* girl for a while." My voice catches.

Jordana's quiet for a second. "Don't even worry about that. We've been friends for too long."

I take a deep breath. "Well, remember that perfect senior year I was supposed to be having? It has kind of come to a screeching halt."

"Already? What happened?" She sounds genuinely upset for me, which in and of itself makes me want to cry.

I walk toward the common room, which is on the first floor at the front of the house, right next to the kitchenette. Hopefully it has a door that locks. But Jess is already in there on one of the two couches, watching a movie on her laptop. "Aren't you the lucky one with a single?" I ask.

"Yeah, but I haven't given up hope that someone will watch with me one day," she says, not taking the hint. "Until then I have to settle for educating through osmosis." She turns back to her movie. A giant oil tanker takes up most of the screen while a dry voiceover spouts off statistics. Looks riveting.

"Hello?" Jordana's voice comes through faintly over my phone. I glower at Jess and back out of the room.

Outside on the porch I sit down on the steps and rest my forehead on my knees. Even though it's late, the temperature hasn't cooled much, but a faint breeze stirs the air. "How much time do you have?" I ask.

When I get through the whole sordid story, Jordana is silent. "What? What are you thinking? That I had it coming? That my friends are disloyal jerks—what?"

"Slow down," Jordana says. "Would you believe me if I said all of the above?"

"Kind of a cop-out but, I guess."

"What's up with this Lila person? Do you think Whit would be this spun out if Lila weren't at Winthrop?"

I consider that. "I don't know. Whit always made her out to be a conniving one-upper. I'm sure Whit feels like I made her look stupid. She probably had Lila believing that I was some fabulous A-list party girl."

"Hmm. Maybe she's making a big deal out of it so Lila understands that she didn't knowingly exaggerate," Jordana says.

"You mean so Lila knows that Whitney didn't lie to impress her? Unlike me?" I ask.

"Harsher than I was willing to go, but yeah."

"Maybe." Embarrassment in any form is not something Whitney takes lightly. Ever.

"And Leo?" Jordana asks.

With my toe, I trace an *L* in the dirt below the bottom step. "He's really angry with me. We've never had a fight like this before. The thing that kills me is, I did tell the truth! When I first got here and met everyone, my mom was still doing great. Should I be punished in every way possible just because the film business is fickle and things don't always work out? Is it not enough that my family life is grim and that I had to work a ton of hours at a mostly mindless job? Am I really obligated to tell everyone that my mom's business took a nosedive?"

"Definitely not ..." She trails off, and I know what she's thinking.

"But if I told Leo, he'd expect me to be honest about it with everyone."

"Why? Is his life an open book?"

"Yes. Because he's perfect."

"Well, that's annoying," Jordana says. My responding laugh is halfhearted at best. "What?" she continues. "It was annoying when he was your boyfriend, and it's even more annoying now that he's holding his perfection over your head."

I straighten. "He's still my boyfriend. And that's not what he's doing. Is it?"

Jordana sighs. "No. From everything you've told me, he doesn't seem like that guy. He just doesn't get it."

"Do you think he's going to break up with me?"

"I don't know, but if he does, that'll be his one imperfect act."

That actually makes me smile. We're quiet for a minute. "Thanks for trying to make him the bad one, JoJo."

"That's what friends are for," she says.

"What about you? Tell me that your year is going better than you thought it would."

"Nope. It's unfolding exactly as expected. Except Joe Brill asked me out."

"That's amazing!" I say.

"I'm going to let you think about that one for a minute," Jordana says.

Realization dawns. "Oh, second grade, nose picker?"

"Bingo."

"Well, that was a long time ago. But this just means college is going to be spectacular for you," I say. It better be. Jordana deserves it.

We hang up, and I force myself back into the dorm. As I pass by the common room I notice that everyone's in it, including a goth girl I've seen around but never met and a girl wearing faded jeans and a gauzy peasant blouse whom I've never noticed before. I stick my head in out of curiosity. Everyone's conspicuously quiet, trying to look busy. I'm about to introduce myself, but then I see that the front window's wide open and realize that they must have overheard every word of my conversation.

"You guys were eavesdropping on me?" Even though privacy is typically scarce at boarding school, it's pretty gutsy to listen in on someone's private phone call so blatantly.

They all exchange glances, each hoping that somebody else will be dumb enough to speak first. "Isn't it kind of better this way?" Raksmey finally asks. "Now you don't have to tell the story a million times."

Unbelievable. "Just so you know, I had no intention of telling any of you any story, ever!"

I storm up the stairs but not before I hear someone whisper, "She's better than Netflix." A few of the others shush her.

As soon as I get to my room, I crawl into bed. Opal is seemingly not completely oblivious, because she makes sure to let me fall asleep before she comes back.

CHAPTER NINE

Out of habit, I sit with Olivia and Elizabeth the next day in calculus. I've made a concerted effort to conceal the bags under my eyes and even managed to put on a cute outfit. When class is dismissed, they start chattering about how Lila supposedly dated some famous actor over the summer. Though I don't mean to, I let out a snort.

Olivia stares at me. "The Hamptons may not be Hollywood, but they're not exactly sleepy."

I'm confused by her defensiveness, since Winthrop's the only place she's lived in the US. "I just meant, Lila's kind of a lot, don't you think?" I ask.

"That's how Whit's always described her," Elizabeth says.

"True," I agree. "But it's a little odd how she's come in and taken over."

Elizabeth sighs. "We don't want to get in the middle. Just do a good job on the Calendar, and I'm sure things will go back to normal between you guys."

I nod, wondering if they're going to say anything about the whole waitressing thing. They don't, which somehow stings more than if they confronted me about it. Maybe it's my job to bring it up, but it sort of feels like they don't care enough to get involved. Not just with my fight with Whitney. With me.

We've reached the Canteen steps, and I spot Leo several people ahead of us. From his profile I can tell he's smiling. When he notices me, his face falls, but he doesn't wait for me or even acknowledge that I'm right here. "I'm going to run back to my dorm for a minute. I forgot something."

They exchange a look. "You're going to have to be in the same room as him at some point," Olivia says.

So they do know about that. "If you know, why haven't you said anything?"

Olivia shrugs. "Like what?"

"I don't know. How about, 'Sorry your boyfriend, who you're in love with, said he needs space'? 'We still love you even if Leo's confused'? Something like that." I glare at them, and at least they both shift uncomfortably, even if they don't actually seem ashamed.

"Obviously we all feel terrible for you," Elizabeth says. "But honestly, none of us knows what you're going through. If you felt you had to fabricate stories—"

"I didn't give you guys an up-to-the minute, blow-by-blow chronicle of my life. That doesn't make me a liar."

"But you let us keep thinking you were doing something you

weren't." Olivia turns to Elizabeth. "This is exactly why Whit said not to invite her to dinner last night." As if I've spontaneously gone invisible or deaf.

"She *what*? And I'm confused, you all just agreed?"

"Calm down, it wasn't personal. She wanted it to be celebratory, and then she told us that you and Leo broke up and said she didn't want you to feel forced into being cheerful," Elizabeth says.

"How big of her," I snap.

They sigh in unison. "Sorry. It just seemed like either choice would be a bad one, so we went with what Whit said," Elizabeth explains.

"She's your best friend, maybe you should take all this up with her," Olivia says.

Awesome best friend. "Thanks for the advice. I'll do that." Somehow I don't remember my friends being this spineless. "And by the way, Leo and I didn't break up. Giving each other space is not the same thing."

They shoot quick glances at each other. "That's not what that looked like just now," Olivia says. "And we hear that he's telling people you broke up."

"That's crap. You know Leo. He would never overshare about his personal life."

Elizabeth shakes her head. "We're just repeating what people are saying."

"I appreciate the heads-up," I say sarcastically.

On the way back to Abbot, I stare at the ground, furious that the rumors have gotten so out of control. My eavesdropping new dorm mates have to be the culprits. I have to admit, for socially disconnected dorks, they got the word out with impressive speed.

I spot Whitney and Lila sitting on the Field, the expanse of lawn next to Buckland Library, where everyone hangs out in warm weather. They're sitting on the grass, legs outstretched, leaning back on their elbows, with a dozen or so male admirers hovering.

I take a detour and navigate over there, stepping over backpacks and dodging wayward Frisbees. "Whit, I need to talk to you," I say when I'm standing practically on top of them.

She shields her eyes from the sun to look at me. Lila studies me for a second, then turns her attention back to Ben Waters. God, drool much? Then, with a theatrical sigh, Whitney gets to her feet. "In private," I say.

We walk a few yards away and lean against the waist-high stone wall that separates the Field from the academic quad. "Why didn't you tell me about dinner last night?" I ask. "Don't you think it would've been nice for me to spend time with friends after all this drama?" I stare at her hard. "And don't tell me it's because I wouldn't have been able to cope with everyone celebrating."

Whitney brushes nonexistent grass off her skirt and sighs. "Okay, you want to know why? You've created a credibility issue. Not just for yourself, but for me. Lila thinks I'm an idiot and that you've had me fooled since the beginning."

I shake my head, confused. "First of all, you know that's not true. Second, since when do you care so much about Lila's opinion?"

"I need her to know that I'm in charge here. Winthrop's my school, and I don't need Lila thinking she can just come in and take over." *Too late,* I think. She looks over my shoulder, I assume to make sure Lila's still occupied. "I've told you how she is," she says in a hushed voice. "Lila already thinks Winthrop's quaint—and not in a good way—because it's basically in a hamlet. But I've always told her that hanging out with cool, interesting people makes up for it. If she thinks I've been befriending losers, not that I'm saying you are one, she won't hesitate to spread the rumor back home."

"So?"

"I know you don't talk much to your LA friends—if that's even where you live—"

"Will you *stop*?"

"—but I still spend time with my city friends and probably will for the rest of my life. The Upper East Side is small, and Lila's family hosts the big end-of-summer party out in the Hamptons."

"And, what, because I waitressed, now she won't invite you?" The whole thing sounds highly improbable.

"If she makes a big enough stink about this year being pointless—and let's face it, she's not going to suddenly discover a love for academics, so for her it's going to be all about meeting important people—my whole family could get uninvited. We're the ones who suggested she come here. And my dad will absolutely blame me if that happens."

Far be it from me to claim to understand the ways of socialites in training. "Well, can't you just watch the movie again? My mom's name is on the opening credits. Or check IMDB?" Even as I say it, I'm cringing. Is this really the level we're willing to stoop to so we can convince Lila that I'm worthy?

Whitney's shoulders slump. "I'm trying to get her off the topic, but she's like a dog with a bone. When she senses weakness, she goes straight for it. By the way, it doesn't help your cause at all that Leo dumped you when he found out. And now you don't even have the hot-boyfriend thing going for you."

After a speechless minute, I finally come to my senses. I can't even address the Leo part. "Have you completely lost it? Guess what? I don't live on the Upper East Side, so I really don't have to care what Lila thinks."

Whitney shoots a startled glance in Lila's direction while motioning for me to keep it down. She looks at me with pity. "Not yet, maybe. Look, it's in your own best interest to lie low for a while. Everyone will just assume you're nursing your broken heart—which is totally understandable. Then Lila will have a chance to settle in and hopefully warm up to you."

"And if she doesn't?"

"We'll cross that bridge when we come to it. *If* we come to it. I mean, you're my friend. She'll get on board at some point." Whitney gives me a wry smile but then returns to her spot without a backward glance, rearranging her skirt and hair until they're picture-perfect.

"Nobody here would ever do that," Opal protests when I confront her. She and Raksmey are sitting in our room, doing homework on the second freaking day of school. Opal's on the floor, and Raksmey sits behind her on the bed.

"We might have overstepped out of concern and because

we're trying to get to know you, but we're not gossip mongers," Raksmey says.

"Then why does everyone keep saying that Leo and I broke up?"

"Maybe because you did," Raksmey says. Opal reaches back to give her a light slap on the leg.

"But is that something you're telling people?" I ask.

Opal sighs. "We already told you: no."

"Believe it or not, we had lives before you moved in," Raksmey says, earning another slap from Opal.

They look at me with so much sympathy that I know my desperation must be coming across loud and clear. Suddenly I don't know what to do. I run outside and sit on the porch, praying that no one else comes by. Every single person who's mentioned Leo to me thinks that we've broken up. The realization that I might have fooled myself into believing something completely different from what Leo meant feels unbearably humiliating.

I watch the path, ready to escape if anyone approaches. Not that I have any idea where I'd go.

CHAPTER TEN

That afternoon I slip out of Images of Women in Film before I have to face Remy—or deal with him avoiding me—and join Opal for dinner in Lower Left. She's eating with the Vegan Club (all four members are present and accounted for), but the upside is that no one I know would be caught dead in here.

Opal and her friends mostly ignore me while I pick at my fettuccine Alfredo, which is the closest thing to vegan I could find that would actually fill me up. Having no interest in or obligation to follow the conversation, I just sit there in my own world, staring into space.

On our way back to Abbot, Opal seems a bit disgruntled, which I can only tell because she's walking normally instead of floating. "What's up?" I finally ask.

She doesn't hesitate. "You weren't very polite to my friends. When we eat together as a club, we don't usually let people sit with us if they're consuming animal products."

"Sorry, you should've said something." I am genuinely surprised that Opal's upset.

"They made an exception, since you're my new roommate. I thought maybe being around different people would be healing for you, but you just ignored them."

Right now it feels like I can't do anything right. "It was mutual! I didn't know they expected me to weigh in on where you can find non-GMO soy products."

"A few courteous questions or even 'mmm-hmm's' would've been appreciated," Opal says.

Was she seriously giving me advice about social skills? "Fine. Duly noted."

We get to our room, where Opal promptly plants herself on a cylindrical floor cushion and closes her eyes. Now I get why she wears all those baggy clothes. Sitting practically on the floor, cross-legged, requires nonrestrictive clothing. "Excuse me. What are you doing?" I ask.

"Meditating," she says without opening her eyes.

"Right now?"

"Yes."

I take that as my cue to leave. Gathering my history books, I go down to the common room, which is thankfully empty. I try to focus, to put Leo and Whitney out of my mind. *Twenty minutes. Just try.*

About halfway through my admittedly distracted reading of the chapter on the Great Depression, an aggressive thumping starts emanating through the floor. I can't figure out what it is and wait for it to stop. It doesn't. After a few torturous minutes during which I can't think, let alone read, I get up to investigate.

Following the sound leads me to the musty basement, where we have storage and washers and dryers for those of us who don't use the laundry service. By my last count, that would be only me. My parents cut me off even after I presented a spreadsheet showing that the difference in cost is tiny.

I have to feel my way to the bottom of the steps because it's dark, but the noise, which I now recognize as music, gets louder. At the bottom I find Raksmey gyrating and hopping around in front of a disco ball. The beat is so intense that my heart feels like it'll leap out of my chest. Raksmey doesn't hear me, so I watch her, arms crossed, waiting for her to notice me so I can tell her how inconvenient this all is. As I watch a little longer I have to admit that she's actually got some moves, which is totally unexpected.

Eventually she turns around and yelps in surprise when she sees me. She's a disheveled mess, and her T-shirt's soaked through with sweat, but she's wearing a grin big enough to swallow her head. "Hey! You came to check out Club Raks!" She piles her hair on top of her head and holds it there with her hand.

This is Club Raks? You have got to be kidding me. Looks more like a scary satanic ritual. "Uh . . . I didn't know what it was. I was trying to work in the common room."

"Oh yeah, everyone knows Thursday is Club Raks. It's our agreement. I'm only allowed to do this once a week. You either put up with a little bass or go to the library."

"Really? Because Opal's trying to meditate." Maybe she doesn't care about doing violence to my ears, but she might care about Opal's.

Her brows draw together. "Huh. That's weird. Usually she meditates in the morning. Someone must've really pissed her off."

I give an innocent shrug and wait. I'm not leaving until she wraps up this tragedy.

"You're not gonna join? Dance-off?" Raksmey asks.

It's all I can do not to burst out laughing. "No thanks," I say. "Lots of work."

She nods sympathetically. "How are you doing with ... everything?"

Good thing she didn't say Leo's name, because I might have throttled her. When did it become acceptable to butt into a complete stranger's business? "Fine. Still don't want to talk about it."

"Okay," she says, sighing. "Guess I'll call it a night. You should come sometime. EDM can be totally cathartic."

"Sure," I say, already heading back up the stairs.

Even though it's quiet now, my tenuous Great Depression groove is ruined for good. I go back to my room, where Opal is still meditating. I tiptoe around quietly and lie on my bed with my copy of *Frankenstein*.

I've read the same three pages eight times when Opal opens her eyes. But instead of standing up, she proceeds to do a series of bizarre-looking and -sounding breathing exercises. It's one of the strangest sights I've ever seen, like she's trying to shoot her tonsils out of her nose. I have to stop and watch, which she doesn't seem to mind. "What the heck was that?" I ask when she's finished.

"Breath of fire. It helps with mental clarity and respiratory health," she says.

I stare at her, not bothering to hide my skepticism. If Opal's the poster child for mental clarity, we're all in serious trouble.

Friday doesn't go any better, and by the time classes are over, I'm in a full-blown depression. Staying in bed turns out not to be a problem, since neither Leo nor my old friends have so much as texted to see how I am or what I'm doing.

Saturday night rolls around, and I contemplate forcing myself to shower and get dressed to cover Classic Movie Night on the Field. But then showering seems ambitious, especially since no one will really be able to see me in the dark. Every member of the Calendar is expected to cover at least one campus event and report back on the hits and misses at the following meeting. Otherwise there's no way I'd even consider getting out of bed.

My dejected stupor wins out in the end. I blow off my assignment with the rationalization that Classic Movie Night has been going on forever. The Film Club couldn't possibly screw it up. Plus I doubt anyone will miss me.

Perhaps it's finally dawned on my dorm mates that I don't feel like discussing my personal life with them, because they steer clear of me. Then, on Sunday, I roll over to see Opal, already dressed, standing over me with a cup of tea. "Kombucha," she says. "It's supposed to calm and relax."

"Do I not seem calm?" I should, since I've barely moved the entire weekend. "Thanks, but I'm a coffee girl first thing in the morning."

"That's great, except it's noon." She sets the mug down on

my desk while I experiment with sitting up. "You should start doing yoga with me," she says.

"I really don't think so."

"I practice six days a week. That's how much you have to do it to get the full benefit."

"Okay, you lost me right there. I don't do anything six days a week unless it involves nutrition or hygiene or sleep," I mumble.

"Sometimes not even then," she says.

I stand up, drape my bathrobe and towel over my arm, and grab my shower caddy off the dresser. I can take a hint. "Sorry for any inconvenience my imploding social life may have caused you," I call over my shoulder.

When I get back, she's still there, sitting on the floor drinking the tea she brought for me. I unwrap my hair from its towel turban and start getting dressed. Or at least changing into different sweats. It's weird to get naked in front of someone I don't know, but it's not like she's paying attention. "What's up with you and floors?" I ask.

"Chairs are bad for you," she says. I don't even know what to say to that. "So going back to yoga—"

"Aren't we done talking about that? I was pretty sure we were." I turn my back to her, which is very clear "I'm ignoring you" body language, but she's not getting it.

"What do you do as your athletics requirement?" she asks.

This is a majorly sore subject. I spent my first year trying out for various teams and not making any of them. It's not like I didn't play on all the neighborhood rec teams growing up, but my interest in any one sport was never strong enough to warrant the intensive summer camps and private coaches that so many of the Lincoln girls benefitted from.

"Aerobics," I tell her.

"You mean like our grandmothers used to do? With leg warmers and stuff?" Opal asks. Great. Even the yoga freak thinks I'm lame.

"I wanted something that I could do in an hour that wouldn't take up my weekends," I say.

Opal holds up her hands. "I didn't say a thing. Why do you need your weekends?"

"I don't know, because I like doing other stuff!"

"Like what?"

It's like living with a four-year-old. "Like going to football or soccer games."

"Ah. So watching other people's sports." Opal nods, and though she has that same serene smile as always, I see right through it.

"Don't think I don't know you're judging me," I say. "By the way, just so you know, yoga won't be getting its own network or making it onto ESPN anytime soon either."

Opal actually laughs at that. "I'm just saying, you could try it and still get credit. I've been trying to start a yoga club, but it hasn't gone anywhere, so they let me do it as an afternoon course. The yoga teacher they had forever left last year. Attendance isn't great, but it's better than before."

"Gee, I wonder why they won't let you have a club. Seems like Vegan Club is a rollicking success."

She shoots me an annoyed look. "Good things take time to

build. Besides, yoga is the perfect thing to help with your im-balance."

"Look. I showered. I can take care of the rest of my *imbalance* by myself."

It's ironic that I once would have listed the close companion-ship of dorm life as one of my favorite things about boarding school.

Ha.

CHAPTER ELEVEN

Ever efficient, Ms. Randall already has my file onscreen when I walk into her office. She toggles between my transcript and my schedule. "Sit down, Skylar," she says. "This is a college counseling meeting, so we'll be focusing on that today, not your personal life."

This is easily worse than going to the dentist. If she wasn't warm and fuzzy before, she's positively glacial now. "I assume you've already registered to take the upcoming SATs?"

"Yes, I'm set." I didn't quite bomb the test last year, but my scores are definitely nothing to brag about.

"Did you take another prep course over the summer as we discussed?"

I nod, hoping she can't see through my lie. Not only did I not retake a prep course; I never took one to begin with. Neither a class nor a private tutor was in our budget. I just pretended that I was studying with a tutor, but really I was working with a practice book and doing the exercises and tests on my own.

"Were you able to visit any colleges over the summer?" Ms. Randall asks.

"Um, a few. Stanford, Berkeley—"

"Those are both reach schools," she reminds me flatly, like I wasn't already aware that I'll never get into either of those schools. My parents' faith in me is well-intentioned but shows just how out of touch with my reality they are. "Astronomical reaches."

I gulp and hope my voice doesn't shake when I speak. "I know. We just wanted to cover California schools while I was home for the summer." And we didn't have to pay for plane tickets, which was a plus, even if driving there took over half a day.

Ms. Randall sighs. "While I admire your thoroughness, it's important to keep this process grounded in reality."

"Yes." I know she's right. I even told my parents that visiting those schools was a waste of time. Even though it's a tough contest lately, this might be one of the more agonizing moments of my life. "We also saw UCLA, USC, Occidental, UC Santa Barbara . . ."

She nods grimly. "I suggest you see about arranging on-campus interviews for a few of your safety schools." She goes on to tell me what schools those might be—as it turns out, a pretty unimpressive list. Some of them I've never even heard of, certainly none that justify the tuition bill my parents have been paying here. I fan myself with the paper in my hands, suddenly hot with guilt and shame.

"As we've discussed many times, attending a school like Winthrop is no longer a guarantee of admission to top universities.

Students don't realize that it's sometimes smarter to stay at their local school and stand out than to come here and be average." Ms. Randall looks almost mad at me as she lets her point hit home. I want to shrivel up and die in her tweed-upholstered guest chair. "I see extracurricular activities are still limited to the Social Calendar. It isn't a lot to build on, but at least you've taken on a leadership position this year."

Even though I'm furious with her right now, I silently thank Whit for appointing me VP. I'd tried out countless other activities, but nothing stuck.

"How are you finding your classes? Can I expect at least B's in all of them?" Ms. Randall asks.

Uh. I wonder if this is my opening to brag about being on top of my reading. "Yes."

"Maybe some As?"

"Maybe," I squeak. I can count on one hand the number of A's I've gotten since I started here.

My lack of conviction irritates Ms. Randall. She takes off her glasses and rubs her eyes. A gesture of defeat, even though it's only ten a.m. "Skylar, I'm going to tell you what I've told you since day one: get involved. Late is better than never, I promise you. I don't know what's kept you from trying. Despite the best efforts of myself, the faculty, and your house counselors, you've never fully embraced the opportunity you have here."

I'm doing my best to look her in the eye, but it's not easy when someone's eviscerating you. There's no way I'm going to admit to her that I felt paralyzingly stressed-out by the deadlines when I tried working on the *Winthrop Times,* or that I got fired after two weeks of hosting my own show on the student radio station, or that I was told by a senior that I had no eye when I tried photography as a first-year. "I just . . . haven't found my passion yet."

Ms. Randall leans forward, arms crossed, resting both elbows on her desk. "Well. One has to look for one's passion. It's not going to come up and smack you on the head." She pulls up her calendar, and we schedule another appointment. "Within the next week I'd like an email update about which colleges you'd like to speak with. I'll need to approve your list. You might not get all the interviews you want, but adding any kind of positive to your application package is worth a try."

"Don't you think I could apply to some smaller East Coast schools that might not get many applicants from California? What do they call that . . . geographical diversity?" I ask. I must have an advantage somewhere.

She snorts. "Being from Los Angeles might have made you somewhat unique here, but it doesn't make you interesting to the real world."

Yikes. And that's the last thing I'm going to say today.

"Your word for our next meeting is *confront*." Just like last time, Ms. Randall offers no explanation for her word choice.

I can't get out of here fast enough.

Outside Parsons I actually have to sit on the steps to recover. Being forced to listen to an itemized list of all my shortcomings and failures, which I usually try not to think about, is a special kind of torture. If she wasn't so well loved by the administration and the trustees, Ms. Randall could have a very promising career as an interrogator at Guantánamo. Maybe she reserves her extra special powers for seniors, because she's broken me down before, but it has never been this bad.

The thing I'd never explain to Ms. Randall or anyone else is that when I got to Winthrop, I could tell immediately that I was outclassed. We're told it's a fresh start for everyone, because we all start ninth grade together and most of us have never met anyone else in the school.

Well, the truth is, you don't get to leave who you are behind. And while my friends might be wealthy and spoiled, they're also sophisticated and intellectual. They tried to hide it, but I could tell they were surprised when I said the only place I'd been internationally was Cabo.

Their time and activities have been curated at a whole different level, one that goes way beyond just regular privilege. And they all carry themselves with some mysteriously unshakable confidence, like they already know they're going to rule the world one day.

I'll never forget my first Opening Convocation. Ms. Allen, our head of school, gave a speech in which she said, "Look to your left. Now look to your right." We all did as she instructed, then she continued, "One of those two people won't be here at graduation."

Nervous laughter shot through the room, but from that moment on, I was terrified that I would be one of the people who wouldn't make it.

Over time, though I've managed to hang on, it became obvious that, other than strong middle school grades and good recommendation letters, I really didn't have much of a resume. All I had to offer was movie magic. For a while, at least, that seemed like enough.

CHAPTER TWELVE

Wednesday is the first all-school meeting of the year. The entire student body and all of the faculty gather to hear announcements and speeches. We stand shoulder to shoulder, moving inches at a time as we try to squeeze our way into the chapel. There's no room to maneuver, so I have no choice but to file into a pew with my dorm mates.

After more people get seated, Whitney and the others breeze right by without noticing me. My dorm mates all turn toward me to gauge my reaction. I give none. Maybe they were expecting me to hurtle over people to join the Lincoln girls.

Ms. Allen gives the usual welcoming address, wishing us a successful year with new discoveries and challenges. I think I have the challenge part covered.

Then comes the part I've been dreading. Ms. Allen invites all fall varsity team members to join her and start the school spirit portion of the meeting. Players from the various sports leave the pews to take their places in front of the school. While the rest of the school stamp their feet, clap, and hoot, my eyes automatically search out Leo.

He's front and center. His hands are shoved into his pockets in a reserved stance, but his smile is wide and sincere. I watch him get elbowed and patted by his teammates and think that he looks happy. Complete. Unlike me, who's walking around with a huge, gaping hole, not just in my heart but in my entire self.

The frenzy around me reaches fever pitch, but it's like I'm seeing it through a tunnel. People jump and wave their arms, but their movements feel draggy, slow motion. The sound fades out too. I can't rip my eyes away from Leo. Eventually, his gaze lands on me, and I want, more than anything, to not be staring at him. His smile falters, and I recognize the look on his face as sorrow.

Someone nudges me in the side. Jess is mouthing words that I can't make out, but then she gestures toward the aisle. She looks frantic, swiveling her head between me and our other dorm mates, her red ponytail swinging from side to side.

When I don't move, she yanks me by the elbow, then steers me out of the chapel and over to a secluded, grassy area on the side. She lowers me to the ground, where I'm focusing on her ever-present running shoes, when a pair of nonleather Birkenstocks joins us. I stand up, but the sound in my world is still muted, so I see their lips moving but don't hear them until my hearing returns in a sudden rush.

"What?" I yell, then slap a hand over my mouth. "Why are we out here?" I ask at a normal volume.

"Because I can recognize a panic attack about to happen," Jess says. "You locked in on Leo and then basically stopped breathing."

I bury my face in my hands. "Oh god, did it look weird?"

"It was only obvious because everyone else was going nuts," Opal says. I can still hear everyone cheering inside the chapel.

"Well, thanks, but dragging me out here wasn't exactly subtle. Now everyone probably thinks I'm having a nervous breakdown." I replay the scene in my head just to confirm that, yes, I did indeed look like a head case.

"I thought you could use some air," Jess says, eyes narrowed.

"What I could use is to project an image of having some semblance of control over my life! You just made a scene in front of the entire school. If people thought I was sad before, they probably think I'm suicidal now." I can't help it, I a little bit want to kill these two.

"Because hyperventilating in the middle of an all-school meeting would've been a good look," Jess snaps. "Why do you care so much about appearances, anyway?"

"I just do! I may not have a grip, but at least I can look like I'm keeping it together. The last thing I need, from you or anyone else, is pity!" I'm aware that I sound shrill and ungrateful, but fighting for my space right now feels like a matter of life and death.

Opal's face is blank. "Understood. We'll leave you alone. Come on, Jess." They head in the direction of the Canteen with-

out a backward glance. I sit on the grass until the chapel doors open and everyone floods out, all in a hurry to get somewhere. I watch as they pass me by.

That afternoon I sit through the Calendar meeting in Porter Hall, the history and social sciences building, but I'm there in body only. All ten Executive Committee members, plus Lila, are assembled around a long oval table.

"Second to last thing on the agenda is coverage. Everyone here knows which events they're going to this weekend, yes?" Whit asks. Nods all around. She smiles. "So let's go over the events from last weekend." Uh-oh. "Guthrie, how was the Fantasy Club thing?"

"Good." Guthrie, another senior, is a tall, reed-thin boy with wavy, out-of-control blond hair. "They hosted a Harry Potter–themed lunch. A couple English teachers and some other staff came, but it was mostly students. People had capes and wands. It was dope."

"Thank you for the summary, but was it well attended? Did people seem into it?" Whitney looks at Guthrie expectantly. It's only her first month as president, but she's taking on the job with a zeal that none of her predecessors possessed. Can't say I'm surprised.

"Um, yeah. Maybe like ten people showed—"

"Ten people?"

Guthrie watches in dismay as Whitney scribbles in her notebook. "Or maybe more like fifteen. I'm telling you, it was cool.

They had decorations. We should let them keep doing their thing," he says. Whitney continues to make violent scratching motions with her pen. Judging from Guthrie's forlorn expression, he knows he's been overruled. "They're not hurting anyone," he finishes lamely.

Whitney smiles. "Next! Skylar, how was Classic Movie Night?"

Time to improvise. "Fine! Have to give it to the Film Club, they're consistent and reliable."

She makes a harrumphing sound. "Was it packed?"

"Mmm, same as usual, I would guess." I'm dying for her to move on to the next person.

Lila flits her eyes in my direction. "Actually, I wanted to raise an issue with this event. I know I'm new here, but I found it strange that they were selling concessions when it doesn't mention that anywhere in their application for this year."

"They were?" Whitney whips around to face me. "We specifically turned down that part of their application because there was always so much litter all over the Field the next morning."

"Right, I know," I begin, hoping that some amazing excuse will occur to me. "I guess I just didn't notice."

Lila arches an eyebrow. "Really? All their members were roving around with bags of popcorn and drink bottles on trays. Everyone was eating."

"Well, no one complained about the Field the next day, right? So on the positive side, they must've gotten the message and done a better job cleaning up," I say. "Plus, I know it's expensive to get those old movie imprints, and they're not allowed to

charge admission. Can't blame them for trying to recoup their costs."

Everyone's doodling or shuffling papers, restless and wanting to keep the meeting going. But Whit's lips draw into a thin, tight, stubborn line. "Were you even there, Skylar?"

I sigh. Busted. Yet again. There seems to be no end to my downward spiral. "I'm sorry, no." There's no way I'm going into detail about the depression that had me sleep most of the weekend away. It's a miracle that I've managed to show up for classes this week.

"It's okay. I was there. I can give you the rundown." Wonderful. Lila swoops in to save the day.

"Thank you, Lila. It's nice to see that our newest member is on the ball."

Lila proceeds to give an excessively detailed report about Classic Movie Night, even describing the audience's reaction to *Ghostbusters*. When she's done, even I have to admit that I've been effectively outplayed.

So when Friday night comes, there's no messing around, no depression-fueled excuses to hide in my room. I go straight to my coverage event, which is a play in the black box theater. The black box is a small room that is painted pitch-black from floor to ceiling. The stage and the small set of risers are also painted black. It's meant for intimate, more experimental shows, and though I don't attend many, I can safely say that this show is more experimental than most.

Two boys sit cross-legged on the stage, talking about the most mundane aspects of their lives. They face each other and acknowledge that they can see each other, yet they're both talking on old-timey rotary-dial phones, the kind with the curly cords. Oh, the irony. I get that it's a commentary on how silly our modern attachment to technology is, but still—yawn.

I type notes into my phone as I watch, determined to give Whit the type of granular reporting she seems to crave. We're supposed to minimize our critique of the work itself, so I skip over how it's a total snooze fest. There are exactly six audience members, including myself. The Calendar will not approve.

A guy a few seats away leans over the empty chairs between us to tap my knee. He wears all black and is trying really hard to grow a goatee. "Do you mind?" he whispers, gesturing at my phone. Apparently the glow from the screen is ruining the moody atmosphere we're going for. I put it away and try to commit the rest of my notes to memory.

The play runs almost two hours, and by the middle I'm getting antsy. One of my legs has fallen asleep, and I have to keep jiggling it, much to the annoyance of Mr. Goatee. This is yet another faction of the Winthrop population I don't understand. Who finds this stuff interesting? It's nonsensical pretension at best.

Then I see one of my dorm mates lurking at the side of the stage. The goth one, of course, whose name is Samantha, if I remember correctly. She's tall and big-boned and offsets her all-black wardrobe, clunky boots, and multiple silver ear piercings with femme fatale crimson lipstick. She must be some sort of stage manager/production person, because she watches the show intently, like something might actually happen. It doesn't.

By the end, I'm fascinated about how it is that the two actors have remained cross-legged for this long without losing it. It's a testament to the will to create bad art.

Since it's such a small space, there's no real end to the play. Eventually the actors just stand up and take an awkward bow. We clap, some in a more heartfelt manner than others.

Samantha climbs the risers to where I'm sitting. "What a surprise to see you here," she says.

"I'm here from the Calendar," I say.

"Figures."

I roll my eyes. "Sorry I can't pretend to like bad plays."

She climbs back down without saying anything else. Everyone seems to be staying for some sort of sad cast party, so I make my way to the door and grab a program on my way out. I peruse it quickly to see if I want to make notes on anything and notice that Samantha is actually the playwright. Sigh. My streak of stepping in it continues.

That night everyone in the dorm ignores me. Word about my little outburst after the all-school meeting had already gotten around, and I'm sure Samantha wasted no time bad-mouthing me. Even nice-girl Yasmin has a pinched look when she encounters me in the bathroom. Whatever. If this is what has to happen in order for me to get a little breathing room, I'm not sorry.

CHAPTER THIRTEEN

Whit sprints up to me on my way into the Canteen the next morning. "I was coming to find you," I say.

She looks radiant rather than sweaty in her running clothes. She puts a hand on my shoulder and doubles over, trying to catch her breath. "Lila wants to be VP. We're going to have a vote," she blurts out.

I snort. "Yeah? Why have a vote? Why don't we just give it to her?" I start walking into the building but notice that Whit's not following. "You're joking, right?"

She exhales in a huff. "You kind of forced my hand by not doing your coverage. Lila found some random stipulation in the bylaws about officials being required to do as much coverage as every other member."

"Give me a break. I missed one event—one that has pretty much run itself for years. And you're the one who told me to lie low!"

"I didn't say disappear and become a slacker!" Whitney says. I can't tell if her face is red from running or if she's really angry with me.

"I've been part of the Calendar just as long as you have. I *should* be VP."

"Lila's pretty eager right now, and you're very distracted, which is me putting it nicely. Maybe it's for the best. You can finish dealing with all your stuff."

"No, you don't understand. I need this. Ms. Randall's on my case about my college applications, and this is all I have to put on them." I'm practically begging, but I don't see another option.

"It's up to the rest of the committee. I can't stop the process." Whitney shakes her head—in apology or disgust, I'm not sure which—and walks ahead of me. "You coming?"

"Hell, no." Forcing myself to sit through a meal of superficial pleasantries was already going to be painful. With this new information hanging over my head and knowing that everyone knew about it before me, there's no way I can fake it.

I turn, exit the campus, and walk down Main Street into town, where I head straight for my favorite coffee shop, Perk Up. After hesitating only a moment before buying myself a five-dollar latte, I settle in for what turns out to be a very long session of staring out the window. If anyone from school comes in, I'm too catatonic to notice.

I already know what the outcome of the vote will be. My friends already think I got the VP position strictly because I'm Whit's best friend. Or was. Everyone wants our senior year to be epic, and Lila's already proven that she's willing to be super agro and un-fun about the events. If I'm not power hungry and controlling enough for them, then Lila can have at it.

Senior year should be special, but these events have been done a thousand times. We're confined to the same campus spaces; we still have to rely on the clubs and dorms to bring good ideas. Everyone here is busy, and I personally think Whitney's expectations are unrealistic. Not every event is going to be the best ever.

What it comes down to for me is not having the title for my college apps. It'll definitely affirm Ms. Randall's belief that I'm just taking up space at Winthrop. Also, I won't be able to pretend my friends aren't throwing me under a bus for a newcomer. If I still lived in Lincoln, they'd have to be comfortable with backstabbing me to my face, but since I don't, they don't have to deal with the fact that they're traitors.

As furious as I am with my friends, I'd still rather be with them than with my new dorm mates.

Yasmin spends all her time either crying in front of some horrible romantic drama or in Groton Music Hall practicing her cello in one of the studios, which are the size of a walk-in closet. No wonder she's a little off.

Jess is attached to her computer and always spouting off about various conspiracy theories. I endured a lengthy conversation between her and Opal about how the government is trying to poison us through the food supply.

Bettina, who might be mute, favors peasant blouses and denim skirts or else overalls, and pins her hair up into high topknots, disappears for long periods of time, and comes back covered in all kinds of gross and colorful substances.

Raksmey bops around in giant headphones, dancing to music no one can hear (or stand) but her.

And Samantha shoots me hate glares whenever she sees me, then wanders off with a notebook and pen in hand, probably to go write another horrific play.

Definitely not a lot to get excited about around here.

But what starts off as welcome solitude quickly turns into feeling like I'm being systematically frozen out. I try not to care, but so soon after Leo's rejection and my old friends' indifference, it feels surprisingly personal.

"We all tried to be nice, but you weren't receptive to it, so we're just honoring the wishes you made so clear," Opal says when I try talking to her.

"Oh my god, can I live? Am I supposed to feel guilty because I'm in a bad place?" I ask.

"Why are you upset because we're giving you what you want?" Opal asks.

"Because. You're doing it with such attitude," I say.

Opal tilts her head and gives me a flat look. "Really? If I tell everyone they need to tone down the attitude, you really think that's going to make you more popular?"

Ugh, she so didn't get it. "I don't want to be popular here. I like being left alone but just not so aggressively."

She shakes her head and leaves the room.

. . .

The next Social Calendar meeting is a full meeting, meaning that all fifty members are present. There's a representative from each dorm, plus the Executive Committee. Samantha's here from Abbot, bored out of her mind, still giving me death looks. There is a vote for VP, just as Whitney had warned me. At least she has the decency to avoid eye contact with me as she reads out the results. Three out of four people have voted for Lila.

I am completely embarrassed, but before I slink off, I confront Whit. "I have no reason to be part of the Calendar if I'm not going to be on the Executive Committee," I say.

She sighs. "You're determined to self-destruct. Don't expect me to stop you."

Okay, this was not the response I was expecting. *Why not?* I want to ask. Why isn't she fighting me on this and trying to convince me to stay? "Just so you know, if you're so worried about Lila taking over, letting her snake VP from me probably wasn't smart."

"If she brings hard work and good ideas to the committee, it'll make us all look good," Whitney says.

"She knows nothing about this school or the people in it. Besides, it's my position. She already has my room, what's next?" I don't add that she's already taken my best friend. "Why did she stop at VP? Why didn't she just go for president?"

Whitney glares at me. "You brought this on yourself, Skylar. If you'd just done what I told you to do, this wouldn't have happened."

When I get back to my room, I'm so distraught that I'm about to do something I've been so determined not to do. I reach for my phone, pull up Leo's number, and stare at it for a long minute. "What are you doing?" Jess asks. She's in the room studying with Opal on the floor. Seems she's bought into the whole "chairs are bad for you" notion.

"Nothing," I say, still staring at my phone.

"Yes," she says, standing up. "You're about to send Leo a regrettable text."

"No, I'm not." I put the phone down and glare at her.

"I know that look. Don't do it," Jess says.

"If she wants to do something stupid, let her," Opal says.

Ugh. I'm so over fighting with everyone. "Exactly. You do you and I'll do me. Just because we're living together does not mean we're insta-friends. Especially since I didn't even choose to move here."

Opal and Jess both look at me dispassionately. "What some people perceive as butting in, other people think of as caring," Opal finally says. "But take all the time you need."

"I don't get it," I say. "Why *would* you care? I'm here for a year. We would've graduated without ever having said a word to each other if I hadn't been assigned to this dorm."

"True," Jess says. "But you're here now."

I'm tempted to scream into my pillow. I look at my phone, which now sits at the end of my bed. But I don't let myself pick it up.

CHAPTER FOURTEEN

Insomnia takes over my life and makes me even less functional than when I was just sad. Although I spend hours sitting at my desk with my books open, my work slides, making my promise of getting all B's seem like a fading possibility.

I'm dragging to get ready for aerobics while Opal changes out of her salwar kameez (I've been imperiously informed that this is the correct name for her caftans and matching pants) and into spandex Lululemon workout clothes. I can hardly believe what I'm seeing.

"Why do you look like that?" I sputter, waving at her perfectly toned, amazing body.

"Like what?" Opal glances down at her six-pack abs and muscular ballerina legs. Even her arms, while rail thin, are defined and strong.

"Oh, you know, like a freaking swimsuit model?"

Opal smiles shyly. "Yoga and a vegan diet. It works."

"If you have all that"—I can't stop pointing and staring— "why in the world would you hide it under those baggy clothes? I mean, do you know what would happen to your social life if you showed it off even a little?" I have so many questions.

"I'm totally happy with my social life the way it is," she says.

"Have you ever even been on a date?" I ask.

She frowns at me. "Do you want to come or not?"

I finish getting dressed and walk with her to the gym. I may be depressed, but I'm not an idiot.

By the time we're done, I'm sweating like mad. Somehow, even though my arms and legs feel like overcooked noodles and I never realized before how unbendy I am, I feel fantastic. Kind of light and clear, like I've been running a really high fever and it's just broken. Aerobics never made me feel this way.

"Next time I'm going to have to bring a towel," I say on our way back to Abbot.

"Next time? You mean you're going to grace us with your presence again?" Opal sounds snippy, but she's smiling. "I told you, it's better than Zoloft."

"You know, you're going about it all wrong. If you want to start a club, I can probably help you," I say.

"Really? Student Council said I need at least ten members for a charter. I've tried a million different things—"

"Leave it to me." What people don't realize is that the most obvious solutions are usually the best ones.

• • •

Parents' Weekend sneaks up on me this year. None of my friends' parents came last year, so I'd assumed it would be just another regular weekend for most of us seniors. But it turns out a lot of people are feeling nostalgic and want a chance to visit campus one more time before their little darlings graduate high school.

All my dorm mates disappear with their families for things like the Head of School's Coffee, a performance by the a cappella group the Of Notes, or meals at expensive restaurants in Boston. Everywhere I go I'm surrounded by grinning parents dressed in sports coats and loafers, wrap dresses and slingbacks.

This is one of the few weekends when the library is guaranteed to be empty. Since the silence of my dorm is driving me a little batty and the risk of running into Leo is low, I pack up my laptop and walk over there.

When I turn onto the path that runs between the Field and Main Street, I spot Whitney getting into a town car with her parents and sister. And Lila. She never mentioned that her family was coming. I don't realize I'm staring until Whitney happens to glance in my direction. We make eye contact, and she gives me a small wave.

Every other year, she would've insisted I go with them. The Lamberts always invited me to tag along when they came for a visit. One time my parents even gave permission for me to spend a weekend in Boston with them. We went to a Celtics game and had dinner at a fancy French restaurant called L'Espalier.

I wonder if any of them has asked about me or is curious about where I am. But they don't notice me. I struggle to keep my face neutral as I wave back and watch them drive away.

· · ·

"How'd it go?" I ask Opal when she gets back from her first Yoga Connection class. She's glowing, grinning from ear to ear.

"It was great! The roster's almost full. A lot of boys came."

"Really? Like who?" I ask, although I'm really not surprised. After a lot of cajoling, I finally got Opal to pose for the club photo in her Lululemon gear. But she still balked when I showed her the flyer with a picture of her sick body and the headline that read SAY HELLO TO YOUR FUTURE.

"Believe it or not, it seemed like a lot of jocks," she says, tilting her head. "They were all pretty coordinated and in good shape. Not flexible, though. Maybe you should switch to the morning."

Her meaning doesn't slip by unnoticed, but I ignore it. "No way. Then I'd still have to do aerobics. But I'll come sometimes." No part of me even wants to think about another boy, let alone put myself in a situation where I'd potentially have to hang out with one. That's the problem with having a perfect boyfriend: everyone else pales in comparison.

"Why did we cap membership at twenty-five? I can teach way more people than that."

"Exclusivity is very enticing. When people are knocking down our doors, we can open up to new members." I'm actually getting excited about this. This is how I imagine it feels to start a new dance club or the latest exercise trend in Hollywood.

Opal gives me an appraising look. "Thank you. I've been trying to start this thing for the last three years. It never occurred to me that I should try a more basic route."

"Like I said, sex sells." She rolls her eyes. "The key is to get them in the door. Then you'll have a captive audience for all your nonsense."

"How long do you think until I can spring chanting and veganism on them?" she asks, all excited.

Um, never? "At least a couple of months, probably," I say. No need to burst her bubble while she's enjoying this victory.

"Marshall couldn't believe this came together so fast," she says, referring to the school president, which is Winthrop's version of student body president. "I've put in the application so many times before, he was sure it was going to be another vain attempt."

"Well, you showed him," I say. Marshall's well liked by everyone, but in my personal opinion he can be a teensy bit affected.

Opal heads off to take a shower, humming along the way. I finish getting dressed and realize that, for the first time in weeks, I feel almost okay. Maybe Opal's right about yoga.

CHAPTER FIFTEEN

I realize too late that it's Club Raks night. As I stand in the dorm foyer, trying to figure out a plan B, Bettina comes downstairs wearing a grimace and carrying a giant tote bag. Of all my dorm mates, she's the one I've had the least interaction with. She's not all in my face like the others; she kind of just fades in and out, like a cartoon ghost.

"Hi, Bettina," I say. "Cute overalls."

Usually she blows off my comments, responding only with a smile or a perplexed look. "If you need an escape, you can come work in the art studio with me," she says. "It's quiet."

I'm trying to figure out why she's suddenly inviting me somewhere when she says, "What you did for Opal made her so happy." We don't say another word as we walk to Albright.

I haven't set foot in the art building since first year, when I took Visual Studies, the art survey requirement. It has a famous art gallery attached to it that I've never visited. The head of school uses it to host lavish fund-raising parties, so it's closed a lot of the time. Leo tried to take me there early in our dating life, before he realized that when it comes to art, my taste runs more toward pop than fine.

Bettina leads the way to the studio, a brightly lit room with white walls and large white tables with high stools around them. There are colorful splatters of dried paint on the floor and table-tops, and drying racks along the wall.

There's a boy here, wearing headphones and drawing. He looks up when we come in and gives Bettina a warm smile, but his gaze only skims over me before it returns to his paper. I don't know why I feel so offended that this angsty art boy, with his band T-shirt, hoodie, and black Vans, basically dismissed me. Because if he's who I think he is, he was involved in a big drinking scandal sophomore year and therefore probably has issues.

I shake my head and take out my laptop. *Focus. I will now attempt to write a paper on Frankenstein.*

"Film class," he says.

"Excuse me?"

"We're in Dr. Fan's film class together. That's how we know each other," he says, still not looking up.

For some reason this irritates me. Maybe he assumes that getting busted makes him interesting, but my curiosity is mild at best. And besides, I'm positive that it took place in the privacy of my own head. "Oh. Nice to meet you," I say from under the table as I plug in my laptop.

Fortunately, the grating small talk ends there. The next time I look up, I actually have a decent outline for my paper written.

Bettina's been busy too. A dozen white plastic grocery bags have been stretched flat on the table in front of her. She's bending plastic drinking straws into loops and securing them with clear tape. "What are you making?" I ask.

She blinks, as if she's just coming out of some kind of trance. "Hot-air balloons."

"Really? That's so cool! What are you going to do with them?" I catch art boy smiling at his paper, his headphones now slung around his neck. "Is something funny?" I ask.

He shakes his head. "Just happy that Bettina has another fan." He flashes me a mocking grin, pushing his wavy brown hair off his forehead.

"I'm planning an installation where I launch them all at the same time," Bettina says. I must look confused, because she adds, "And record it."

"But how will you get them back?" I lean over the table to look at the bags. She's painted little skulls adorned with floral vines. They're cool but creepy looking.

"I might not be able to," she admits.

"So all this time and effort and it'll just be gone in an hour? What's the point?" Seems like a waste if you ask me.

"It'll be beautiful," Bettina says, like a short burst of beauty could be the point of what appears to be a ton of work. "What are you working on, D?"

"I'm having a show later this term," the boy says.

"That's huge," Bettina says.

"It'll look good on my art school apps." He turns his attention to me. "What about you?"

"Me?" I ask.

He looks around. There's no one else in the studio. "Yeah. What's your story?"

"Uh, I'm not an artist, if that's what you're asking. I just have a paper due tomorrow and needed a quiet space," I say.

After studying me for a minute, he says, "Well, if Bettina brought you here, you must be all right." Bettina shoots him a wry smile.

Are arty people usually this standoffish? My lack of experience in this arena throws me a bit.

We resume working. A couple hours later Bettina and I walk back to the dorm. "That was Declan," she says, like it matters.

"Yeah? He seems quite fond of you."

She raises her eyebrows. "But not like that."

"Is he the kid who got busted sophomore year?"

"Yes." But she doesn't offer any other information.

Now that I don't have to go to Social Calendar meetings, I feel unexpectedly free. Sure, there's kind of a phantom limb–type pain, but it's offset by the fact that I won't have to cover any boring events on the weekends.

Everyone is already seated in the common room by the time I get to the dorm meeting. Dr. Murdoch goes over house rules and the schedule for dorm duty, which consists of cleaning chores. My first assignment is vacuuming, which isn't as bad as, say, cleaning the bathrooms.

"Now that we've covered that, we need to come up with ideas for our first Social Calendar event," Dr. Murdoch says. "Abbot House is on the schedule for the week of October fifth."

Well, nothing like waiting until the last minute to plan. Looking around the room, I can tell that no one really wants to deal with this. Abbot is notoriously lame with its events, and erasing this stigma would require divine intervention. This ought to be a raging success.

"How about afternoon tea?" Yasmin eventually volunteers. "You know, a traditional English one, with scones and finger sandwiches?"

"Okay, we don't live in a Jane Austen novel," Samantha says. I'm just glad someone else said it. "Why don't we start a book club where everyone reads books written by faculty members? Then we don't have to reinvent the wheel every time it's our turn to do something."

"Um, 'cause we don't want to bore everyone to death?" I say. "No offense, Dr. Murdoch."

"None taken," she whispers. "Although I do have a book on ancient Greece coming out next month."

We all let that pass without comment.

"How about a weekend-long Ultimate Frisbee tournament?" Jess says.

An hour later the suggestions have gone so far downhill that Yasmin's English tea idea actually starts to sound good. The plan is to take over the Study on Friday afternoon and offer everyone refreshments and a chance to socialize. Whatever, it's their funeral. I don't plan to attend, much less help out with it.

Opal clears her throat. "One more item on the subject of the

Social Calendar." For some reason everyone's looking at me. "As you know, each dorm has to send a representative to present the dorm's proposed events. For the past couple years it's been Samantha, but this year we'd like to make a change. I hereby nominate Skylar to be the Abbot House rep. All in favor, raise your hands."

All six hands go up. Samantha looks elated, and I realize too late that I've been ambushed. How did I not see this coming? "I don't think this is such a smart idea. I'm not on great terms with the Calendar at the moment, and I don't think my presence will increase support for our events. In fact, my association might even have a negative impact," I say.

Opal and Jess look at each other. "Nice try," Jess says. "Whenever we have to come up with something or turn in a proposal, we're a disaster. You're obviously the most familiar with that world, so it will save us all a lot of time and agonizing if you could just shortcut it for us."

"Look, the Calendar doesn't rely on our events to be big draws," Opal says. "We just want to get through it unscathed. Getting any kind of turnout is hard, and we know that no one thinks Abbot is a hottie dorm or anything." Seriously? A hottie dorm?

I look around the room and recognize that I really am the only candidate for this job. They're all blinking at me, just so incredibly lost. Maybe I can at least facilitate the process. It seems like expectations are realistically low enough. "Fine," I mutter.

Everyone jumps off the couches, ecstatic. Even Dr. Murdoch. For me, there actually is an upside, which is knowing how much this will get under Whitney's skin. She might be able to turn all our friends against me, but she's not rid of me yet.

CHAPTER SIXTEEN

"I thought you quit," Whitney says when I show up at the next Calendar meeting.

"My dorm needed a rep, and I agreed to step up," I say.

"For once," she mutters.

"Uh, okay," Lila says, stifling a laugh. I ignore her.

"We've been waiting on your paperwork forever. What's the holdup?" Whitney asks. She thrusts her hand out, and I give her our application with a sweet smile.

Lila grabs the proposal from her and peruses it with a scowl. She reads the important parts out loud.

"So you're actually going to close down the Study?" Elizabeth asks.

"Obviously anyone can come in, and instead of making them pay for food, we'll provide it." Now that I think about it, there is an aspect of this that's genius. There's built-in attendance from those people who'd go there after class on Fridays anyway.

"But it's going to be themed?" Olivia asks.

I nod. "Traditional English tea. Everyone will still get their caffeine and sweets but also be able to try some other stuff."

"Okay, fine, approved," Whitney says, waving her hand. That's easily the fastest that any Abbot event has been green-lit.

"So you're no longer in a leadership position with the Social Calendar," Ms. Randall says when I'm back in her office.

"I am, just in a *different* leadership position." I try to keep the defensive tone out of my voice.

"A *lesser* leadership position," she says, glaring at me. "How did this happen?"

"It's a long story. But honestly, Abbot needs me. No one there knows how to navigate this part of campus life. I feel like I'm leading them out of the social dark ages." As I say this I realize that it's true. Abbot does need me. I know better than most that the Calendar's ways aren't always the most straightforward. I actually feel like I'm doing a good deed.

Ms. Randall, however, is unmoved by my new charitable streak. "That was the one noteworthy item on your applications."

You don't have to tell me.

She looks over the list of colleges where I'm thinking of applying. "You were supposed to do some soul searching and narrow this down. This is still a rather scattershot list. Going by this, I can't tell if you want a large or small school, urban or rural setting, what types of programs you might be interested in." She looks at me, the disappointment written plainly on her face.

"I—I actually worked very hard on this. I don't know the answers to some of those questions, so I thought I'd apply broadly in hopes that I would figure it out by the time acceptances come in." After hearing how flaky (and maybe optimistic) that sounds, I gulp and hope that she lets it go.

Ms. Randall sighs. "Another thing colleges look for is desire. If you can't even show or explain why you want them, they're unlikely to want you."

I nod, frantically, nonsensically. I can't handle another session of character pummeling at the hands of this woman. Just can't. Might literally die if I have to. She looks at me for a long moment. "When I said 'confront,' I meant that you need to confront the reality of your situation. You've made certain choices over your time here, and only you know why you made them. All of that, all of those decisions, have led you to where you are now. That's what *confront* means. That's not something I can help you with."

"I am trying. To figure it out."

She sighs again. "That's a start. While you're figuring it out, we need to work on this list. You have to make some more choices. Just basic ones, like where you might want to live for the next four years. Nothing dramatic. Can you deal with that?"

I nod again, less crazily this time.

"And how is your SAT prep going?" She glances at her monitor. "Okay, given your math and science grades, you're not a likely candidate for the ACT. SATs it is. Well?"

"I've been studying," I say. If cracking open the practice book counts as studying.

"Fine. Then your word for this time is *creativity*. As in, we're going to need some for your applications." Ms. Randall smirks. She just can't help herself.

When I get back to Abbot that night, I want to scream as soon as I hear the sounds of heavy bass reverberating through the floors. It's Club Raks night. Bettina's heading out the door.

"Studio?" she asks. I've sought refuge there a couple times. For some reason, her silent presence makes getting work done easier. Plus the bright lights of the studio force me to stay awake. And since I'm still tossing and turning most nights, I need all the help I can get. But tonight I'm too tired to walk all the way back to campus.

"Next time for sure," I say.

Bettina gives a wry half smile. "Declan's going to be dis-appointed."

I roll my eyes at her attempt at humor. Declan's been at the studio every time I've gone there with Bettina, and one time he sat next to me in Images of Women, but otherwise he barely acknowledges me.

My internal organs rearrange themselves with every thump of the music. Everyone caters to Raksmey's need to hold a dance party for one each week, but I'm hoping I can get her to turn it down just a little. When I open the door to the basement, the spike in volume is an assault. I venture down with my hands over my ears.

Since my last foray down here, Raksmey has hung multiple strands of fairy lights from the ceiling so that they crisscross and arc down into the space. She beams when she sees me, then grabs my wrists and drags me down the final few steps. I stand there, horrified, while she hangs on to me and continues to jump and wriggle around. But then a song I actually recognize comes on. Jordana and I danced to it back in middle school, but it's been remixed, with samples and a much more aggressive beat. It sounds so good that I start bobbing my head.

"Yeah! I can't believe it!" Raksmey shouts. "All it took was some old-school music!"

For the next forty-five minutes, I whirl around the darkened basement with an insane junior. When it's almost time for lights-out, I'm drenched, my heart's pounding, and my limbs feel gangly from all the flailing.

"Welcome to Club Raks," she says when she turns off the music. "Never would've pegged you for a dubstep fan."

"Oh my god, that was ridiculously fun," I say. "Am I the first person to come down here?"

"Yep. In two and a half years, no one has been brave enough. Maybe I have to get some ecstasy."

I laugh and hope she's joking.

We unplug the lights and walk up the steps. Raksmey hip-checks me as a way of saying good night, and I stumble into my room, only to be confronted by a giant greenish-gray cricket on the floor. Seriously, the thing is as long as one of my fingers. I barely notice when Opal walks into the room, toweling off her freshly washed hair. "What are you looking at?" she asks, coming up behind me.

"Possibly the ugliest thing I've ever laid eyes on."

She peers at the cricket. "Oh please. Clearly you've never been to India. I've seen cockroaches twice as big as that guy . . ." She continues to prattle on while I work up the courage to stomp on the cricket. If I miss and it flies or hops away somewhere where I can't reach it, I will lose it. I raise my foot so that it hovers over it. "Wait! You can't kill it!" Opal shrieks, hurrying back over.

"You have a better idea?" I ask.

"Set him free! Practice ahimsa, which means 'Do no harm.'"

"I am not touching that thing."

But I don't have to worry, because Opal scoops it up in her bare hands, as if it's a delicate flower or an injured butterfly. Actually I probably wouldn't touch that either. She sweeps out of the room in her bathrobe, thunks down the stairs, and opens the front door. "Be free, little guy!" she calls.

Yeah. Not sure how long she'll be able to keep the charade of normalcy going with her new club members. But if letting her weird out makes her happy, who am I to stop her?

CHAPTER SEVENTEEN

The Canteen's kitchen is like a medieval torture chamber, all clanking metal, suffocating steam, and shattering glass. Everyone has after-dinner kitchen duty two weeks per year, and this is one of my lucky weeks. It's not hard so much as gross.

The key is to show up early so you have a choice of either feeding the giant industrial dishwasher, which involves scraping plates and putting silverware that has been in people's mouths onto a conveyor belt, or working on the other side to remove washed items, where there's a real possibility of getting scalded. Given my choice, I'm all for risking a little third-degree burn. The sight of all that mangled, commingled food makes me gag.

But of course, I'm five minutes late. I walk into the kitchen at the exact same time as a boy I only vaguely know as one of a handful of students from mainland China. He smirks at me and says, "Race ya!" Even though I roll my eyes at his childishness, I pick up my pace. He reaches the dishwasher ahead of me and exclaims, "Dag! That's cold!"

Apparently both drying spots are already taken. I look at the bin of dirty dishes in front of me. It was a mashed potato night. Extra disgusting. I take a deep breath, prepare to hold it for the next hour, and slip on an apron.

The boy has disappeared to the drying side, whining at someone I can't see. "Come on! You owe me!"

If he thinks I'm doing this by myself while he negotiates, he's sadly mistaken. I round the corner, ready to drag him back by the ear if necessary, but stop when I'm confronted with Lila's cool stare. My first instinct is to turn right back around, but I force myself to stand my ground. "Someone is coming to load with me."

Lila snorts. "I know you don't think it's going to be me."

"Skylar, you can come over here. C.J. and I will load," someone else says.

I turn to see Declan handing off a rack of clean glasses to one of the uniformed kitchen staff.

"What? Don't volunteer me for shit. If you're giving up your spot, I'm taking it," says the boy, who I'm guessing is C.J.

"Don't be a jerk," Declan says. "Let her dry."

"Sure! Maybe Skylar can entertain me with some tales about the movie biz," Lila says, twirling her hair. She hasn't lifted a finger since I've been standing here.

"Get to work!" Martin, the head chef, snaps his meaty fingers at us. "I'm not above keeping you late, and I'm sure you all have study groups to get to."

"Some other time," I mutter at Lila before returning to the other side.

Declan joins me a moment later. He watches me jam my hands into rubber gloves and start haphazardly throwing plates onto the conveyor belt. "You know, I was offering to be polite, not to ruin your life," he says.

"I know that," I say through gritted teeth.

He stands there, observing me as I continue doing a barely passable job. "Ah. That explains why you're in such a rage."

"I'm not— Look, it's not you. Sorry. She just gets under my skin." I slow down and try to summon some rationality. "But thank you. For trying to be nice."

"You're welcome."

We settle into a routine, with Declan doing most of the scraping and me dumping out the drinks and organizing items for the machine. But what starts off as comfortable becomes monotonous.

Someone on the other side pushes the emergency stop button, which holds us up for a few minutes. How hard is it to unload a dishwasher? My money's on Lila being the button pusher, although, to be fair, C.J. didn't seem too well acquainted with menial labor either.

Declan and I just stand there, gloved hands raised, waiting.

"So. How's the drawing coming?" I finally ask.

Declan snorts. "It's up and down. Thanks."

I guess he doesn't want to talk art with me. Fair enough. "What did you think of *Grease*?"

"Basically unwatchable, but I'm not sure movies have gotten that much better."

"Seriously? You know it's a classic, right?" The machine starts up again, followed immediately by a shriek. Declan and I both shake our heads.

"I am aware," he says.

"What didn't you like about it?"

"Um, that the girl had to change everything about herself to get the boy."

Okay, that was not the answer I was expecting. We still haven't discussed it in class, but after the screening a few of the other boys cited corniness as their number one objection to the movie.

"Well, he changed for her too. He went out for all those sports. What did you think about that?"

Declan smirks. "Right. And as we all know, cute girls have a thing for jocks."

I doubt he's referring to me but feel myself reddening anyway. I fumble for a subject change. "So where do you live?" I ask. The dishwasher grinds to a halt again.

"Come on! Are you serious over there?" Declan yells. He turns back to me. "Thatcher."

"Really?" I scrunch my nose, trying to picture it. He's not exactly what I imagine when I think of Thatcher Hall guys. Not that I ever think about them much. He's quirky and fairly thin, so, I would guess, falls on the less athletic end of the spectrum, but he doesn't fit the awkward/spastic profile that the dorm is known for.

When the conveyor belt doesn't start moving, Declan stalks over to the other side. "It's not that hard, you guys," I hear him say. "We send the dishes through, you pick them up and stack them."

Lila utters some indignant-sounding reply. C.J. just laughs.

The motor whirs, and with a jerk the dishes resume their journey. Declan comes back. "She's a treat," he grumbles. "So, yeah. You were expecting something more . . . what?"

"Huh?"

"Thatcher."

"Oh, I don't know. Nothing, I guess."

He smirks. "You seem to have a lot of questions for me all of a sudden." He glances at the clock on the wall. "Unfortunately, I have to go. Maybe we can pick this inquisition up at the studio next time."

He holds out his hand for my apron, which I slip off and hand to him.

I'm still standing there, doing I don't know what, when Lila and C.J. pass by on their way out. C.J. flashes me a peace sign, but Lila stops, her hair frizzed up and mascara running. This is the most unattractive I've ever seen her look. Being swindled out of drying continues to yield pleasant surprises. Still, I wish I'd had the good sense to get out of here quicker.

"I am going to kill Whitney," she says. Before I can even think of a question to ask, she forges on. "She never even mentioned that I'd have to work at this god-awful place. When people first talked about Canteen duty, I assumed it was voluntary."

This girl takes diva to a new level. "It's only for two weeks a year—"

"*Two weeks?*" Lila's mouth hangs open in horror. "You mean

I'm not done after this? And dorm duty on top of that? Who does this to *children*? It's as if they don't realize that we pay tuition to go here." Her eyes travel over me, and somehow, even without her saying it, I know she's thinking that some of us don't actually pay tuition. I suppose the dots wouldn't have been that hard to connect. "This would never fly at my old private school."

I give a small shrug. "What do you want me to say? Sorry." *Not sorry.*

"And this Calendar thing. I mean, sure, it's kind of amusing, but there's no way it's worth me spending a year out of the city for it. And there's practically no datable boys in the entire school!"

I have no idea who or what I have to thank for this massive overshare. "Have you talked to Whit?" I ask, more out of morbid curiosity than genuine concern.

Lila sniffs. "She keeps trying to convince me that it's better than I think and that the best stuff is yet to come. I have never seen someone who has so completely drunk the Kool-Aid."

"I think she genuinely does love it here." For some reason I feel tears pressing behind my eyes as I say this. Thankfully Lila's too self-absorbed to notice anything that subtle.

I get another one of those looks. "Well. Obviously Whit doesn't always have the soundest judgment."

She strides out before I can think of a retort. Or smack her upside the head.

CHAPTER EIGHTEEN

Yasmin has transformed the Study, with its greasy burger smells and beat-up furniture, into a proper English garden party. We blanketed the room in doilies and tablecloths with a muted floral pattern. It doesn't look merely English; it looks Victorian. I marvel over the tiered silver pastry stands and ceramic teapots while I reach for a cucumber finger sandwich. Before I can pick it up, I feel a sharp crack on the back of my hand.

"Are you insane?" Yasmin shrieks. "Those are for the guests!"

"Okay, sheesh!" I say, rubbing the welt on my hand. "We're not allowed to eat at all?"

"Maybe if there are leftovers," she says. I wonder if my Nona Rose would count this as fasting. She knows I don't usually fast for Yom Kippur, which doesn't make her happy, but my dad says I'm already in the doghouse for forgetting to call her on Rosh Hashanah.

Raksmey drags me away before I get slapped again. "You have to understand," she says. "This is a dream come true for Yas."

"Yeah, I've noticed she's a bit obsessed with romance."

"You have no idea. Don't ever tell her you like a boy. She'll plan some elaborate scheme to catch him for you. And that's exactly how she'll phrase it, too. Like he's a fish."

I have to smile at that. Yasmin is hopelessly, embarrassingly naive, but she's also a little bit adorable.

"Okay, people! Showtime!" Yasmin flutters her hands at Opal, who stands by the entrance. Opal throws open the double doors. There's actually a line outside. People push their way in, and I can't believe Yasmin has actually managed this. But then I see that the guests are starting a line by the register so they can order from the Study menu. I walk over to them.

"I'm sorry, but the Study is closed today. You're welcome to stay for tea, though. It's free." I whisper all this as discreetly as I can. Yasmin doesn't need to know that her guests are here by mistake.

One boy looks at his posse, shrugs, and loads up a plate. He lifts the lids to a few teapots, takes a sniff, and replaces them. "Where's the coffee?" he asks.

Yasmin scurries over. "We aren't serving coffee. It's not traditional."

"You can get coffee in the dining rooms," I say quickly. "We'll be happy to hold your plate for you."

The boy takes a small pot of clotted cream and overturns it on his plate. He smears it around with his scone and then pops the whole thing in his mouth. Yasmin cringes in disgust. "Good, but it needs coffee," he says through a mouthful of scone crumbs. He motions to his friends, who've all been testing out the food. They abandon their plates and head for the exit.

Yasmin stacks their dishes with clenched teeth. "Let me take those," Samantha says. She carries them toward the kitchen, but I see her sneak an uneaten pastry off one of the boys' plates. Gross.

I look around. Another group seems to be taking tentative bites out of some finger sandwiches. "Who made the food?" I ask.

"Martin from the Canteen kitchen. Making tea is one of his favorite pastimes," Yasmin says.

"But judging from everyone's faces, he's not very good at it," I venture.

She glares at me. "The food is delicious. These people just don't have refined palates."

"We can't verify one way or the other. You won't let anyone taste the food."

Yasmin ignores me and storms off. I think she's taking this a tad personally.

An hour later the room is still practically empty. Almost everyone who's walked through the doors has stayed less than ten minutes. Yasmin starts greeting people with "Hi. Welcome. There's no coffee." Some don't even bother to sample the food after that.

Sid and Wyatt come in and walk right over to me when they spot me. I feel like I've been busted doing something wrong. "What's up with this?" Sid asks.

"It's an afternoon tea hosted by Abbot House," I say, like tea is an event any teenager would kill to attend.

He gives me a sidelong glance. "Okay." He helps himself to some éclairs and cheese-and-pickle sandwiches. "This shit is disgusting," he says. "How did you get suckered into this?"

I'm highly aware that my dorm mates can overhear everything and that Sid's implication is that I'm somehow above this sad tea. Apparently he hasn't been tracking my downfall like most of the rest of the school has. "I live in Abbot now, and we only had a week to put something together," I say lightly. I can feel Yasmin's glower boring a hole through the back of my head. Maybe I'm supposed to defend this train wreck until the bitter end, like a captain going down with the ship, but I can't bring myself to do it.

I have no idea why these two aren't turning tail and leaving like everyone else. That would make me so happy right now. "If there's no coffee, what do you have?" Wyatt asks. Oh god, they're staying.

"Earl Grey, chamomile, or lavender!" Bettina calls out from the counter. I cringe inwardly. But Wyatt gamely gets himself a pot and a teacup and sits on a couch. Sid seems to have found some kind of tart that he's not mad at.

The realization that I miss these guys hits me suddenly and without warning. My fraternity brothers were a big part of my life. Well, maybe not Sid. I'm about to go over to catch up with them when Leo comes in. We make eye contact for a brief, wholly awkward second. "Hey," he says, and turns his back to me, walking toward Sid and Wyatt.

My facade of calm crumbles. I grab some dirty cups, bring them back to the kitchen, and throw them crashing into the sink. The door swings open, and Opal scurries in. "Okay, everyone heard that. We borrowed these dishes from the Winthrop Society. If we break them, we have to pay for them."

"Sorry, they slipped out of my hands."

She gives me a knowing look. "You have to pull it together. We're not even halfway through the tea."

"This thing is a total joke. I should've figured. Everyone knows English food sucks. I can't believe that Leo, of all people, has to be here to witness my final descent into loserdom."

Her expression hardens. "I'm no expert on guys, but if you don't get out there and act normal, you're going to regret it. Besides, we need everyone out there so it looks busier."

Somehow, even through my haze of despair, I can see that she's right. So I take a deep, cleansing breath as instructed and open the door. As soon as I step out, Leo gets up and comes to the counter with a tentative smile. I struggle to keep my face neutral. "Sorry about that a minute ago," he says. "I was a little caught off guard."

"That's okay." I clear my throat and attempt a smile. "How've you been?"

"Okay. You know, just busy with the team and all the usual stuff. What about you?"

"I'm fine. Took up yoga. Got booted from my position on the Calendar."

"Sorry," he says.

"About which part?" I ask. He laughs, and even though I've missed his laugh so much, it sounds hollow.

"So this is pretty cool," Leo says, looking around at the depressingly empty room. "Something a little different from the usual campus stuff."

"Uh-huh." He's being totally sincere, but it's fairly obvious that English tea is unlikely to become a recurring event.

I wonder if this will be the moment he finally tells me what's going on. I know he wasn't planning to run into me (at least, I don't think he was), but it's been a month, and I've given him all the space a person could possibly need. I haven't even texted him once.

"So you're liking Abbot okay?" he asks. I deflate a little bit.

"Well, it's . . . fine." For some reason I can't stop using that stupid word. "It has its moments."

Leo nods emphatically, like I've said something really revealing. "Awesome. That's so good to hear. Any other updates? College stuff?"

I must be giving him a weird look, because he's starting to look scared. Which is when it dawns on me that he's not going to say anything about him and me.

"Not really," I say. "Ms. Randall's stressing me out, but that was a given."

He snorts and nods again. "No kidding." Seriously, I could be having this exact conversation with someone I just met. But before I can decide whether or not to raise the subject of us, he reaches for my hand and gives it a quick squeeze. "I wish we had more time to catch up. But it seems like things are going okay, and I'm really glad."

Sid and Wyatt are already heading for the door, pausing to wait for Leo. None of them look my way as they exit.

CHAPTER NINETEEN

The slog continues into the next week. I get a 79 on my history test and a B– on my *Wuthering Heights* paper and pull my hamstring. This is a pain that no one should have to suffer through. I blame Opal for pushing me too far in a forward bend, but she insists it's because I have emotional blockages due to not fully expressing myself with Leo.

Despite analyzing it every imaginable way, I don't know what I could possibly do. If Leo's not ready to talk, forcing him would just weird him out. So I'm back to staring at my phone.

One morning after I haven't slept at all, I tag along with Opal to Yoga Connection. It has definitely grown since the first couple meetings. She keeps the studio warm and dimly lit, and due to the early hour, there's almost no talking. Just being in the room feels calming.

I move at a slower pace because of my hamstring, lying flat

on my back, reaching my arms and legs in opposite directions. Someone unrolls a mat next to me. "Hey," he whispers. I lift my head and smile when I see Remy standing there. It's a habitual response; we haven't spoken since the day he ditched me. I turn my head away from him and pretend to watch Opal working with a student.

The style of yoga she teaches is especially active and athletic, so there are a fair number of jock types practicing. Still, I'm surprised that Remy's here. We all go through a set sequence at our own pace while Opal patrols the room and adjusts us. I sneak peeks at his poses, and he looks proficient enough that I'd guess he's been coming for a little while.

An hour later we're finished. I slip out of the studio and am walking toward the girls' locker room when Remy calls, "Wait up, Skylar." He's loud enough that if I ignore him, everyone will know it's deliberate. So I turn around.

"Everything okay?" I ask when I see the worried look on his face.

"Yeah. Just feels weird not to see you much," he says. "We were friends too, you know."

How touching that he remembers. "I guess Leo got you in the divorce. Aren't you worried about what he'll say if we start hanging out?"

His body sags, like he's profoundly disappointed in me. "That's not how he rolls. You know that. Besides, it's not like he wants to start listening to all my girl troubles."

I smile. "Okay, but if we're going to keep being friends, you might actually have to eat with me sometimes."

His cheeks turn pink, but at least he doesn't deny that he blatantly blew me off that time. "You know how it is: the team sits together during the season."

I nod. I do know how it is.

"What happened to you?" Declan asks as I limp to the seat beside him at the next screening for Images of Women in Film. We had bonded a little during the rest of our Canteen-duty week—mostly over a shared dislike of Lila and an annoyance with C.J.'s tendency to slack.

"Yoga injury."

He tilts his head as if he wants to know more, but then the lights go out and opening credits for *Desperately Seeking Susan* start rolling. This is one of my mom's favorite movies. She's almost as passionate about it as she is about *Over It*. Seeing it gives me a sharp pang of not exactly homesickness, more like worry about what's going on back home. My parents call me every week, but we never talk about anything important. I don't feel like it's my job to know about their lives as much as it's their job to know about mine. But they're clearly already maxed out.

Declan's still watching me, so I force back tears and try to act normal.

But when the lights go back on nearly two hours later, he turns toward me. "Did you think it was going to be a sad movie?"

"I've seen it before. Probably at least five times." I close my notebook and put it away.

He nods slowly. "Oh. Then everything okay?"

He's looking at me with so much concern, like he really wants to know, that I almost break down and tell him. Not everything, just about how this particular movie at this particular moment is giving me an unshakable feeling of melancholy. So of course I say, "Yeah. Why wouldn't it be?"

"Okay. If you say so. You coming by the studio after dinner?" he asks.

"Maybe." I haven't even thought that far, but with a calculus test at the end of the week and a paper for this class due on Monday, it probably wouldn't be a bad idea. We stand and pack up our stuff.

"Is there a story behind why you've been working there instead of your dorm or the library?" Declan asks.

"Sorry. Does my non-artiness cramp your style?" I know that's not what he meant, but don't I have a right to be there? "Bettina invited me that one time, and I actually got a lot done." He shrugs and nods. "I've seen you work there on non-art stuff," I say. "Is it because you hate your dorm?"

He gives a surprised half laugh as we walk out of the building. "No. Why would you think that?"

"I don't know. Isn't Thatcher known for having a lot of geeky personalities?" I'm distracted, looking through my bag for my phone. I know Leo probably hasn't decided to suddenly text me, but you never know. Other kids whip past us.

"Thatcher might not be jock central, but that doesn't mean it's lame. They're smart, nice guys. Most people like that kind of thing," he says.

"Well, yeah, but everyone here is pretty smart. Don't you think?"

Declan stops walking. "So what are you trying to say?"

"Huh?" I look up from my bag. "No, nothing. Just that I can relate to not feeling in sync with your dorm. The Abbot girls are nice and smart, like you said, but, like, I don't consider myself one of them."

He stares at me hard enough to make me squirm. "Well, I do consider myself part of Thatcher," he says.

"Okay. Great. That's nice for you." I break eye contact but sense he's still staring at me. "Why are you looking at me like that? You have to admit, Thatcher has a certain . . . flair."

He resumes walking. "I can't figure you out. I know the Webster guys are your friends, but I used to live in that dorm, and I can say firsthand that the Thatcher guys are way more solid."

"I wouldn't exactly say I'm friends with the Webster boys. And I was just repeating a commonly held opinion. It's not like I've given it a ton of thought." I know he lives there, but I think Declan's being overly sensitive about Thatcher.

"Sorry, I just get bummed about misperceptions." He doesn't make an excuse and bolt, but we both go silent. Eventually I make some inane comment about the weather turning colder, but the return to small talk feels stilted and unwelcome.

It's a cowardly response, but I don't know what else to do. I see Opal in the distance, mumble a hurried goodbye, and then rush to catch up with her.

CHAPTER TWENTY

Jess barges into our room while I'm doing some last-minute cramming for my calculus test. "I need to start a documentary screening series," she announces.

"Yeah, good luck with that," I say, flipping through my notebook.

"You have to help me," she says.

"I don't even like watching documentaries. How am I supposed to convince other people to watch them?" I ask.

Jess grins. "I don't know. But if anyone can, it's you."

I groan, but Jess only waves her hand dismissively. "You'll think of something. Opal says you helped her realize her dream of starting a yoga consciousness at Winthrop, and I figure that has to be harder than getting people into documentaries."

"Okay, Opal's nuts. Yoga consciousness—are you kidding me? People just want a hard body and some feel-good stretches.

The minute she tries to introduce chanting or her wacky dragon breathing, the jig is up." I shake my head. It's like no one here understands people.

She plops into the chair in front of me, willfully oblivious to the fact that I'm trying to pass my classes. "There must be some angle we can take."

She clearly isn't going to let this go. "Why don't you start with existing clubs? Ask them if you can show their members a documentary on a subject that would actually be relevant to them. It would have to tie in thematically. Then, when word gets around that you actually show interesting documentaries, you can start your own series and show whatever you want."

"You. Are. A genius!" Jess stares at me wide-eyed before leaping up and kissing me on the cheek. "Oh my god, where should I start? I could show that food one to the Vegan Club!"

"Sure, all four members. Way to think big!"

"What about something on how health care costs are sky-rocketing and bankrupting the average citizen?"

"Who're you going to show that to? Know your audience. Winthrop students are more likely the offspring of pharmaceutical giants, not people who struggle with their co-pay."

Her brow furrows. "Then what's your idea?"

I seriously want to scream. "I don't have an idea! I'm trying to study." Why won't she take no for an answer? "Start broad. Why don't you show a sports-related one to one of the teams?"

She lights up. "I love that! There's a really controversial one on concussions and brain damage. I could show that to the football team."

"Great idea. I'm sure Coach Hewitt will love you for it. The whole team will be skittish and afraid to take a hit. Rally Weekend, not to mention our winning record, will be in the toilet." I raise my eyebrows. Not big on common sense, this one.

"Okay, maybe not that one, but there are plenty of nonscary, inspiring sports ones. So it's still a great idea. I knew I came to the right place!"

It's like I'm talking to myself.

But within the week I see flyers around campus for a showing in the auditorium of a documentary on the Oakland Raiders. At least she managed to pick one that isn't too polarizing or out there. She's listed my name as one of the two founding members of the Documentary Club, and a murderous impulse flashes through my body. She says she got around the ten-initial-member rule by saying that we won't require a set space and time until we reach it. Even though I feel a bit railroaded, I am impressed that she got this off the ground so quickly.

The Calendar meeting is already in progress by the time I arrive. I've been summoned here, presumably to get reamed for Abbot's tea.

"The Halloween Masquerade Ball is approaching fast, and we need to plan some events around it for the people who are antisocial and don't want to get dressed up," Whit says.

"We need people to step up," Lila says. Everyone groans. People only like to work on the big stuff.

What the hell? I'm fairly certain that none of the Abbot girls have ever set foot in one of the big school dances, and I'm clearly not in the right frame of mind to socialize. Planning something for the nonparty crowd should be a no-brainer. Plus, it gets me further entrenched in the Calendar, so it'll be harder for Whit to pretend I don't exist. "We can do something," I say.

Lila snorts, and Whitney stares at me in disbelief. "Oh, don't worry, we're getting to you," Whitney says. "In what world is it a smart idea for you to do another event on the heels of your catastrophic tea?"

I recite the answer I prepared. "There was nothing inherently wrong with the concept. We just overestimated the taste level of our fellow students."

"Yeah. That was the problem," Lila says sarcastically. "Nobody covered the event, because Whit thought we could trust you to coordinate a tiny affair like that. But obviously she was wrong. Again."

That last word hangs in the air. Whitney winces a little at Lila's words. "And by the way, you're not coming to the ball?" Whit asks.

I shrug. "I don't have a date. I'm fine with lying low."

"It's our last year," Olivia says, protesting.

"I know, but I can take one for the team." Maybe if I act like I'm still a part of all this, we can get past our differences.

"That's very generous of you," Lila says, suddenly looking much happier. "I'm sure you can put the tea behind you and figure out something cute."

"We'll go ahead and put Abbot in the calendar for October thirty-first," Whitney says.

But when I get back to Abbot and tell the girls what I've committed to, they have a collective meltdown. "Maybe we didn't make it clear, but we want less social responsibility, not more," Jess says.

"You're going to have to handle that one on your own," Samantha says. "We don't want any part of it."

"Well, it's not like you're going to the Masquerade Ball! Did you have something else on your busy agendas?" I can't believe the amount of pushback I'm getting on this. No one will be checking up on us, because they'll be too busy with the ball. We can pretty much do whatever we want. And we get credit for doing something when no one else wanted to. I fail to see the downside.

"Washing my hair," Yasmin says.

"Doing my chem lab write-up," Raksmey says.

I turn to Jess. "You owe me. You're using my name to start your club, so the least you can do is back me up on this." She groans. "Come on. It's an easy way to get Abbot on the social map with no pressure."

Everyone looks at Jess, waiting to see if she caves. She finally meets their gazes. "One more event. I guess it couldn't hurt."

That's the spirit. I don't know why I'm pushing them. If they're content to languish in social obscurity, maybe I don't need to rock the boat.

I put the whole thing out of my mind and leave the dorm on Thursday night as soon as I hear Club Raks gearing up. Though

I'm actually tempted to join her, I put myself on autopilot and head toward Albright. I haven't spoken to Declan since our awkward moment after film class the other day.

I'm passing the cemetery when someone pounces on me from behind. I scream and whirl around, fists raised. It's Jess, and she doesn't seem troubled that I'm about to beat the crap out of her. "Sorry," she says with a smirk. "Didn't know you scared so easy."

I shake my head and resume walking. "Where are you going?" I ask.

Jess grins. "Believe it or not, I have a date. Vince Romboli from the football team asked me out after the screening."

"No way." I stop short. Vince, while not exactly popular (football players don't have the same kind of status here that they seem to at other schools), is kind of a player, and not just in the football sense. I'm more than a little concerned.

"Yes!" She bounces happily on her toes.

"You sure he's your type?" I ask.

"You mean hot? Uh, yeah. Don't worry, I know he's got a reputation as kind of a ladies' man, but I'm not completely clueless."

I'm not sure I agree with her, but she's too excited to hear anything rational at the moment.

"Dude, you should've come," she says. "I was so nervous."

"Apparently you did just fine."

"Will you come to the next one? I'm doing what you said and starting out with interesting but not necessarily contentious ones." She sounds both hopeful and somewhat desperate.

"I'll try, I promise. I have to actually work to get good grades." I'm getting cranky just thinking about all the studying I have ahead of me.

"We all do. If I can help in any way, just ask. I work on the *Winthrop Times,* so I'm great at editing, not so useful on the science-and-math front," Jess says. "Opal's better at those."

I sigh. "Walk with me. What are your ideas for the next one?"

Jess starts prattling on. Maybe we're inspired by the sight of Albright, but we agree on one about a working-class couple who managed to amass one of the most impressive modern art collections in the world.

"But who's going to go to that?" I ask.

"A lot of artsy people go to this school. Plus it's just a cool story. You'd like it."

"Does this mean you're going to help me with Halloween?" I ask, narrowing my eyes.

"I already said I would, didn't I?" Jess widens her eyes in an attempt at innocent cooperation.

I give her a look. "Where are you meeting Vince?" Date place options around here really suck.

"The gym. He's finishing his workout, but then we're going for a quick run and maybe the Study after."

That sounds like a legit first date (for a boarding school), so I nod my approval. Vince isn't a completely terrible person, so I don't know why I'm acting weirdly and unexpectedly protective of Jess.

She drops me off at Albright, more excited than I've ever seen her when her face isn't stuck to her laptop screen. Maybe the Documentary Club wasn't such a horrible idea after all.

CHAPTER TWENTY-ONE

Two hours later I'm settled into the studio. I've worked and reworked my section of the physics lab report to death, and my brain has turned to mush. I email the draft to my lab partner so she can look it over.

Bettina's lost in her own little world of hot-glue-gunning and paint pots. Across the table from me, Declan's eyes never leave the paper as he sketches, headphones on, absorbed in his drawing.

He didn't acknowledge me when I came in, so, as far as I know, he's still mad about my insinuating that the Thatcher guys are uncool. I've been fine with ignoring him back, but now not talking to him is starting to drive me insane.

I lean over to take a closer look at his drawing, then walk around to his side of the table. He smells like pencil shavings and wintergreen gum. I pull one of the ears of his headphones away. "Is that me?"

He slides the headphones down around his neck and looks at me, so unembarrassed that he's almost mocking. "Well, you are sitting right there."

My cheeks color. He's extremely talented, so there's not much for me to complain about. His rendering is flattering but not obsequious. As he shades the areas near my eyes, my good intentions to apologize evaporate. I feel too exposed to say anything.

I slip away to Bettina's side. The plastic bags have multiplied over the last few weeks and gotten even more colorful and elaborate. "You're procrastinating," Bettina says.

"Nope. I'm waiting for my lab partner to email me back. I'm allowed to take a break, aren't I?" I've been working really hard in monk-like silence for the entire night.

"Have you ever done this before?" I ask.

Bettina shakes her head, then rips a piece of packing tape off a roll with her teeth. "This is an original installation."

"Then forgive me for asking, but how do you know it's going to work?"

She glares at me. "It's pretty straightforward in terms of the balloon science, but I have no clue as to how it's going to look."

"Don't you want to test it out? I mean, you're spending so much time on it. You should make sure it'll work." I'm trying to be helpful, but from the way she's looking at me, it's obviously not being taken that way.

"That's part of the discovery, the artistic journey. If there's no risk involved, it's not art," Declan says. Evidently he's done ignoring me.

"I want to experience the rush of uncertainty and seeing them all go up together for the first time," Bettina says.

Who knew artists were such adrenaline junkies? Not quite sure I agree with her, but it's her time and energy, so fair enough. "Do you know when you're going to release them?" I ask.

She studies the different designs laid out across the table. "Whenever they're ready."

"And you're fairly certain it's going to work?"

"There's no logical reason why it wouldn't. And besides, the worst that happens is that I don't get the recording for my video portfolio. I still have time to come up with something else."

As I listen to her talk, I'm getting an idea. It might be a terrible one, but I can't seem to stop it from coming out of my mouth. "Do you think they could be ready by Halloween?"

"Possibly. Perhaps," she says.

"Because I have a great idea."

Bettina stares at me, a flat look through half-lowered lids. "Do tell."

"We make a party out of it. It's a perfect event for Halloween, and as you know, Abbot is on the hook to host something." I talk fast, hoping to bombard her with so many reasons that she won't have a chance to think better of it. "Also, you said you want an element of risk. Well, what ups the ante more than a live audience? It's like those tightrope walkers who walk between skyscrapers. Everyone is psychically pulling for them to succeed, and all that cosmic group energy is part of the journey, like you said. And enjoying it with a crowd will only add to your emotional high."

Her expression is skeptical. "And what if it doesn't work?"

"That's actually a great idea," Declan says. "And you'll totally pull it off. No fear."

I smile at him, grateful for the support and relieved that we seem to be getting past my slipup. "We'll make it clear that it's meant to be experimental art," I say. "People will eat it up. They'll feel like they're part of something unique and special."

She actually seems to be buying the nonsense I'm spewing. "So people are just going to stand around and watch me send them up?"

I think fast. "I'll have snacks of some kind, of course—Halloween themed, like popcorn balls and caramel apples. It'll be big. Where were you planning on doing this?"

"The athletic field?" she says, nose wrinkled.

"Kind of generic, don't you think? Won't look interesting on video. You need a more cinematic setting."

Declan actually looks impressed by me, but an anxious look flashes across Bettina's face. "The Field would be ideal, but I'm guessing there'd be too much incidental traffic that could screw things up," she says.

"Hmm. Yeah, that's not quite right either." Then, a sudden stroke of genius: "What about the cemetery? It's always empty, and it'll be amazingly creepy and atmospheric. Oh my god, it's perfect!" Now I'm not even making stuff up. It really would be perfect. The cemetery would transform her art installation into a staged show.

"You mean near the Mausoleum?" Bettina asks.

The Mausoleum is actually a mausoleum. It entombs a handful of members of the Lawrence family. I have no idea who they are, but their burial site is a very popular make-out and smoking spot. I'm kind of surprised Bettina knows of it. "Sure," I say. It's the only area without a lot of trees in the way.

Bettina's mouth twists sideways. "As long as all I have to worry about is my balloons, I'm in. You have to handle everything else."

"Done!" I say. I'm actually ecstatic about this latest brainwave. If it works, it's going to be brilliant. If it doesn't, well, that'll be nothing new for the Abbot girls.

CHAPTER TWENTY-TWO

My next meeting with Ms. Randall is more of the same. This time her crusade starts with the upcoming SATs. "We'd like to see your score come up by at least one hundred and fifty points. Does that look doable based on your tutor's assessment?"

I make a noncommittal gesture, halfway between a nod and a shrug.

She shakes her head. "That does not fill me with confidence. If you can do that, as well as present solid grades for the term, it'll give us a bit more to work with." Hints of both doubt and desperation creep into her eyes.

"I have been working hard, as I always do—" I say, but I stop. Defending myself is useless unless I have the grades to back it up, and at this point I don't. I'm pretty sure that whichever college accepts me will have to be a big believer in potential.

"Is there anything of interest that you'd like to mention?" she asks.

"Well, things are very different for me this year, as you can imagine. I've actually had some fun experiences," I begin.

"As long as 'fun' translates to items that can strengthen your application, I'd love to hear," Ms. Randall says. I wonder if she knows that every time she speaks, I get more afraid to say anything. But I regroup and forge ahead.

"I helped my roommate, Opal Kingston, start the Yoga Connection, which is a club she's been trying to get off the ground for the last few years." I wait to see if she has anything encouraging to say about that, but she stays silent. "And I have a sort of advisory capacity in Jess Frazier's new Documentary Club. Both of those have proven to be surprisingly popular." Ms. Randall keeps waiting, apparently unimpressed. I take a deep breath. "I'm also spearheading a Halloween event that will showcase Bettina Massey's artwork. It's unique, and I predict that it'll be a huge success."

Ms. Randall removes her glasses and drops them on her desk with a crack. I prepare myself for another downsizing of my already fragile ego. "Ms. Hoffman. You do realize that these examples, while demonstrating some proactivity on your part, are completely dependent upon your classmates' talents?"

"Uh, of course, but we worked together . . ." I can't finish the thought. This woman is never going to think I'm good enough to be here.

"When working on your essay," she says, abruptly changing topics, "remember to keep the focus on your own accomplishments and not your mother's." We'd agreed that I'd write about my internship with my mom's company, and it's clear she's not thrilled about this approach but can't think of anything better. Neither can I.

She misinterprets my nervous expression. "I know it's hard to juggle applications with a senior course load. That's why we asked students to have most of this finished before returning to school."

Well, believe me, I tried. Waiting tables in the hot sun all day didn't leave me with as much energy as one would think. But I don't say any of this. I just wait for her to get bored.

We keep staring at each other until I think maybe I'm just supposed to leave. "Don't you want your word for next time?" she asks.

Not really. "Okay."

"Your word is *prepare.*" Mentally I add *for the worst.* We both know that's what she means.

Following that meeting, I have a demoralizing FaceTime call with my parents. "We got an email from your college counselor. Seems like she thinks you're a bit behind in the process," my mom says.

"Don't worry," I say. "I have it under control. I've had to reevaluate some of my choices, but there are plenty of colleges out there."

"We just want you to be happy, honey," my dad says. They sound nervous but distracted. I give them a brief summary of my next steps.

Then, out of nowhere, they mention that they're borrowing money from my grandparents to help with the mortgage. That pretty much kills any further discussion about college.

"But otherwise things are great!" my mom says. "We had a garage sale and made over five hundred dollars."

"Any bids on the house?" I ask.

"Our realtor suggested we take it off the market for a while. When a property hangs out on the listings for too long, there's a stench of death about it," my dad says.

"Have you found a new screenwriter for the *Over It* sequel?" I ask.

My mom's jaw tightens. "Not yet. All the hot young writers don't want to work on anything that feels the least bit dated. But enough about us. How are you? How's Leo?"

"Fine," I say, forcing a smile. Wow, every single one of these subjects has the stench of death about it. There's no safe topic. "Just a lot of work all the time, soccer, keeping busy with Calendar stuff. The usual." My voice quavers, and I'm sure there's no possible way that I'm convincing anyone.

"That's great, honey!" my mom chirps. "So glad you're taking advantage of your last year!"

I use the opening sounds of Club Raks as an excuse to get off the call. After the day I've had, flailing around and sweating it out to aggressive music doesn't sound half bad.

"What happened to you today?" Raksmey asks when it's time to turn off the music. We've spent an hour dancing our faces off.

I sigh, sweeping sweat-drenched strands of hair behind my

ears. "A little of everything. I need to figure out how to get a good score on the SATs, but I can't afford a tutor or even an online prep class." Saying the words *can't afford* aloud feels so foreign that my tongue tangles over them and my high from dancing immediately dissipates. "It's probably too late now anyway."

Raksmey beams, not even registering my discomfort. "Why didn't you say anything earlier? I'm thinking of taking them too."

"Why? It's only fall." She's a junior, and most people wait until spring of junior year to take them.

"Yeah, but I'm the master of standardized tests. I figure, why wait?"

"You're not even going to start with the PSATs?" I ask. I've never heard of anyone being cocky enough to do that.

"Growing up, I was always in after-school tutoring programs, and the teachers were college students, total geeks who got off on things like gaming tests."

I roll my eyes. "I don't think you can game the SATs."

"Well, not literally," she says. "But trust me, there is a system, which means there is a strategy, which means that I can figure it out." I must look skeptical, because why wouldn't I be?

Raksmey exhales in frustration. "It's multiple choice, is it not?" she asks. I nod. "That means the answer is right in front of your face."

"Have you even been studying?" I ask.

"Here and there. I mean, if I bomb it, which I won't, I can still take it in the spring."

She has a point.

"It'll be like a test party. And helping you will help me too. So when do we start?" she asks, practically bouncing on the balls of her feet.

"Last year would've been a good time," I say, suddenly feeling the full weight of the dire predicament I'm in. "I've been studying on my own but not consistently and not in the most organized way."

Raksmey lays a comforting hand on my arm. "We can only work with what we have. Amazing things can happen in just a few weeks. Onward!"

I have no reason to believe her, but her confidence settles me a bit. If nothing else, it feels better to not have to be in it alone.

CHAPTER TWENTY-THREE

On Halloween morning I beg Opal to come to the Canteen to help me make food for Ghouls and Graves. That's what I've decided to call this latest brainchild. Jess is at a track team meet and, despite her promises, has successfully avoided helping me so far. "I sort of already have plans," Opal says.

"What could be more important than making sure Bettina and her art appear in the best possible light?"

She doesn't respond or elaborate on her plans, so when Remy arrives at Abbot, I assume he's here to see me. But I would be wrong.

"Okay, you're signed in," Opal says to him, her cheeks flushed rosy pink.

Remy winks at me before they go upstairs. "Excuse me. What is this?" I ask, following them. Obviously I have a right to know. I've known both of them longer than they've known each other, and if it weren't for my flash of brilliance about the Yoga Connection, they wouldn't have even met.

"Remy wants to learn about the *Yoga Sutras*," Opal explains. Sure he does.

"You mean the sex thing?" I ask.

Remy shoots me a horrified look. I guess stomping on his game is sort of mean. He's a good guy, not to mention very handsome, and I actually think he deserves someone sweet like Opal. "It's not a—"

Opal puts a hand on his arm. "She knows. She's just being awkward."

"Well, am I allowed in the room?" I ask, continuing to fly in the face of all decorum.

"God, Skylar," Remy says.

"Of course you are," Opal says through gritted teeth.

I decide to take them at face value and follow them to the room. Popcorn balls can wait. I don't disapprove, exactly, but I feel acute discomfort at having my worlds collide. One should have a say if one's friends are suddenly going to start intermingling.

Sure enough, Remy and Opal sprawl on the floor, poring over some smelly old book. Every now and then Opal erupts with some Sanskrit chant. And though it's positively adorable, I about burst out laughing at Remy's mesmerized, smitten look.

Eventually my humanity returns. "Off to bake," I say. "Won't be back for a few hours. At least. See ya!" I enjoy their baffled, cringing expressions as I slip out the door.

I spend the rest of the morning with Martin, the Canteen

chef, elbow deep in popcorn and corn syrup, rice cereal and liquefied marshmallow. Of course I grumble and complain, but it's actually pretty fun.

"Am I invited to this soiree?" Martin asks.

"I'll save you a front-row seat," I say. "It should be pretty good."

"No offense, and I do love tea, but I have a feeling this will be much more popular with your fellow students," Martin says.

"Sure. All this sugar is like teenage crack. But I bet they'll have plenty of sugar at the Masquerade Ball," I say. "Last I heard, there was going to be a bulk-candy wall."

"Ah. Not to worry. You'll get the forward thinkers at this. The dance is a friendly old standby, perfect for those who prefer tried-and-true."

"And inferior outside catering," I say. Martin winks at me, and suddenly I feel a lot better. I like the spin he put on it, like Abbot might be ahead of the curve on this.

We arrange the treats on industrial baking sheets, with puffy tents of wax paper held up by toothpicks covering them. Martin affixes note cards to each tray that read PROPERTY OF GHOULS AND GRAVES. EAT AND DIE.

"Thanks, Martin. If I did this on my own, I'd probably give everyone food poisoning. You definitely saved the day."

He smiles. "Happy to help. I love a good dark-horse story."

I wince but then realize he's right. For the first time in my Winthrop experience, I'm a total underdog. No one expects me to succeed at this or anything else. The thought is sobering, and once again I wonder how it is that I've gone from the girl who had the perfect, coveted life to the scrappy long shot in just a couple of months.

While I set up card tables by the Mausoleum for the food and sweep off some flat grave markers for seating, Bettina works quietly and efficiently, with only a handful of impressively foul-mouthed outbursts. She sprints to the studio a few times for what I imagine to be hot-glue-gun emergencies.

Attendance is still totally up in the air. Jess ran an announcement in the paper. I posted flyers around campus and even got a one-sentence mention in the Social Calendar e-newsletter. I highlighted the treats and the fact that costumes are welcome.

At a certain point I just can't watch Bettina anymore. I go back to Abbot. Remy's gone, but Opal's putting the finishing touches on her Bride of Frankenstein costume. Her dark hair is pulled back in a tight bun, and she wears a body-hugging, long-sleeved, floor-length white column dress and a thin layer of pasty gray foundation with greenish smudges on her face. She looks amazing. Naturally I picked everything out.

"Did Remy see you in that?" I ask. She ignores me.

I change into my Minnie Mouse costume, which is really just a sweet red-and-white polka-dot dress with a pinafore, black patent leather Mary Janes, lacy white ankle socks, and Minnie Mouse ears, which I've had since my first trip to Disneyland.

"What do you think?" I ask.

"Why do you get to wear something . . . nonconfining, while I have to wear this?" she asks.

"Because you live in nonconfining. We're both doing something different."

Opal scowls and slips on her Birkenstocks. At least her feet are hidden by the dress. I don't know what she's grumbling about. If she showed up to the Masquerade Ball in that, Remy would have a lot of competition.

When the first people arrive at the Mausoleum, I immediately panic. Bettina continues assembling balloons and determining their optimal placement. Sometimes this means moving them a matter of inches, staring for a few minutes, and then moving them back. But oddly enough, people are riveted by her artsy meditation.

There are several dozen balloons. I have no idea how she found time to make so many. Each one is more intricate and colorful than the last. Bettina said letting them go is part of the process, but I think seriously about stealing one to keep. "Can we get this going?" I ask. "I said we'd start at six."

She tilts her head and looks at me like I'm insane. "We have to wait until dark. Otherwise it won't make any visual impact."

I want my head to make impact with the marble wall of the Mausoleum. Of course she's not going to change her plan just to help me not look like a complete idiot. I consider telling people to leave and come back later, but I know once they go, it's all over.

So I stall. I socialize, push snacks like my Nana Rose would, use my phone to look up trivia on some of the obscure dead people around us and quiz everyone.

By the time the sun sets, we have a decent crowd of about twenty-five people, and I'm grateful that Martin talked me into staying to make extra batches of Rice Krispie Treats. The Masquerade Ball has already started, and I fully expect people to leave within the next few minutes. It's completely dark, and I resist the urge to micromanage Bettina, but when she decides to light the candles that power the balloons, I collapse with relief.

"You okay?" Jess asks.

I clutch her arm. "This is so incredibly painful. The wow factor has to happen now. If these people have hung out all this time for nothing, there's going to be a riot."

"You're being way too dramatic. Ooohh!"

We crane our necks as the first balloon floats up, a bright, glowing orb in the sky. Finally. The birthday candle illuminates the rich colors Bettina used, so that the painting looks like a gorgeous stained-glass window. This was worth the wait.

Now the crowd is on their feet, looking up, mouths open. I'd offer my help, but Bettina looks like she's in a trance, and I don't want to break her concentration. I make sure Samantha's recording.

Interestingly, she's not the only one. People are taking photos and videos on their phones and posting them or texting them to friends. Soon even more people arrive.

Bettina sets up her next round of balloons. There's almost no wind, so the first group hovers within sight. They illuminate the cemetery like a massive, delicate chandelier. Everyone's talking and laughing but keeping their voices low, mindful of Bettina working.

As more people join and claim spots on the ground or the

steps of the Mausoleum, I get a nagging feeling that the ball may not be going perfectly. Whit's reaction won't be pretty if the gym isn't filled to capacity, much less if she finds out that people flocked here.

When we've blown through the treats and apple cider and it's standing room only, I busy myself with collecting discarded cups and napkins. Then I spot Leo in the crowd.

I drop the stack of paper plates I'm carrying and make a bee-line for him. Seeing him out the night after a game is so unusual that somewhere in my confused head I think he must be here to see me. He looks startled when I tap his shoulder but breaks into a smile that I can't help returning.

"What are you doing here?" I ask.

"You can see these all the way from the quad," he says, gesturing up to the sky. "Lots of people came this way to check it out. It looks cool from far away, but being up close is phenomenal."

"Thanks," I say, with what I hope is a combination of modesty and satisfaction.

Leo looks confused. "Was this your idea?"

"Well, I didn't make any of the actual balloons, but hosting it here on Halloween, that was me."

"That's the part that's so genius." Leo's looking at me like I just grew a second head. "I can't think of a more perfect time or place."

"Glad you like it." My tone is light, but I'm aggravated. Why's he so surprised that I'm capable of planning and organizing an event like this?

"And look—practically half the school is here." He gestures at the still growing crowd.

Oh yeah. That small problem. Leo catches my distressed look. "That's good, right?"

I sigh. Confiding in him feels so natural. "It's just Whit and that girl Lila."

He frowns. "The friend from New York?" He puts the "friend" in air quotes.

"Yeah. They're running the Calendar and expect everyone to produce exciting events, just not as exciting as theirs."

Leo nods. "But once they hear how into it everyone was, they can't be too mad. They might even be impressed that you thought of something so out-of-the-box."

I sincerely doubt it, but Leo's encouragement is sweet. I'm trying to keep my feelings in check, but I'm grateful that, in some ways at least, we can pick right back up where we left off.

With nothing else to say, we stand and enjoy the party. People sit on blankets, huddled close for warmth. Except for the temperature, the vibe reminds me of a beach bonfire—relaxed and convivial, even though there are people here from all different sectors of Winthrop life.

Samantha walks by, and I grab her arm. "We need more food," I say. She holds out a big bag of gummy bears.

"Great, but that's probably not enough for everybody." I grab a handful, shoving them into my mouth. They feel bigger and slipperier than normal gummy bears.

"That was ill-advised," Samantha says.

And now I taste why. After chewing and swallowing, these

leave an alcoholic after burn. They've been soaked in vodka. Sneaking alcohol was a regular occurrence in Lincoln, but until now I thought Abbot was stuck in the Prohibition era. Since I haven't had so much as a beer in a very long time, my head swims minutes after I've swallowed them.

Suddenly I don't feel quite as nervous. In fact, this could be the perfect time to ask Leo about where we stand. I take a deep breath. "So I know we really haven't had a chance to talk about—"

"Uh, Skylar."

I lay a hand on his arm, determined to keep going. But then, in my peripheral vision, I see a hand snake its way around Leo. I turn to look at him squarely. He shoots me an apologetic look before my gaze returns to his waist.

A girl with long, wavy dark hair and bee-stung lips smiles at me, but it comes off as more of a grimace. "Hi, Skylar," she says.

I vaguely recognize her as a girl from Baldwin House who's on the swim team. Convenient. Opposite seasons. Her name's not coming to me, but who cares when her name from here on out will be The Bitch Who Was on a Date with Leo.

"Oh, sorry, this is—" Leo begins. I interrupt him immediately. The less I know, the better.

"Wonderful. Well. Feel free to eat, drink, and be merry!" Forget that the food's been devoured or that what I just said is really more of a mangled Christmas sentiment. I whirl away, hoping that I made the most graceful exit possible under the heinous circumstances.

I glue myself to Yasmin and Jess. Shockingly, they have

enough sense to not ask me what's going on. I must look like I've been struck by lightning. When Samantha passes again, I grab another handful of gummy bears and down them. "What's up with you?" she asks.

"You can only have two or three," Jess says. I sit down and bury my head in my arms. "Oh no," she says.

I don't know why I'm so shocked that Leo's on a date. He's Leo. I guess I thought he might have cared to at least tell me where we stood first.

"Hey." Someone taps me on the back. I look up and manage to smile when I see Declan. He's slightly blurry, but I'm inexplicably happy that he's here.

"I didn't see you," I say, standing up.

"That much is clear." Declan looks amused, and I wonder if he can tell that I'm swaying.

"When did you get here?" I ask.

"Not that long ago. Had to come see our girl do her thing." He nods at Bettina.

"That's really nice of you. You're such a good friend," I say. Declan hadn't said for sure that he'd be here, but now I realize that it wouldn't have been complete without him. Only he and I have been able to watch this process and know how amazing it would be. I reach out and loop my arm through his.

He looks down at me, unsure but keeping me steady. I take a deep breath. "Sorry I was rude about your dorm. I don't know those guys, and it was wrong of me to judge."

"It's okay," he says, chuckling and patting my hand. "I understand now that you were just making conversation. Badly, but still." I blink up at him, grateful that someone really seems to get me.

"Usually my social skills are flawless," I say.

Declan smirks. "Debatable."

"No, it's true! Ask anyone. Well, not just anyone. I mean, this isn't how I really am."

"Oh? How are you really?"

"It's just, I've been kind of . . . not able to put my best foot forward." I peer into his eyes, willing him to believe me.

"How drunk are you?" he whispers. I shrug, throwing both of us off balance. "Yeah, let's just sit back down until some of that wears off," he says. "For the record, this you isn't so bad."

Declan sits and guides me down next to him, but I still land with a plop. I rest my cheek on his shoulder and marvel at how much more comfortable my heavy head feels.

"I have to ask. Does your hanging all over me have anything to do with your ex being here? I mean that and the fact that you're totally inebriated?" he asks.

"Ugh. He's still here? With that girl? Why won't he just go away?" I bury my face in his arm.

"So is that a yes or a no?" Declan mutters. I pretend not to hear him.

Bettina lights her last balloons. The crowd's quiet again. Collectively we know that something special is coming to an end and that we're the lucky ones who were here to witness it.

CHAPTER TWENTY-FOUR

"You know that was phenomenal, right?" I say to Bettina the next morning as we get ready in the bathroom.

"Why were you flirting with Declan?" she asks, glancing at me in the mirror.

"I was? That doesn't sound right." I scrunch my eyes, like I'm trying to picture it, when of course I know exactly how long my head was resting on his shoulder. "Well, I was drunk. That could've had something to do with it."

She shuts off her faucet and turns to face me. "Don't do that to him."

"What? I'm sure he understands. We all know he's been around drunk people before."

Bettina glares at me. "Getting busted was a really terrible time for him. Do me a favor and don't bring that up."

"I would never," I say with a furrowed brow. Rubbing

people's mistakes in their faces would be pretty hypocritical of me. Bettina packs up her caddy and leaves.

Monday night, when I get back to Abbot, I go straight to the kitchenette freezer. "This really isn't going to help you," Yasmin says, pausing by the door with Jess.

Usually I don't like an audience while I have a tub of mint chocolate chip ice cream stuck to my face, but I turn around anyway. "What are you guys doing?" I ask.

"I have to run to orchestra practice, but *she* has another date with Vince," Yasmin says, smiling proudly at Jess.

I swallow a cold lump of ice cream. "Seriously?"

"It's casual," Jess says. "He says he likes running with me because it's getting him into better shape. And maybe we make out a little after."

"That's great," I say, but I know it sounds hollow. Does everyone but me have a life? I lick the inner edge of the container, which makes Yasmin wrinkle her dainty nose.

"Listen, maybe you should talk to Leo," Jess says, looking concerned.

"Yeah. Maybe he'll bring his date." I put my ice cream down. My appetite is gone.

"You can't give up that easily!" Yasmin says. "It's not over, because you haven't fought for him. All good romance requires a grand gesture, and you haven't made one yet."

"Nor do I intend to."

They exchange glances, and I glare at them.

"For all intents and purposes, you lied to him," Jess says.

"I know this already. So what's your point? I already apologized."

"But maybe by now he's had enough distance that he'll actually be able to hear you," Yasmin says. "Besides, I'm sure he misses you."

I might be talking to a crazy person. "Are you serious? Did it look like he was missing me when he had his arm around that girl?"

Yasmin looks unfazed. "Appearances can be deceiving. For all you know, he's just trying to fill the huge hole you've left in his heart."

My laugh comes out strangled. "I wish I lived in your world, where it's sunshine and puppies all the time."

"Trust me. Grand gesture." Yasmin nods at me, her conviction unwavering. "We have to go, but we're not done talking about this. Think of some ideas, and we'll review them later."

"Glad to see you put the ice cream down," Jess adds before they walk out.

The front door slams a second later, and I feel more friendless than ever. Everyone is out of the dorm. I'm tempted to go find Bettina in the studio, but I have a feeling I'm not welcome there at the moment.

I drag myself to my room and take out my essay for Chinese class and my English-Mandarin dictionary. I'd written it in simplified Chinese characters, not realizing that the assignment was for traditional characters. Baker Laoshi, who's usually one of my favorite teachers, only gave me a day to redo it and penalized me with a third of a grade. It's a pain, but for the most part it's busywork, which is about all I can handle.

By the time Jess and Yasmin return, I've actually come up with what I think qualifies as a grand gesture to show Leo how I feel.

"That's it?" Yasmin asks when I tell them the plan. We're in Jess's room, which has no decor, unless you count a few running posters with inspirational quotes on them.

"Sorry, did you think I should spell out SKYLAR + LEO in flower petals on his lawn? Or hire a skywriter to proclaim my love in the airspace above the Field?"

"Ignore her," Jess says, grinning at me. "Yasmin's always in a bad mood if practice doesn't go well."

"I'm a perfectionist," Yasmin says.

"Why are you in such good spirits?" I ask Jess, narrowing my eyes at her. "Never mind. I don't want to know."

She smiles even wider. "We started our run at his dorm and barely got to the bird sanctuary before we were all over each other."

"Okay, I get it. Hashtag blessed. God, I wish I could bleach my brain. Didn't I just say I don't want to know?"

"Prude." Jess laughs. "There's nothing wrong with going to the soccer game this weekend—"

"But it's uninspired," Yasmin interrupts. "Half the school is going to be doing the exact same thing."

"But the point is, I used to go to every game, and I think he'll realize how hard it was for me to show up on his turf, no pun intended."

Yasmin shakes her head and sits on Jess's bed to begin her stretches. Before I met Yasmin I had no idea that being a serious cellist required a whole fitness regimen to avoid injury. "You know him best," she says. "But just so you know, I was willing to play a private candlelit concert for the two of you."

"That's very sweet, but I'm pretty sure that would be weird for all of us," I say.

I'm a little discouraged that they don't seem to have much enthusiasm for my plan. But now that I've been thinking about it, I realize that I'm sick of waiting. I can't stay in limbo forever, and if Leo and I are truly over, I need to know.

I finally get up the nerve to go to the studio a couple of nights later. I don't know who I'm more nervous to be around, Bettina or Declan. Fortunately, Declan's not there. Bettina's hard at work on a clay sculpture. As far as I can tell, she hasn't taken a single second to bask in the runaway success that was Ghouls and Graves.

"On to the next thing already, huh?" I say, plugging in my laptop.

She shrugs, and while it could be modesty, it feels more like indifference. "Unlike many artists, who grow attached to their work and obsess about its importance, I'm more about the fluidity of the cycle of creativity and consumption."

As usual I have no idea what she's talking about, but I nod. I may not get it, but I admire her ability to keep moving forward. "Where's your biggest fan?" I ask, and immediately wish I could take the words back.

"Why? You need someone to make you feel better about Leo?" she asks.

Ouch. Maybe there's more between them than I realized. Usually I'm better at reading situations. "Why don't you two just go out already? You obviously have some kind of arty connection."

She sighs, wiping her clay-encrusted hands on a wet rag. "I'm gay, and Declan knows." Oh. My face gets hot. It's not like I don't know other gay people, but I feel like the world's biggest idiot. "Besides, we're friends through his ex-girlfriend, and she's still not over him."

I struggle to stay on topic and not get distracted by the fact that Declan has a past. "I'm sorry. But I mean, nothing happened. He knew I was buzzed, and he was just trying to help me. Trust me, I am not looking for a rebound."

Bettina rolls her eyes. "Just try to be aware of other people's feelings."

Her reproach stings, like she thinks I'm willfully insensitive or something. Maybe heartbreak hasn't had the best effect on my personality, but it's not as if I'm not trying.

CHAPTER TWENTY-FIVE

Once again I've been called to the Calendar executive committee meeting, this time to answer "serious questions" they have about Ghouls and Graves. This meeting happens downtown at the Golden Palace, Winthrop's answer to Chinese food. For some reason this restaurant is a favorite among my fellow students. Whitney and I and the other Lincoln girls celebrated all our birthdays here. I guess they still probably do.

On my fifteenth birthday we decided that we were grown up enough to get a little rowdy. We stayed for hours, ordering Shirley Temples, begging the waiters to spike them, and laughing so hard when they got mad. I almost smile, remembering it now. Whitney gave me a silver necklace with a tiny bean pendant from Tiffany's. "I'm sick of you borrowing mine all the time," she said before giving me a hug.

Despite all the good times, the best thing I can say about the Palace is that the food is salty, greasy, and fairly cheap.

I duck under a low-hanging red paper lantern and take a seat at the long table where the Executive Committee is already eating. They've ordered several pu-pu platters—many more than the number of people here can actually eat—and pick at things like fried spring rolls and sesame beef skewers. The Palace is not actually owned or operated by Chinese people, which explains the existence of such things on their menu. It does not appear to be a spiked Shirley Temple kind of night, which makes me wonder why we're bothering with meeting here.

"First let's cover the Masquerade Ball. Since most of us were there"—Whit darts a glance at me—"we don't have to go into too much detail."

Elizabeth takes a deep breath. "It was a beautiful event. We had the most exquisite decor we've ever had, the menu was perfect, and the music was on point." I read her tone as defensiveness laced with confusion.

"We know," Whitney says. "You did everything perfectly. There's no one to blame here. It's just one of those flukey things." It doesn't escape my attention that she's abandoned ownership of the ball.

"I'm sure it was fantastic," I say to Elizabeth. "I would've loved to have been there."

"For all the hype it was definitely on the sleepy side," Lila says. Whitney raises an eyebrow and gives Elizabeth a nervous look. "Anyway, let's talk about Abbot's balloon party," Lila continues, snatching a fried prawn with her chopsticks. She makes it sound like we were making balloon animals for a kid's birthday. "We heard turnout was better than anticipated."

I'm smart enough to know that I'd better tread carefully here. "I mean, we had nowhere near ball numbers or even weekend-dance numbers, but still, it was surprisingly well attended. We weren't expecting much, so anything felt like a huge win."

"Obviously none of us came," Whitney says. "We're only going by the few grainy photos published by the *Winthrop Times,* but it seems like nothing disastrous happened."

"Nope. Not at all." Unless you count Leo showing up with a date.

"I guess there's no accounting for taste," Lila says. "It just goes to show you that most Winthrop students are simpletons. We hand-deliver a perfectly executed Halloween celebration, and they'd rather go off and watch plastic bags fly around."

Everyone giggles nervously, and I'm surprised that they all tolerate Lila insulting our school. I wish I could take back the encouraging words I said a second ago and stab them with my chopsticks.

"I don't know, guys," Guthrie says. "I actually stopped by. It was pretty brilliant. And everyone kept talking about how chill and communal it was."

"Ugh, whatever," Whitney says.

Of course she'd be bitter about people cutting out of the ball for any reason, but I am surprised that she's not at least a tiny bit pleased that something new went well. "I thought you'd be happy that Abbot managed to deliver something people actually wanted to go to," I say. "You're always on about how certain dorms don't pull their weight."

Everyone looks to Whit to gauge her reaction. "True enough.

But if people could maybe learn to calibrate their events better, it would benefit everyone. I mean, competing with the main offering on the schedule is never a good idea. Balance is key. I would think you'd know that by now."

"I had no way of knowing Ghouls and Graves would be such a hit." Or that the ball would be so lackluster that it would send people running.

"God," says Whitney. "No one in their right mind would've predicted that so many people would geek out over a bunch of balloons. Next year it would have to be scheduled for a different night, clearly. And then we'd need to implement some improvements." She looks at some of the members who are juniors. They scribble frantically in their notebooks.

I straighten up, alarmed. "Oh. Actually this was a onetime thing. Bettina's graduating, and it wouldn't be right for someone to copy her idea."

"Well, if she's graduating, I guess it's convenient that she won't be here to police it," Whitney says, narrowing her eyes. "Besides, it's not as if she owns the copyright on balloons."

"Maybe not, but people will know. Faculty, other students. And it's unethical to do it without her express permission." I'm starting to get pissed. Bettina worked hard on this project, and I'm not going to sit here while people talk about stealing it.

Whitney snorts. "You're preaching ethics now? So not only did you ruin Halloween, but you've done it with something that can't even be useful to us in the future?"

I shrug. "Sometimes you can't catch lightning in a bottle."

"Let's not waste any more time on this," Lila says, staring at me. "It's over. We can't use it. It was utterly pointless. Next."

When the bill comes, I take out my wallet to contribute to the pu-pu platters. Some of the others ordered entrees, but given my budget, I'd refrained.

Whitney frowns over the very lengthy itemized receipt. Lila snatches it out of her hands. "Just split it," Lila says. "It's so much easier." Everyone tosses their credit cards over.

"I brought cash. Can you tell me how much I owe?" I ask.

Whitney doesn't look up, just sighs and taps on her phone. "Thirty-two seventeen, including tax and tip."

There's forty dollars in my wallet, total. But beyond that, there is no way I'm paying that much for a couple strips of sesame beef. I almost lose the nerve to speak up, but I've already infuriated everyone, so I really have nothing to lose. "Sorry, I barely ate. Can I just throw in twelve?"

Again Whitney keeps her gaze on her phone. "Fine. I'll subtract your twelve dollars and recalculate everyone else's bill."

No one objects, but they do avoid looking in my direction. Maybe everyone would be happier if I were actually invisible.

I'm the first to leave, but Whit corners me just before I reach the door. "How could you do that, not only to the Calendar but to me?"

"What?" I ask, confused.

"You deliberately upstaged us and ruined the ball! You never shared the details of your idea and kept talking about it like some quaint little surprise." Her arms are crossed, and her pretty face is twisted into a scowl.

"You mean, if I'd said 'balloon art,' you would've known it was going to be a campus-wide phenomenon?" I ask.

Whitney snorts. "Let's not get carried away."

Her derision makes me abandon any humility. "You heard Guthrie. People are using the word 'spectacular' to describe it," I say.

"Next time you propose something, you better be ready to disclose it fully," she says.

"Fine. But as we all agreed, Ghouls and Graves's success wasn't predictable. Instead of wasting your time doing damage control on a bad event, why not celebrate the success of a good one?"

I continue out the door. If Whit ever thought of herself as my friend, I don't see how she could be this unsupportive and threatened just when I finally feel like I did something right.

Opal has the unfair advantage of being able to talk my ear off when I have no place to hide. Like when I'm in bed, head buried under my comforter, trying to sleep. "People really want us to do something for Rally Weekend. No one wants another formal dance."

"What do you mean? The Cotillion is a hundred-year-old institution."

"Yes, and it shows. People are ready for something a little more progressive than velvet and corsages," Opal says.

The Beecher School has been Winthrop's main rival forever. Each fall Rally Weekend centers on a football game where student spectators from each school trade insults through witty poster slogans. Alumni take over the Winthrop Inn, faculty assign less homework, and students party, watch the football game, and hook up at the Cotillion. It's tradition.

My plan for Rally Weekend is to stay in bed and wait until it's over.

"Come on," she pleads. "Consider all the poor souls at this school who hate the stuffy culture of Rally Weekend. The Cotillion is hellish for us."

Opal's point makes some sense. Funny, I never thought about what all the unattached people did over the weekend. I never had to worry about it—at the very least, I went with a boy as friends. Now that I'm on the other side, needing a date for a football game and a school dance seems ludicrous.

Once I utter anything resembling an agreement, Opal will hold me to it, so I say nothing.

But the next morning I surreptitiously check the Calendar schedule. As luck would have it, our next turn in the rotation falls on Rally Weekend. Although part of me doesn't want to admit I'm seriously considering this, I already know what I'm going to propose.

When a boy I've never spoken to before passes me a note in US History, I know that Abbot has gained some weird alternate-universe-type momentum. He has a pierced eyebrow and wears black steel-toe boots with shorts, even with the forty-degree temperatures we've been enjoying recently. I unfold the paper while Mr. Karchmer isn't looking. GHOULS AND GRAVES WAS RAD, it reads. THOUGHT ORIGINALITY WAS LONG DEAD AROUND HERE.

I shrug and offer a modest smile before folding the note and slipping it into my bag.

But he's not done. He falls into step behind me after class and talks my ear off all the way to the Canteen. "You guys should do something for Rally Weekend," he says. "This place needs more interesting options. And Rally Weekend is the perfect time to make that statement."

"Have you been talking to Opal?" I ask.

"Huh?" he says.

"Never mind. Nontraditional isn't exactly my forte."

"Well, anyone who thought to pull off Ghouls and Graves has my complete respect. I thought you were the brains behind it, but I guess I heard wrong."

He takes off for Lower Left (of course), and I find myself wanting to call him back. "You weren't wrong," I want to say. "That was me. I can do it again." I sigh.

Suddenly the prospect of upsetting Whitney and the rest of my old friends seems not only like a good idea but a necessary one.

CHAPTER TWENTY-SIX

Operation Get Leo—which Yasmin insists on calling it—is in full effect by midweek. There's a home game, and though half the school's going, there's a guaranteed way to get Leo's attention.

Much to Jess's and Yasmin's annoyance, I ban them from the game when the day comes. "Opal's going to watch Remy, so I won't be totally unsupervised," I argue. "She'll make sure that I don't wimp out." Opal nods solemnly.

I put on my old red Uggs and a red Patagonia parka. I always made it a point to wear red to games so it'd be easy for Leo to spot me in the stands amid the swaths of green and white, Winthrop's school colors. When we get to the soccer field, I choose a spot about forty-five degrees to the right of the goal.

Sure enough, right before kickoff his gaze lands on me and stays there for a few seconds. My phone buzzes with a text from Yasmin. *Has he seen you?*

I type back a quick affirmative response.

As the first half progresses, I find myself so caught up in the action, I almost forget about Leo. Remy's out there hustling and outmaneuvering the opponents. Opal grips my arm. The whole team plays at the top of their game, and I'm just as exhilarated as the rest of the crowd when Winthrop's up three to one at halftime.

But when Leo shoots me a questioning glance from the sidelines as the coach is going over plays, my stomach twists. That was not a happy-to-see-me look. I consider making a run for it, but Opal puts a hand on my shoulder. "Don't even think about it."

Fortunately, my presence doesn't seem to be much of a distraction. Leo's saves are otherworldly. In fact, what I'm assuming to be annoyance at me might be making him play even better than normal.

But I realize that I don't know what normal is for him anymore. A summer and half a season have passed since I last saw him play, and for all I know his skills have elevated this much.

When the second half comes to a close, I really don't want the game to end—and not just because I'm afraid of what I have to do. I've missed being a part of all this.

Winthrop wins over Millard Day, five to three. The teams do the customary handshakes, with the keepers leading, and then head straight to the locker rooms. Leo lingers behind, and I know he's waiting for me.

"Great game. Glad to see I didn't throw you off at all," I say when I get down to the field.

"Hey. Thanks for coming." He gives a half smile but has a flat, faraway look in his eyes. My outfit gets a once-over. "I'm assuming your coming wasn't a spur-of-the-moment thing."

"No. I don't know if you're ready or not, but I want to talk."

Leo nods, looking at his feet. "About Miranda?"

I shake my head. "Don't need to know her name." I take a cleansing breath. "But I do need to know if you're ever going to forgive me." I blink rapidly, trying to hold back tears.

He sighs and wipes a hand over his face. "Of course I forgive you. This isn't about me being mad."

"Then what?" I say. It comes out like a croak.

"I told you. We were so serious about each other, but you didn't trust me enough to tell me. It made me wonder if I was wrong about what we were to each other."

"You weren't wrong. You know I love you. But I was embarrassed and afraid. I still am. So you weren't wrong about that either. But how I feel about my family has nothing to do with you. Living with all their anxiety and disappointment has been so hard, and it's really not my favorite subject. Basically I'm guilty of wanting to enjoy the parts of my life that were still great, and that included you."

"I guess I can understand that," Leo says after a minute. "But it's kind of a lot to work a whole full-time job all summer long, never mention it, and actually say you're doing something else."

"Yes. But it wasn't so much the waitressing I wasn't mentioning as it was my parents' silent feud or their constant, delusional reassuring that things will be back to normal any minute now. I was trying so hard to keep it together. If I'd started venting about my life, I would've driven everyone insane. That wouldn't have been good for anybody."

"It's nice that they want to give you everything, but yeah, that sounds rough." He actually does look sympathetic, which makes me think that I may have finally gotten through to him.

"So what now? Are you seeing that girl?" Ugh. Miranda. I don't think I've ever hated a name more.

He nods, and suddenly I can't swallow. "We've been hanging out for a month or so."

"Is it . . . I mean, is it . . . serious?"

Leo sighs. "I don't know. I'm just seeing where it's going for now." His mouth tightens into a resolute line, and I know that's it. Game over.

"Okay," I manage to get out. "Well. Thanks for listening." It's a meaningless, hollow thing to say, but that's exactly how I feel at the moment.

Leo grabs the rest of his gear and smiles sadly before walking toward the gym. I, on the other hand, am rooted to the ground. The stands are now empty, and the wind starts to whip, snapping bare tree branches in the distance. When the field lights eventually blink out, I start back to the main campus.

I'm in bed for all of one minute when the door flies open. It's Opal, with Remy in tow. "Oh no," Opal says when she sees me curled up.

"Guys, I can't handle this right now," I say.

"Haven't we already done this?" Opal asks.

"Yeah, Skylar. Nothing new has really happened," Remy says.

"He confirmed he's seeing that girl," I say.

"Miranda?" Remy asks.

"Why does everyone keep saying her name?" I groan into my pillow.

Opal approaches my bed and sticks her face right up next to mine. "I'm giving you twenty-four hours to snap out of this. We have work to do." She pinches my arm—not hard enough to hurt, but I yelp anyway.

"Ow! That's not ahimsa!" I love throwing Opal's yoga-speak back at her.

"Sounds more than reasonable to me," Remy adds. Traitor.

What's wrong with these two? This is so not how to treat someone who's had her heart ripped out. They leave with mercifully little fanfare.

I wake up a few times during the night, with Opal's words reverberating and bouncing around my brain. The next morning I don't feel any worse than I did before. In its own way I suppose that's a win.

Luckily, I don't have time to overanalyze, because the SATs happen this weekend. For the two weeks leading up to the exam, Raksmey and I woke up at six a.m. "The test starts at eight," she said. "We want our brains to be sharp and ready to go by then, so we have to get used to functioning at the early hour." She's like a standardized-testing personal trainer.

Dragging myself out of bed was more than half the battle,

but once I did, I just attached myself to Opal and let her steer me to Yoga Connection. After about a week of this torture, I find that I did indeed adjust to the wake-up time. And there's something nice about not having to dash to class as soon as my feet hit the ground.

So on the morning of, I'm sitting up in bed, waiting while Raks picks out my outfit. "Now, I know some people show up to finals in pjs or sweats and think they're being cute in their all-nighter attire," she says, continuing to rifle through my closet. "F that. You need to get in a take-no-prisoners frame of mind. Like, 'I'm here to conquer this test, and no one better get in my way.' And for that you can't be too comfortable."

"Okay. What kind of clothes say that?" I ask.

"Do you have a suit?" she asks.

"Are *you* wearing a suit?" I ask, giving her a suspicious look.

"No, but I don't need to. I don't respond to costumes and adornment as much as you do. Clothes directly affect your mind-set, so you need to look the part."

I'm kind of startled that she's read me so well. "I'm not judging," she says, misinterpreting my look. "I get it now. It's how you express yourself."

"Actually I do have a suit." I have a couple of my mom's hand-me-downs, which I wore when sitting in on development meetings. That seems like a lifetime ago. I brought one for college interviews.

"Well, get it on!" Raks says.

Soon I'm standing in front of the full-length bathroom mirror, checking myself out in a black pantsuit, white blouse, and sky-high heels. The suit's a bit wrinkled, but it mostly steams out after Raks hangs it in the shower. She studies me. "You look sharp," she concludes. "Now we need breakfast."

At the Canteen she continues to order me around. "Don't talk to anyone. You're in the zone unless your mother's dying. Anything else can wait until after. Pick something high in protein."

"You're being extreme." But actually I'm not complaining. Her intensity, while weird, is motivating. And with any luck, effective. Needless to say, my preparation last time included none of this.

I do as instructed and bring my one cup of black coffee and two soft-boiled eggs to a table at the edge of the dining hall. I avoid eye contact with everyone, which is hard, because I'm causing a bit of a stir in this suit. I've seen boys wear sport coats to finals, but maybe I should've taken Raksmey's advice with a grain of salt.

When we get to the gym, people are already seated in the rows of desks that fill the room. Kids from the local public school are also here to test, so it's going to be a full house. I take a seat in the middle and practice my cleansing breaths. My palms are clammy, and my clothing feels a bit constricting. I don't dare remove my blazer for fear that this facade of control I have will immediately crumble.

Just like last time, the test supervisor does the introductory spiel, followed by the proctors' handing out the test booklets and pencils. "You may begin." I break the seal on the booklet and keep my head down until time is called, thrilled that I had a chance to run through my answers a second time.

During the break I walk around to get my blood pumping

and clear my head, my high heels clicking conspicuously on the wooden floor. But I still don't talk to anyone. I know myself. I'd get too anxious comparing answers or talking about how difficult or easy we found that first section.

I see Elizabeth gabbing with Lila. Opal, Jess, Leo, and Whitney were happy with their scores from last year, so they're not here. How I envy them.

When the break ends, we file back into the gym. The next four hours both drag and zip by, and then we're done.

I stand up and unbutton my blazer, stretching and cracking my spine. I have no sense of how I actually did, and I'm more than a little grateful that results won't be available until after Thanksgiving break. But there's no doubt that I felt more on top of it than last time. Maybe it's limited progress, but I think it counts.

CHAPTER TWENTY-SEVEN

I stumble out of the gym, squinting and shielding my eyes against the bright sunlight. I feel like I've been in a cave for several days.

My toes feel pinched inside my high heels, and all I can think about is taking them off. I'm starving and stare longingly at the Canteen, trying to determine whether I have enough time to run back to Abbot and change before lunch closes. I decide I can make it and turn toward the dorm but end up smacking into someone and knocking her over. After helping the girl up and profuse apologies on both sides, I notice Declan sitting on the steps of Porter Hall, looking at me, shaking with laughter. Other students crowd the steps, elbow to elbow in fleece jackets or thick wool sweaters, but no one else seems to have noticed.

Declan and I haven't spoken since Halloween, not even during film class. As much as I hate to admit it, what Bettina said made me think twice about being overly friendly to him. Even though Leo and I are now definitively over and my pride could probably use a little restoring, I wouldn't do that to someone. Despite what Bettina may think of me.

Still, his laughing at me seems like a reasonably good ice-breaker. I walk over and stand beside him until he slides over to make room. I sit down and slip my heels off. He's still laughing. "Let me know when you're done," I say.

"I'm sorry! It wasn't even that funny." His face buried in his arms and quivering shoulders would suggest otherwise. "But you're so tiny and look all fancy, and then you take some chick out. . . . Okay, it was pretty funny."

I roll my eyes. "Did you already eat?"

Declan nods and stands, finally collecting himself. "But come on. Let's get you a sandwich."

"I should change. I've gotten my fill of weird looks for the day," I say, gesturing down at my suit.

"Skylar Hoffman, shy away from being noticed?" His tone is mocking but not mean. "Unheard-of."

"Ha ha." But I decide he's right. So I stand up.

Inside the Canteen, I do, in fact, get a record number of looks. "You'd think they'd never seen a suit before," I grumble.

"If it was from Brooks Brothers, you wouldn't be having this problem," he says after a glance at me.

"It's my mom's," I say, like that should explain everything.

He starts down the deli bar, piling veggies and cold cuts on a plate. "You vegetarian? Allergic to anything?"

"Oh, that's for me?"

"I already ate, remember?" he says. I watch as he toasts the bread, then assembles a delicious-looking sandwich, which he cuts in half and wraps in napkins. "Let's go."

"We're not eating here?"

Declan shakes his head. "That suit is attracting too much attention."

We walk out of the building and back to Porter Hall. I'm just about to point out that it's kind of chilly for a picnic when Declan motions for me to follow him to a side entrance into the building. Our footsteps echo in the deserted hall. He takes the stairs two at a time all the way to the third and top floor.

"Are we even allowed to be in here on a Saturday?"

"Probably not." At the far end of one wing, he opens a door, and we go up yet another set of stairs. Judging from the cobwebs and musty smell, this one is seldom used.

"How did you know these were here?"

"I used to babysit a fac brat. They know every inch of this campus." I try to picture Declan babysitting some teacher's toddler and can't stop the smile that threatens to consume my face.

"What?" he asks, exasperated. "I like little kids. And it's good money."

"No, it's cute. It's just, I don't know, you wear a lot of black." I'm completely joking, and to my great relief, Declan smiles.

We get to the top of the stairs and climb out onto the wooden attic floor. The space is completely empty and spans the entire length of Porter Hall, with a ceiling that slopes under the gables. Shafts of late-afternoon sunlight stream through the tiny windows, giving off a dusty, low level of light.

"This is amazing," I whisper.

"You haven't seen the best part," he says.

We walk toward the center of the building. Declan spots an old skateboard and jumps on it, kicking off and riding it to the other side. He looks unexpectedly comfortable on it, even while holding a sandwich.

There's a lone couch facing an enormous stained-glass window that overlooks the quad and the Field. I curl up on it while Declan rolls back over. "This was a pain in the ass to get up here," he says, tapping the couch with his foot.

"You put this here? What for?"

He gestures out the window. "This is the best reading spot on campus."

From the outside you almost can't tell the window's here. Or maybe I just haven't spent enough time gazing at the tops of these buildings.

Declan's right. Winthrop never fails to impress me with its beauty. Even now, though its trees are bare and the grounds no longer have the deep green of early fall, it's still breathtaking. From up here you can see just how far the campus extends, and everything feels possible.

"Can you teach me to skateboard?" I ask.

He answers me with a shrug, so I get up and wait next to the board. Exhaling a loud sigh, Declan comes toward me. "Let's try standing on it. Baby steps."

"Your confidence in me is overwhelming." I put one foot on, but when I try to lift the other, the board slides out from under me. Declan holds his arms up so I can hang on to them for balance. I manage to do this without looking him in the eye. When he tries to move away, I immediately start wobbling and jump off. "Try again," he says, holding his hands out. So I do.

After a minute of me just standing and balancing, he says, "I don't actually skateboard."

"Then why am I up on this tiny piece of wood, entrusting you with my life?" I ask, jumping off. Declan steps hard on the back of the board, flipping it up and catching it from the top. "You look natural enough."

"I used to snowboard. And do BMX biking."

"You mean, like tricks and things?" I ask. Declan nods. "And you don't anymore?" Another nod. "Why not?"

"I decided I was done competing." He says it with such finality that there doesn't seem to be more to the story. At least nothing that he's willing to get into with me.

"How long have you been coming up here?" I ask.

"Since sophomore year. That was the year I did a lot of thinking. Like, too much thinking."

I wonder if he's going to say anything about getting busted, but he doesn't. I lean against the wall, my head resting against the window frame, watching life below. "And they've left your couch here all this time?"

"I doubt anyone even knows it's here."

Gazing out the window, I feel peaceful and removed, like I'm finally getting to catch my breath. The adrenaline that carried me through the exam seems to get sucked from my body all at once, leaving me heavy and sluggish.

I move to the couch to sprawl out next to Declan. "I thought I knew all there was to know about this place," I say.

He nudges me with his knee. "Guess you were wrong."

CHAPTER TWENTY-EIGHT

Whitney sits poised to type on her laptop. "I know it feels like we just got done with Halloween, but as we all know, Rally Weekend is fast approaching, and with the number of guests we'll be hosting, we need everything to be flawless. The main events are obviously the Friday-night pep rally and bonfire, and on Saturday night the Cotillion. And with all the sports going on, all we need is to come up with a few things to offer those people who won't attend any of the above." The entire table shares a knowing smirk.

Olivia raises her hand. "I've received a few emails about the Cotillion ticket price being too high."

They've priced tickets at a hundred and fifty dollars a pair, bumped up from a hundred last year. Single tickets are eighty-five, not that anyone buys them. I suppose it's mostly safe to assume people have that much money, but still. Yet another reason for me to be glad I'm not going.

Whitney shakes her head. "Don't worry about it. People gripe about the price every year, but they always come."

"For the nonrallying, what about a poetry reading?" Lila asks. "Or how about a chess tournament?"

"I like how we periodically support alternative activities when it's convenient to our agenda," I say.

"Your holier-than-thou shtick is getting tired," Whitney snaps back.

Everyone ignores us. "Lila's on the right track, but the hard part is getting people to be responsible for anything," Elizabeth says. "Most of the active planners want to do the Rally Weekend stuff, not get stuck hosting the . . . other stuff."

"Skylar, you actually don't need to be here," Whitney says. "Since Abbot did the Halloween thing, we took you off the schedule for Rally Weekend."

"What? No, we have something to propose, and we want to do it," I say. "Abbot will host an underground dance club in the black box theater."

Lila snorts. "Isn't one dance enough? And that doesn't exactly sound like the type of thing that will appeal."

I narrow my eyes. "People will love it. Trust me."

"It really doesn't matter whether it's a good idea or not," Whitney says. "Abbot got bumped from the schedule. You're not back on until winter term."

This is news to me. "Didn't you just say that we're having trouble getting people to step up?"

Elizabeth nods reluctantly, sneaking a sideways glance at Whit.

Whitney meets my stare. "Since Rally Weekend is crucial in

so many ways, we decided to assign some of the more seasoned planners to these events."

"I'm quite confident we can handle it," I say. "Besides, we're offering up a fun, inexpensive, uncomplicated option. We can use the sound system that's already there, and I have the DJ and all the music."

"Where'd you find a DJ?" Whitney demands.

"Don't worry about it. We don't even need decor. The atmosphere in there's perfect for what we're going for. We'll just use a couple of the spots."

Everyone looks at Whitney for the final say. I can barely refrain from doing an exaggerated eye roll. "Sorry, but no," she says. "It sounds too derivative."

I can't believe what I'm hearing. "Was Ghouls and Graves too successful for you? Is that it?" I'm asking in an ironic way, but when anger flashes in her eyes, I realize that she's afraid of the competition. Right then I know there's no way I can win this battle. At least not in any straightforward way.

"Unbelievable," Opal says when I fill everyone in. "She's stonewalling us. What do we do about that?"

I groan, feeling the onset of a massive head-and-face ache. "We have to go over her head somehow."

"Do you have a copy of the bylaws?" Raksmey asks.

"Yeah, I can email it to you when I find it," I say.

"Go look now," Raksmey says. After just a few weeks of being my SAT tutor, she mistakenly believes that she has authority over me in all areas.

"No," I say, glaring at her. "It can wait."

"Come on. I know her password," Opal says. The two of them flit out of the common room, exhibiting zero qualms about breaking into my personal email account.

I clutch the sides of my face and massage my temples.

"Do you really think we can make this work?" Bettina asks.

"Yes," I say. "In the way that your art brought something totally unique to this school, I think that Raks's club kid-hipster aesthetic will do the same."

"Anyway, what do we have to lose?" Samantha says.

"A lot, actually," I say. "I've thought about this. If we can engage the people who feel left out by all the staid drivel that the Calendar puts on, we'll have made a difference. We all deserve to feel like we belong here."

Bettina and Jess look at each other. "We didn't even have to bite her," Samantha says. I think she's kidding.

"God, you guys, ease up," Jess says. "Maybe it was rough going at first, but getting pushed out of your dorm senior year would be really traumatic for anyone."

"Thank you, Jess," I say.

"And then she had to grapple with the fact that she's not one of the cool kids anymore," Jess says.

"What?" I say, indignant. "I'm still cool. Just not, you know, popular."

Jess shoves my arm, laughing. "That's like me saying, 'I'm still rich, just cut off from my family money.'"

I snort, but Samantha looks at Jess with concern. "They still haven't gotten over that?"

"Well, I did destroy about five hundred thousand dollars'

worth of inventory. Wholesale." Jess has a rueful smile, but I can tell she's not kidding.

"What are you talking about?" I ask.

"Thanks to Opal's influence, Jess is a conscientious objector to her family's furrier business," Bettina explains.

"Yeah, so she spray-painted an entire warehouseful of minks," Samantha crows.

"Some of them were fox and rabbit," Jess says. I can tell she's still pretty proud of her stunt. "And that's when they cut me off."

"That's crazy. On both sides," I say, wide-eyed.

Jess shrugs. "They think I was just rebelling because they sent me away for school. They also let me spend a night in jail, to scare the crap out of me. It wasn't exactly shattering, though, because, let's face it, Barrington's hardly the big bad city."

I'm still trying to wrap my head around the fact that Jess is old money. No wonder nothing ever fazes her. "How do you pay for everything?" I know it's nosy, but she doesn't seem to mind.

"I work at an indie movie theater in the summer and on winter and spring breaks. The owner's a cool guy, and he lets us in for free when we're not on the schedule. As you know, I love movies, so it's pretty painless."

"So you're kind of in the same boat I am?" I'm trying to understand how she feels about her whole life changing. Okay, so clothes clearly weren't her thing, but there had to be something.

"Not exactly. My education is guaranteed to be paid for, and my big brothers slip me money sometimes. Especially the one who doesn't work in the family business. He gets it."

"But don't you miss anything?" I ask. "Or you have school and movies and that's enough?" Whit would be lost without her money. She once ordered a new laptop from her phone while we were running.

Jess rolls onto her stomach, her brow furrowed in concentration. "I miss traveling. My parents go away every summer and leave me home with our housekeeper. At least Lucy's chill. She's lived with us since I was in third grade."

"What about all your friends? Don't they pity you?"

"Ha! The ones I still have kind of do," Jess says.

"That, more than anything, is something I just could not take," I admit.

"Oh, your old Lincoln friends pity you, just not so much that they'd actually want to do anything to help you," Jess says.

"Seriously. Do you really need friends like that?" Samantha asks. "I mean, keep your fucking pity. Not everyone gets to live in a bubble their whole entire lives."

"Or wants to," Bettina adds.

I guess I never thought of it that way.

By the time I venture upstairs, Opal and Raks have printed out the bylaws and spread them out all over the floor. There are so many pages, you'd think the Calendar was a UN committee. "Got it! Right here," Raksmey says.

They glue their heads together for about five minutes, and

then Opal claps her hands. "Simple! We just have to get approval from the school president."

I groan. "That's not going to be easy."

"Marshall's still torn up about Whitney?" Opal asks. Marshall Buck, school president, is Whitney's ex-boyfriend. Even though she's less than kind to him, he's not over her, and everybody knows it.

"There must be a way to persuade him," Opal says.

"I'm willing to try, but I don't want you guys to be disappointed if he doesn't help us," I say.

"Don't be such a bummer," Raks says.

"He'll see our side of it," Opal agrees.

I would give anything for their confidence.

CHAPTER TWENTY-NINE

One afternoon Raksmey and I plot the official public debut of Club Raks over a couple of pizzas at Andrea's. This is also my way of thanking her for helping me with the SATs. I'd tried to buy her an iTunes gift card—just a token—but this was the only form of payment she'd accept from me. Anyway it's way cheaper than a prep class or a professional tutor would've been.

"But we're not going to call it Club Raks, are we? That's just our own nickname for it, right?" she asks.

"Why? Getting cold feet? Not confident enough in your skills to attach your name to this?"

She knows I'm just messing with her and smirks. "Not at all. I'm just worried that it won't mean anything to anyone."

"It will when it's over. Besides, I like that it's our little inside joke. Do you have a plan yet?"

"I just want it to be a big, happy, inclusive celebration where everyone loses their minds," she says.

"Okay. That's . . . descriptive." I bite into a steaming hot slice and pull stretchy strings of melted cheese away from my mouth.

"I want everybody to dance and not feel self-conscious," Raksmey says. "You know how at most dances everyone moves around like they know they're being watched and judged?"

I laugh. "Yeah. Because they are."

Raksmey nods. "Well, I want the opposite of that. So it has to be kind of hard to see, so that people can really go off in there. Maybe we could get a strobe instead of using the spots."

I don't want to break it to her that a big selling point with our plan is that we can do this whole thing on a shoestring budget. "I might know someone who has one, come to think of it," she says.

"Really? Just lying around in their dorm room?"

She gives me a look. "You'd be surprised at what those boys in Thatcher get up to."

Marshall Buck is tall, broad, and muscular, with fine white-blond hair that looks like down. From his striped rugby shirt and jeans right down to his Y chromosome, he is the proto-typical Winthrop school president. Whitney dumped Marshall at the beginning of last year for a fling with a lacrosse player. Marshall was so devastated that he hasn't dated anyone since. From what I've heard, he's attempted to mend his broken heart by throwing himself into crew, water polo, and of course the Student Council.

"What's up, Skylar?" he asks as I slide into the seat across from him at the Student Council office. Naturally he has a wooden placard with his name and title etched into it perched on the edge of his desk.

"This is nice," I say, pointing to it. Can't hurt to appeal to his ego.

"Thanks. The staff got it for me." And by "staff" he means the rest of the Student Council. But my bet is that he bought it for himself. He's the kind of guy who will one day get himself a WORLD'S BEST DAD mug for Father's Day to keep on his giant mahogany CEO desk. "What can I do for you?"

So much for warming up to it with small talk and my half-baked plan of flirting with him to grease the wheels, so to speak. Not that I even know how to flirt anymore.

"Well, believe it or not, I am here in an official capacity," I say. "My dorm wants to plan something for Rally Weekend, but we got bumped from the schedule." I know appealing to Marshall's concern for the underrepresented isn't the way to go. Instead, I focus on how Winthrop should be grooming the next generation and that Raks is only a junior and should be given the chance to step up.

"Her name hasn't come up before," Marshall says.

"Exactly. But she's a top student, has real leadership potential and excellent organizational skills, and she could be your discovery."

He gives me a knowing look, and I wonder if I went too far. As far as I recall, his bullshit detector was never that finely tuned. One flattering word or charming smile from Whit would get her almost anything she wanted.

"You put me in an awkward position," he says. "No one has used that clause in the bylaws in almost fifteen years. I looked it up."

"Even better," I say. "You're a pioneer! A visionary!" Okay, I'd better stop it, because now he's smirking at me. "Well, it is a way to leave your mark anyway."

Marshall sighs. "People will assume I'm doing it to dog Whitney."

I don't have the heart to break it to him that the only person who still thinks about him and Whitney is him. "No one will think that," I say. "In fact, since there's no reason not to approve this, people might assume that your not doing it is because of her."

"What happened between you two?" he asks.

"Nothing," I say, too quickly. "I guess since we don't live in the same dorm anymore, it's only natural that we grew apart."

Marshall's at least pretending to peruse my letter of request. "Is it Lila?" he asks. His casualness is so studied that I assume he'd heard the same stories from Whit that I had.

"No. She's a bit of a handful and kind of possessive, but Whitney and I aren't getting along for our own reasons." I watch him flip my letter over and back again. "You have the added ammunition that Abbot was supposed to be on the schedule. Everyone knows you're a stickler for rules and that you believe in doing the right thing."

He smiles, but it's perfunctory. "Okay, you've appealed to my vanity three times"—four, but who's counting?—"which means I at least owe it to you to consider this thing. Leave it with me, and I'll email you by the end of the week."

Dang. I thought I had it in the bag with that last one. But I know better than to push it. He shakes my hand before I go, which I think means he'll take it seriously.

"I thought you said you'd be able to woo him to our side," Jess wails when I give everyone the update.

"I never said anything remotely close to that! I said we used to be friendly and that I might know a few tricks to talk him into it."

"That definitely suggests an ability to woo," Opal agrees.

"He said he's thinking about it. That's not a no, so let's stay positive." I check my email for the fourth time. It feels good to be checking for a reason other than hoping that either Leo or one of my old friends will be reaching out to make amends. Maybe I'm finally starting to move on. I turn to Raksmey. "I'd have your set list ready just to be on the safe side."

"Are you kidding? It's been done for a week. I bought a ton of new stuff, and it is off the hook!" She rubs her hands together in gleeful anticipation.

"Raksmey! We're supposed to be doing this under budget," Jess says.

"Don't worry, I'm underwriting the whole thing," Raksmey says. "If I tried to hand in those expenses, you'd probably fire me."

"Probably?" I say. "Why do you need new songs? You have a million." Seriously. She has a separate computer just for music.

"I told you. For a real dance party, you need just the right progression. It has to build at the right time, with room to breathe. . . ."

As she blathers on about her vision, I realize that it is going to be a huge disappointment to her if this doesn't come together. To Raksmey this isn't merely a way to upend the Calendar or level the social playing field at Winthrop. It's about creating an unguarded moment for everyone to remember. If only the Calendar were made up of such generous, nonegotistical people.

CHAPTER THIRTY

"I know what you're doing."

I'm just about to get on an elliptical machine in the gym when I turn and startle to see Whitney right up in my face. "Using Marshall to overrule me? You have some nerve, I'll give you that," she says.

Honestly, I've been preparing myself for this moment. Whitney has ears everywhere, especially where Marshall's concerned. "This has nothing to do with you and Marshall."

Whitney snorts. "I don't know why you're bothering. Everyone is coming to the Cotillion."

"Great. Then why do you care?" I put my hand on the elliptical rail to deter some guy from getting on it. But Whitney's not done talking.

"I'm not sure what you think you're accomplishing with this stunt, but you're not going to make me look bad. You're just leading your geek friends down a path of humiliation and defeat."

The guy waiting for the machine keeps shooting me irritated glances. I've waited more than twenty minutes to work out, and I'm not about to give up my place in line, so I get on and program the machine. "Again, this isn't about you," I say to Whitney. "I'm sure that's hard for you to believe, but there are good reasons for doing this, and it's too bad you can't see them. I mean, what are you so worried about? Won't you be thrilled if all the people you deem losers stay away from the Cotillion? Aren't we helping you, in a way?"

"Well, not the way you went about it!" Whitney shrieks.

"You left me no choice!"

"Do you know this is the first time in fifteen years that the Calendar's been challenged?" She glares at me like it's solely my fault that this is happening on her watch, instead of acknowledging her role in the whole matter.

"Don't worry. I'm sure that won't be your only legacy."

Jaw clenched, neck stiff, she says, "Don't mess with us, Skylar. It will *obliterate* what little social status you have left."

I smile sweetly. "Because you've been such a bitch to me all year and managed to turn all our friends against me, threatening my social status really doesn't pose quite the threat that it once might have."

"Who are you kidding? You still care. You don't want to graduate without your oldest friends."

"I'll find a way to carry on. And since when does what I want matter? Did you ever take that into consideration when you were systematically freezing me out?"

Whitney sighs. "You needed time in the doghouse. If you stop this nonsense now, it wouldn't be too late for you to come back and finish the year with us."

I can't believe she's trying to dangle our relationship in front of me like it's a carrot and I'm a donkey. "I'll take that under advisement. Thanks."

She tries one last tactic. "We both know that all I have to do is pick up the phone. One night with Marshall is all it would take to turn this completely around."

Gross. I can't believe I was ever best friends with someone so opportunistic and cruel. "If you're comfortable using your . . . *influence* like that, and your ex-boyfriend's dumb enough to let you, then you deserve each other."

I slip my headphones on, increase the resistance to ten, and give her a sarcastically friendly wave. Thankfully she takes the hint.

I know he said he'd get back to me by the end of the week, but when I get back to my room, I'm still so agitated that I fire off an email to Marshall. After listening to Whit and her utter conviction that she controls everything, including me, I'm more determined than ever to show her that Club Raks can be a success.

Marshall,

I think you'd be surprised by how much having something like Club Raks matters to some of our fellow students. A lot of people at Winthrop are engaged academically but not socially, and given that networking has traditionally been one of the great selling points of attending an institution like ours, we are missing a huge opportunity to make Winthrop a more integrated place. They may be geeks, but one day they'll be running the world. And yes, I know it's ironic that I of all people am speaking up for the masses.

Peace out,
Skylar

It takes less than ten minutes for Marshall to reply.

You have my support. Come by my office tomorrow.

Officious to the end, but I'll take it.

Once Club Raks is an official event, it's no small feat to get it off the ground. We've decided to make it invitation-only. Because it's a school dance, we can't *technically* make it invitation-only, but we don't advertise it at all. Instead, we put the first invites in the hands of club leaders who almost definitely never considered attending a Rally Weekend event, and then rely on word of mouth. Just like in certain exclusive clubs, potential guests will need a password. And because it's going to be in the black box theater, we're making it a "blackout party," so everyone has to wear all black to enter.

I'm there when Jess hands out the envelopes at the end of her screening of a documentary on how killer whales are mistreated when used for entertainment. I notice that the three other members of the Vegan Club are in attendance.

On the front of the black envelope, we've printed NO TICKETS, NO DATE, NO WORRIES in silver ink.

"What is this?" "I don't dance." "Rally Weekend sucks." This is just a sampling of the many protests we hear. It's as if we're inviting people to a voluntary waterboarding party.

"Trust me, it won't be like other dances. We want you to come and be yourself. There's no formality, and hopefully no attitude. Just a good time had by all. Spread the word."

The response is skeptical at best.

"I invited Remy," Opal announces in the common room one night.

We all look at her. I knew they were becoming a thing, but everyone else seems thrown for a loop. "Remy's cool, you guys. Out of everyone I used to hang out with, he's the most mellow," I say.

"I agree with Skylar," Yasmin says. "We shouldn't write him off just because he's popular and athletic. And handsome."

"Are you sure you don't want to invite Remy?" I ask. She laughs and sticks her tongue out at me.

"And he won't tell anyone we don't want to come," Opal says. At first I think she's saying this for everyone else's comfort, but she glances at me. Ah. Leo. I'm sure he and Miranda will make a dashing couple at the Cotillion.

"The problem with this strategy is that we have no idea how many people will show," Raksmey says. Of course she's the most nervous; she's put so much into this.

"I know it feels risky and that it'd be more reassuring to have a traditional RSVP system, but keeping it on the DL both adds to the mystery and takes the pressure off. People will come around. If we want to prove that we're offering something different, we have to commit to doing things in a different way."

Honestly I had no idea that rallying the troops took this much cheerleading and handholding. I feel like a general, because I'm the only one who isn't allowed a second of doubt or insecurity. In the moments when I do feel those things, I have to fake confidence. Everyone else is free to be their neurotic selves, but not me.

And the rumors. There's absolutely nothing I can do to stem the rumors. "Lila and Whitney have been telling everyone that they put us on the schedule as a farce." Opal brings this news via Remy.

"So?" I ask. "They obviously consider us a threat. Take it as a compliment and ignore it."

"But people will believe them. Everyone always does," Yasmin says.

I can't argue. I'm living proof of that.

"Look, we have to try, no matter what," Opal says, smoothing down her caftan. "We have karma on our side."

"Not to mention righteousness," Jess adds.

"Even without all that, I'm not worried," I say. "Raks has worked really hard on making this an amazing night for everyone, and I think it will be. If people are going to fall for Lila and Whitney's crap, they were never coming anyway."

They seem satisfied with this for now.

Remy catches me on the way into Images of Women. "Word is that Lila's putting a lot of pressure on Whitney. She wants Whit to use all methods at her disposal to get Marshall to withdraw his support."

I snort. "I doubt it'll take much to convince Whit to go there. How do you know this?"

Remy shrugs. "I hear things. Right place, right time sort of thing. Besides, Lila's not exactly quiet." He grimaces. "Anyway, Whitney let Lila take the reins on the Cotillion, and Lila's pulled out all the stops. She said she wanted to make it a real party, not like these podunk country boarding school affairs we've been having. But now she's supposedly way over budget, and they're using money from Lincoln's dorm fund."

"Isn't that, like, embezzlement?" I ask. "Why doesn't Whit reel her in?"

"Nobody knows," he says. "It's like the Whit we knew no longer exists. Ever since Lila got here, she's let herself be run into the ground."

"Glad I'm not the only one who's noticed," I say.

"I don't totally get it, but you know how it is with people from your past. Sometimes you regress into old roles." Remy lingers outside the building even though the first bell has rung. "Lila asked me to the Cotillion." He kicks at the ground, looking so upset that I start laughing. Remy rolls his eyes. "Glad I can be here to amuse you." He scowls and brushes past me into the building. I almost feel guilty for being such an unsupportive friend, but not really.

On a purely selfish level, I hope I'm there when Lila learns who Remy's dating.

CHAPTER THIRTY-ONE

The night finally arrives, and we're ready to go. Except there's about fifteen whole minutes where it's just the seven of us, sitting in silence, staring at one another and occasionally at C.J.'s strobe light, which flashes sadly on the stage. Club Raks is officially open for business.

We don't say anything. Even Raksmey sits completely still for once. None of us wants to be the first to call it, like we're ER doctors and our underground club is the patient we're trying not to pronounce dead. I know they won't pack it in until I give the word.

So I stand up. "Okay, let's get this thing going," I say.

"Nothing's happening," Bettina points out.

I jump off the stage as Raksmey starts the music. "So what?"

Everybody's up, dancing and singing. We're so loud that I can't imagine we're not being heard halfway across campus.

At some point I spin around and notice Remy. He's standing and waving his arms, but not like he's dancing, like he's trying to get our attention. I'm not about to disrupt things, so I pull him backstage. "What? And, oh yeah, thanks for coming." I'm just being polite. One guest feels even more pathetic than none. Like now there's an outsider here to witness our spectacular failure.

"There's a line of people outside!" he shouts into my ear.

"Shut up!" I scream back, smacking him on the arm.

"You have to let them in! They know the password and everything!"

At the last minute I'd second-guessed the whole password gimmick for this very reason, but it seemed too late to do anything about it. I rush to the entrance of the theater. Sure enough, there are seven people lined up. Okay, so the fire department won't be shutting us down anytime soon, but it's a start.

"Password?" I say breathlessly to the first person in line. I recognize him as one of Yasmin's Thatcher buddies. He doesn't look like he came to the right place, because he's wearing a black turtleneck with black corduroys, but who am I to judge? I'm sure I look totally charming with sweat plastering my hair to my face. He gives me a hesitant smile. "Uh, 'global warming'?" I shouldn't have let Jess choose the password.

I open the door wide and hand him a glow necklace, and our first guest steps in. I note with amusement that his glasses fog up the moment he comes in from the frigid air.

The rest of the line mutters the password before I let them in. Over the shoulder of the last person in line, I see others coming toward the black box and I shut the door quickly.

When I get back inside, I'm elated to see that the dancing hasn't stopped. There are now fifteen of us in all, which still feels pretty empty. Especially when some of us are just standing still. But with some on the floor and some up on the stage, at least the space feels like it's being used. I take out my camera, trying to find angles from which the room actually looks full.

Raksmey was dead on about the lighting and even the glow necklaces she insisted on. The strobe bounces around the room, catching everyone in midflail, so that any one of us could be an amazing dancer. It also casts silhouettes onto the walls, so that there appears to be more movement than there actually is.

Remy nudges me. "You better check the door."

"I want to let the line build a little," I say.

He gives me a look. "Don't push your luck."

So I go back outside. To my utter shock, there are ten more people waiting. "This is so cool," one of the girls says, bouncing on her toes to keep warm. She and her friend wear retro punk chic, complete with tights, black denim shorts, and black vests over black T-shirts.

"Sorry to keep you waiting. How's the rest of Rally Weekend going?" I ask, giving them necklaces.

"Don't know and don't really care," the first girl says. Her friend laughs and nods.

"Well, hope you have a good time at Club Raks," I say.

I personally welcome everyone coming in. Every single person thanks us for going out on a limb and giving them something different to do this weekend.

As the room fills and it begins to feel like we're actually pulling this off, my stress level drops. Raksmey makes a few adjustments to the set list, which I only know because I watched her go through it about seven hundred times. Her tweaks are seamless, because she worked out every possible outcome ahead of time, using something called decision trees. I think she's going with the scenario she named High Voltage. Believe it or not, she still has a level above that one, "for when people go completely bat-shit crazy."

More people join every minute, until we legitimately have to make people wait. Even people dressed in formal Cotillion clothes come by, seemingly willing to wait outside and watch their breath fog in the bitter cold. I feel so encouraged that I even let the all-black-clothing requirement slide.

I'd have to say the biggest surprise of the night goes to the Thatcher guys. For a bunch known more for their Minecraft abilities than their gross motor skills, some of them are serious dance enthusiasts. I wouldn't say they're good, exactly, but I've long believed that, with dancing, spirit matters more than actual coordination.

I spot Opal and Remy making out on the stage steps and immediately wish I could unsee it.

Declan walks toward me and slides a hand around my waist, pulling me toward him. He must have just gotten here. My gaze automatically flits about the room, looking for Bettina, because I know she wouldn't approve. Luckily, she's not nearby. Declan's a good dancer; he keeps our bodies close but not obscenely so. At some point I stop trying to understand what's going on and hand my camera to Yasmin so I can relax and enjoy the night.

Suddenly all the spots and overhead lights turn on, glowing a hot, searing white for just a brief moment. But a second later they fade to yellow, like we're having a brownout in the middle of a California heat wave. Then everything shuts off, and Club Raks goes completely still in stunned, dark silence.

"What the hell?" someone finally asks. That sets off a low rumble of muttering, nervous laughter, and feet shuffling toward the exit. There are squeals and raised voices as the push to get out grows more urgent. I don't smell anything burning and don't hear any alarms, so I'm reasonably sure there's no cause for panic. Still, my heartbeat picks up and my breaths shorten.

A hand grasps mine and holds me back. "Let's wait," Declan murmurs. "Let a bunch of people go out first. We don't want anyone to get hurt."

So I hang with him, leaning against the wall so we don't get jostled in the evacuation.

When we make it outside, a few people have started to walk off, going in the direction of the Cotillion or their dorms, but most stick around, waiting to see if the power comes back. Samantha huddles with a couple theater kids. I hear snippets like "backup generator" and "makes no sense." From what I can piece together, the black box's extra power generator has gone missing.

I look down and realize that I'm still clutching Declan's hand. I let go and shove my hands in my pockets, trying not to notice his questioning look.

Raksmey positions a small wireless speaker on the steps, and with a few taps on her keyboard the music blares on. She's switched playlists to one that's more mellow. It still creates a nice vibe, though, and surprisingly the dancing starts up again. Not quite in full force—it's more like talking while moving and feeling the music. Maybe it's just too cold to sit or stand still.

We stay out there, getting so close to curfew that people heading home from the Cotillion begin to pass by. In the distance I notice Whitney and Lila speed-walking to Lincoln, their dates nowhere in sight. They don't so much as glance this way.

On a hunch I sprint toward them and cut them off. "Where's the generator?"

They both jump, startled. "What are you talking about?" Whitney asks. Strands of hair have slipped out of her topknot, and her lipstick is half worn off. Neither of them looks particularly happy, definitely not like they've been socializing and dancing the night away.

"We maxed out the electrical in the black box. There was a power surge or something, and the backup generator was mysteriously missing."

Whitney bursts out laughing, but Lila crosses her arms in a smug, satisfied gesture. I stare at Lila, momentarily blinded by her enormous diamond earrings. Does she not realize that, as rarefied as Winthrop is, it's still high school?

"What?" she asks. "And when exactly do you think we'd have time to steal a generator? Maybe you haven't noticed, but we've been busy organizing the social event of the year."

"Seriously. Besides, where would we supposedly hide it?" Whitney's nose wrinkles with scorn.

I don't believe them for a second. They'll never admit to doing this, no matter how ingenious or effective, because it shows how truly desperate they are. But I know it was them. "If you're so positive that the Cotillion is what everyone wants, why stoop to sabotage?"

Lila puts a hand on Whitney's arm. "You can't prove anything," Lila says. Whitney shoots a quick sideways glance at her before turning back to me with a frown.

"It would've been huge," I say.

"I'm sure it would have," Whitney says condescendingly as she looks toward the black box, where no doubt our crowd has dwindled to just a few stragglers. "I mean, glow necklaces. How could you lose?"

I stalk away to the sounds of them dissolving into hysterical laughter.

CHAPTER THIRTY-TWO

"We should stage a coup." We're in bed, and the room is dark except for the moonlight shining through the window, but I know Opal's awake and can hear me.

She rolls over and groans. "You've been hanging out with Jess for too long."

"I know. Part of me thinks, *We're seniors, let's just ride out the rest of our year in peace and graduate.*"

"Which is pathetic," she says agreeably.

"But if they're willing to resort to stealing, how can we let that go unanswered?"

"It is kind of amazing. Do they not understand karmic retribution?" Opal asks.

I snort. "I can assure you, karma has yet to make an appearance in either of their lives."

"Even though we didn't get to keep the club part going, it was still a fun night," Opal says.

"Yes, but it wasn't what Raksmey envisioned. She worked really hard on the set lists, and it meant so much to her that everyone have a good time."

Opal sighs. "We *did*." We're quiet for a minute; then she says, "Okay, I'm in. And by the way, Declan's not going to wait around forever, so don't be a moron."

Ugh. I knew she'd been noticing.

"You're a smart girl, Skylar. He's one of the good ones. Leo was too, but maybe you're lucky enough that you get two good ones."

Inexplicably tears spring to my eyes. When I think about how this year has turned out nothing like what I expected, I get so overwhelmed that nothing makes sense. Usually I try to block it out, but I decide Opal's right. It's not too late to turn this year around. "I know," I say with a sigh. She doesn't respond, but I know she heard me. One of Opal's best qualities is that she doesn't gloat when she's right.

The next Calendar meeting is awkward, to say the least. I have a hard time sitting there when our plans to clean house are under way. Our petition is already circulating among the students with the goal of getting the two hundred signatures we need to hold a midterm election.

"I propose we put Abbot on the schedule one more time before winter break," I say.

"So that's why you're here," Lila says. "We thought maybe you were going to blame us for your lame club."

"Denied," Whitney says without even looking at me.

"What would you do?" Guthrie asks, a note of excitement in his voice.

Before I can answer, Whitney cuts us off with a deadly stare. "It's not happening. Abbot's events are chaotic, unsafe, and unfocused. We're considering removing you from the schedule altogether until spring term."

"You can't do that," I say, rolling my eyes. "And the last one would've been amazing if the generator hadn't been stolen."

Whitney looks at Lila. "Oh. I heard the generator was found in the storage area the next day," Lila says, tilting her head.

It had been, but Samantha insisted that it had never been moved before and that no one who works at the black box would've put it away for any reason. Whitney looks vaguely uncomfortable. I get the feeling Lila may have gone rogue on this generator thing, but even so, Whitney seems powerless to control her.

"Anyway," Whitney says, "you're not the only one who knows how to circulate a petition."

I freeze. I can't believe she knows about the petition. Even though I desperately want to bolt from the meeting to find Opal and start organizing, I force myself to sit through the rest of the meeting and act unconcerned. But as soon as we're adjourned, I text Opal and Jess:

Meet @ Marshall's office NOW, b4 dinner.

I get there first, and the office is empty, so I let myself in and pace until Opal arrives. Jess follows a minute later.

"What's the matter?" Jess asks, breathless.

I fill them in on what I learned at the Calendar meeting. "I'm not exactly sure of the details, but I just know they're doing something to keep us off the schedule."

"So what?" Opal asks. "We're more than halfway there on our petition. Once we get the signatures, Marshall just needs to approve it."

Someone comes into the office, and I whip around, annoyed at the interruption. "Did we have an appointment?" Marshall asks.

"No," I say, turning back around.

"Well, then, by all means keep using my office. Uninvited," he adds when we don't acknowledge him.

"Sorry," Opal says. "We're just trying to figure something out."

"I see. Can I be of any help?" Marshall asks.

"Probably. We're trying to take over the Calendar," I say. Opal and Jess glare at me. "What? He's going to find out eventually."

Marshall sits down and stares at me. "You're serious," he says after a minute.

"Deadly," I say.

He groans, slumps down in his seat. "Skylar, why did you save all this spiritedness for my year as school president? Couldn't you have gotten some of this out of your system last year?"

"Skylar was strictly establishment last year," Jess says.

"But now she's enlightened," Opal adds quickly when she sees I'm insulted.

"I'm glad we can all agree that I sucked last year," I say. "But can we focus on the matter at hand?"

"Right. You were saying something about ousting some very well-liked and respected members of our community from their positions on the most influential student-run organization at Winthrop," Marshall says.

"That's a good summary," I agree. "But I wouldn't say the *most* influential." I smile at him, which causes him to roll his eyes and groan again.

"It's an accepted fact that the Calendar impacts students' lives in a more tangible way," he says. "I made peace with this long ago."

"Okay, but we would actually challenge the statement that those students in question are, in fact, likable," Jess says. Opal nods.

"And respected," I say.

"You've had a tiff with your bestie," Marshall says. "Be honest, isn't this a bit of an overreaction?"

"If that's all it was, then yes. But it's truly not personal. It's about the chokehold the Calendar has over everything. They're archaic," I say.

"And un-diverse," Jess says. "Our goal isn't to go wild and introduce all sorts of deviant stuff. Don't worry, Marshall, we know enough about tradition to keep it alive and well."

"We just want a true representation of the students' interests," Opal says.

"What you're proposing doesn't sound completely objectionable, if only it didn't involve taking people's leadership positions away from them," Marshall says. "That's a pretty serious move. Besides, didn't you already make a statement on Rally Weekend?

Maybe the powers that be are on alert now and they'll start being open to other kinds of programming."

"Our event was sabotaged, and I just left a meeting where they openly admitted that they were trying to keep us off the schedule," I say. "You can't expect us to be okay with that."

"If we can get them to let Abbot have the normal number of assigned events, will you stop your petition?" Marshall asks.

Jess and Opal look at me. "No way," I say. "The bare minimum is no longer going to cut it."

Marshall sighs again. "So what exactly is my role in all this?"

"Nothing. Just keep it quiet for now, but consider this your fair warning that we're going to submit this as soon as we have enough signatures," I say. "And obviously sign it when it comes across your desk."

He looks queasy at the thought. I put a hand on his arm. "It only allows us to have the election. Your signature doesn't give us the positions."

He nods. "Okay. I appreciate the heads-up."

CHAPTER THIRTY-THREE

Not many people get excited about finals, but Winthrop definitely has an abnormally high concentration of people who do. Or at least aren't completely rocked by them. I've made it through three exams and turned in my final paper for Images of Women. My brain feels like runny Jell-O, and I still have my Mandarin exam tomorrow. But I can't study for that until I finish my history term paper, which is also due tomorrow, the last day before Thanksgiving break.

I'd already received an extension, but between our petition and studying for other finals, I let this slide until the last minute. So now I'm speed-reading about the Cuban Missile Crisis, hoping to stumble upon some brilliant point that will help me whip my terrible first draft into shape.

Tonight there are a handful of other students in the studio, because everyone's busy with final projects. Bettina left the dorm before me and is isolated in a corner. At least I'm in good company with fellow crammers. I calm down enough to make sense of my notes and the quotes I've collected.

When I look up to think through the concept of brinkmanship, I see Declan standing there, looking at me, unsure of whether or not to sit down. Even though Bettina didn't give me a hard time about it, I have enough of a conscience to feel guilty about dancing so close to him and then acting so crazy about holding his hand afterward. "Hey. You going to stand there all night?" I ask.

He smiles and sets up his work space, first laying out tools and paper, then getting his music ready. I want to say something before he gets into his zone, but the trouble I'll be in if I don't hand this paper in is unfathomable. I keep watching Declan, searching for ways to address the subject that will miraculously not kill the entire night.

Finally he looks at me. "We're cool. There's only one more day until break, and I'm not going anywhere."

Somehow he read my mind and landed on the perfect thing to say. "You're staying too?" I ask.

He smiles. "I mean that figuratively." Oh. I gulp, setting off a flutter of tiny butterflies in my stomach. "But I am staying for part of break. My parents are picking me up Thursday on their way to Maine. What about you?"

I hesitate before answering. "My parents thought it'd be silly to spend the money to fly me home now and then again at winter break." The truth still doesn't come easily, but Declan doesn't blink.

"So we have time," he says.

Hours go by. Declan sketches, and I type. By the time we have to leave for sign-in, I've revised about half of my draft. I still have a late night ahead of me, but at least I made decent progress.

"Come on," Declan says, standing up. "If we leave now, I'll have time to walk you back."

I look around. Everyone else is long gone, including Bettina. "You don't have to," I say.

"I want to," he says.

We leave the building, cross the quad, and walk toward Abbot. "You're going in the complete opposite direction of your dorm," I point out.

"It's okay. I can run back fast if I need to. Besides, Chris isn't the biggest hardass in the world," Declan says, referring to his famously liberal house counselor.

"Since you're sticking around, you want to meet at the squash courts Saturday morning?" I ask.

He turns his head toward me, and I'm glad he doesn't break his stride, because I'd probably die on the spot. The squash courts are a notorious hook-up spot, especially during off hours, and I'm pretty sure Declan knows that I don't play squash. I wish any other place on campus had popped into my mind just then. Attempting to play something just seemed like a good distraction from a potentially uncomfortable conversation.

"I don't play squash," he says.

"Me neither. It always seemed kind of douchey. But I suppose we should try it once before we graduate." I sound like a nonsensical weirdo, but fortunately, he laughs.

"Uh, okay. Eight o'clock?"

"Perfect," I say. A moment passes.

Declan nods, and we remain silent the rest of the way to Abbot.

Luckily, having to finish my paper keeps me from obsessing all night long, but it doesn't help that Opal laughs uncontrollably when I tell her about my proposed meet-up at the squash courts.

"Are you sure you don't want to go to India with your parents?" I ask. She's staying for break too while her parents make a trip to visit their guru.

"I guess the upside is that none of the faculty patrols at that hour," she says. "If you change your mind, you can have your way with him right then and there. Pretty convenient, actually."

"It popped into my head before I could think it through." But she's laughing too hard to hear my protests.

CHAPTER THIRTY-FOUR

The next morning I pass a whooping celebration in the mailroom on the way to my Mandarin exam. Seems that some of the early-action letters have come in. I swallow my rising panic. Some people actually know where they'll be going to college, whereas I still owe Ms. Randall a revised draft of my admissions essay. Which I have yet to start revising.

Saturday morning, before Declan shows up at the squash courts, I practice hitting a few balls. One almost smacks me in the forehead and knocks me out. Who knew those little rubber balls were so deadly? As I'm about to serve to myself again, the door swishes open. Declan holds out a pair of goggles. "You're supposed to wear these."

"I should probably also be wearing a helmet," I say, taking the goggles. "And some protective padding."

He laughs. "Don't worry. I suck too. Why are we here, again?"

I shrug, but I can already feel myself getting defensive. Leo and I never hooked up here, mostly because it's such a cliché. "It's on my bucket list," I explain, lying through my teeth. I don't actually have a bucket list. "When else am I going to live in such close proximity to squash courts? College campuses are huge, and I'll probably be way too busy to just mess around."

Declan smirks at my Freudian slip. "Fair enough. Do you even know how to keep score?"

"Let's just rally," I say irritably.

"Is that what it's called in squash?" he asks.

"Who cares?" I reply, waiting.

We whack the ball around for several minutes. If nothing else, it's a great way to release tension. "I can't believe you actually brought me here to play squash," Declan says. I start laughing, which earns an appreciative smile. "So what other things are on your Winthrop bucket list?"

I swing and miss the ball. "I don't know. It's not a formal list, exactly. Just a bunch of stuff I haven't done that I should probably do before I leave Winthrop, never to return." *Which I'm making up as I go along.*

"Like what?" he persists.

"Like I've never gone skating on the sanctuary pond, or napped at the library, or—"

"What have you been doing for the last three years?" he demands.

I take another swing. "No idea. Anyway, I'm sure I won't get around to most of it, so thanks for helping me out with this one."

We're quiet for a bit, which seems to be key in getting a good rhythm going. Squash is definitely harder than it looks. "I . . . I'm not over my ex-boyfriend," I say. "Not yet, anyway." I hadn't planned to just blurt it out, but there it is.

Declan gives the ball another whack. If he's surprised by my spontaneous proclamation, he doesn't show it. "Ah. Well, that's a shame, but I pretty much knew that," he says. "I won't hold it against you."

My cheeks redden, and I'm grateful that physical exertion provides a plausible cover. "But can we be friends?" I ask.

He shoots me a quick smile. "Of course. We are friends."

Friendship notwithstanding, Declan manages to keep his distance over the next couple of days. Since so few students stay on campus, Lower Left is the only dining room that remains open. He must be working overtime to make sure he doesn't run into me.

"I'm sure he's just exhausted, like the rest of us," Opal says from her bed. Yasmin's curled up next to her, and none of us has moved in hours. My laptop sits on a stack of textbooks piled on the floor so we can all watch a movie together, but we keep falling asleep at different intervals, so we've yet to make it all the way through.

We eventually drag ourselves to dinner and walk to Thatcher afterward. A white frost has settled on top of the frozen ground. Campus is deserted. "Why are we going over there? Are you sure we're invited?" I ask.

"Don't be nervous. Declan will be happy to see you," Opal says.

"It's not about that," I say. "I'm still tired, though. I could go to bed right now and be perfectly happy."

Yasmin looks at her phone. "C.J. says Chris is out for the evening."

"Don't you think Dr. Murdoch's going to wonder where we all went?" I ask.

Opal smiles. "No. She appreciates how easy we are most of the time. Besides, she told me she's determined to get her shopping done before Black Friday this year. And funny, you don't sound like Skylar Hoffman, resident party girl."

"Reformed," I say. "Skylar Hoffman, *reformed* party girl."

When we get to the dorm, the door opens before we can even knock. "Did anyone see you?" C.J. asks, then exclaims, "Hey! Canteen duty!" when he notices me.

"No, everyone else was smart enough to stay inside," I say.

"Let's go." He leads us to the top floor. Once we're there, he holds up a hand to stop and silence us. "Take your shoes off so you don't leave footprints," he says. We obey.

Just as the eerie quiet starts to creep me out, he nods with satisfaction, then walks to the end of the hall, where there's a recessed window, creating a shelf that's about a foot deep. He climbs onto it, reaches up, and grabs hold of a metal ring that's folded flat against the ceiling. It's painted white to blend in, so I never would've noticed it on my own.

C.J. tugs on the ring, and a panel tilts down. He grabs on to the edge and hops down, bringing a whole set of stairs with him.

Shoes in hand, Opal and Yasmin climb on up, like it's no big thing that C.J. just pulled secret stairs out of the ceiling.

"What is this?" I ask, staring up through the hole. Opal and Yasmin have disappeared into the dark, and I can't hear anything.

"Don't ask questions." C.J. follows right behind me and pulls the stairs up after us. A round window lets in just enough moonlight to make out what looks to be a collection of broken, neglected dorm furniture. Then he walks over to the far side, gesturing for me to follow before he knocks on the wall. A panel opens into a room where a few guys from the dorm sit. Declan is stretched out on a beanbag. We exchange smiles, but then I quickly look away.

"Pretty awesome, yes?" C.J. asks, sweeping an arm around the room, which is big enough to comfortably accommodate about ten people. "This is the sacred space that's passed down from graduating seniors to rising seniors at the end of every year." We all contemplate that with the solemnity C.J. appears to want.

There are a couple of mini fridges and an actual bar with bottles of hard liquor sitting on top of it, with speakers set on either side. Judging from the shag carpet, lava lamps, and Grateful Dead posters, this space has been in use for at least a few decades.

Pizza boxes from Andrea's are stacked on the floor. I raise my eyebrows as C.J. cackles, hoists himself over the bar, and holds up a bong. "Herb delivered."

The bong makes its way around the circle a few times, but I

pass every time it gets to me. Paranoia and lowered inhibitions are the last things I need. Yasmin waves it away when it reaches her. "No thanks. Bongs are so unladylike," she says. I notice that Declan doesn't partake either.

"What's going on with the petition? Are you getting your election?" C.J. asks. He's sitting on the floor, leaning back against a beanbag with his eyes closed.

"God, I hope so," one of the other guys says.

I sigh. "We almost have enough signatures. We had to take a break for finals, but I think we'll be able to get it wrapped up next week."

"What about the other petition?" Declan asks. It's the first time he's addressed me directly all night.

"I haven't heard any more about it, but if our petition gets approved, it won't matter," I say.

"If we have the election and don't win, they'll be able to push Abbot off the schedule then anyway," Opal says.

"Exactly," C.J. says. Everyone looks at him and laughs. He's stoned out of his mind. "Wait, what?" He sits up. "I'm saying, I wouldn't be too blasé about it."

"That's not what it sounded like you were saying," Declan says.

"And besides, there's nothing we can do about it anyway," Opal says.

"I'd start thinking of a plan B. Just in case." C.J. lies back down.

Declan and I talk with everyone else in the room but don't even look at each other. I feel like everyone can tell that our awareness of each other is heightened. Finally it gets to be so much that the air actually feels thick. I have to leave.

"I'll walk you back," Declan says.

"No!" I practically yell. "I mean, stay. You're having fun. I'm totally fine."

C.J. walks me back to the stairs, listens with his ear to the crack of the trapdoor, then lets the stairs down. "Thanks," I say.

"Yas brought you, so I assume you can be trusted. She's special. Even the underclassmen who live here don't know about this place."

"Don't worry. Your secret's safe with me." I walk down the steps.

Even though I'm nowhere near Thatcher on Thanksgiving, weight lifts from my shoulders when noon arrives and I know that Declan's parents have come to pick him up.

"You're a total mess," Opal observes.

"Not anymore. Let's go do something!"

That turns into walking downtown and wasting time in CVS, which is the only store that's open. We end up buying a ton of stupid stuff we don't even need—chocolate turkeys, dreidels, playing cards, mini flashlights, and a neon-green, miniature die-cast BMX bike in a bright orange package that says STUNTZ on it. I buy this last item while Opal's distracted. I tell myself that it's just for fun, but I know better.

Dinner that night might be the best Thanksgiving meal I've ever had. My mom makes a valiant effort, but Martin's cooking skills put her attempts to shame. "If I'd known what I was missing, I would've stayed on campus every Thanksgiving," I say.

Opal rolls her eyes and pretends to enjoy her salad, glazed carrots, and roasted Brussels sprouts. Dr. Murdoch seems especially cheerful, and Yasmin says it's because it's usually just the two of them on shorter breaks. Still, she seems more than ready to escape to the faculty table while we take our plates to the kitchen.

I stab my fork into a slice of Martin's decadent pumpkin pie and let myself consider a possible election. I've been careful to avoid thinking about it in depth, not wanting to wind myself up for no reason. Pitting myself against Whitney in such a public way has some very obvious downsides. My dorm mates' reassurance is nice, but at the end of the day it will be me, either failing or humiliating my former best friend.

I'm really not ready for break to end.

CHAPTER THIRTY-FIVE

We've finally collected enough signatures to hold an ad hoc midterm election. My name and Opal's name are listed as candidates for president and vice president, respectively.

"This is insane!" Whitney screams at me, waving her copy of our petition in my face. I'd submitted it just hours before, but I'm not surprised it's already in her hands. Though I am surprised she actually set foot in Lower Left just to tell me off. "You and Opal Kingston do not have what it takes to run this school!"

"Your name will still be on the ballot," I say. "You have a completely fair shot at keeping your position." We have the entire room's attention.

"Awww. Well, the election is so not happening. Marshall buried your pitiful, ridiculous petition!" Whitney whirls away and storms out of the dining room. There's a low rumble of nervous laughter after she leaves.

I send Marshall a text:

> **?**

He responds with one word.

> Sorry.

At least he doesn't make excuses.
I type back:

> Thanks for your support.

"Karma needs a nudge," Opal says

"Have they never heard of democracy?" Bettina asks.

"Maybe we should boycott," I say. "We convince people to stop going to the 'big' Calendar events and only attend those that typically stay under the radar, like the Harry Potter lunch."

"Omigod, that's brilliant! When is that happening?" Jess asks.

"Already happened," I say. "But that's exactly what I'm talking about. We find a way to publicize those events more widely so that students actually get to experience what this school has been trying so thanklessly to offer them."

"Yes! A boycott is a genius idea. Low attendance is like the ultimate form of suffering for the Calendar," Opal says.

"Are you even a real yogi?" I ask. Even though I'm kind of enjoying it, this more aggressive Opal takes some getting used to.

She huffs. "We're attempting to restore some balance in the universe. Shiva would fully approve."

"Okay, so how do we do this? I'm sure we can get a few

people who don't normally go out to show up, but introverts don't just stop being introverts, even for a good cause," I say.

"True enough," Opal says, nodding. "Any type of big event would be introvert repellant."

Jess chews on a corner of her lower lip, deep in thought. "Using the Harry Potter thing as an example, what would've happened if all seven of us showed up?"

"Assuming we all went as Hermione, we'd probably make a lot of boys happy," I say. They all give me a look. "Uh, well, we would've doubled the attendance, probably."

"Great! Let's do that," Opal says.

"I know at some point she mentioned that it already happened," Jess says.

"No, but Opal's right," I say. "If we pick some worthy but unpopular event to support one weekend, they at least might not get to kill it outright. And who knows, maybe we could convince a few more people to come with us. Remy would come, and Yasmin could get her buddies from Thatcher—those guys barely even qualify as real introverts."

Opal pulls up the schedule for the coming weekend. "There's another dance—yawn, the Deadlies are playing." The Deadlies are Winthrop's preeminent hippie jam band. For reasons I cannot understand, they have a huge on-campus following. I'd always wished our school could've produced a really cool band, like Melbourne. Opal keeps reading. "Theater Club's doing *Rocky Horror,* a poetry slam at the Study sponsored by the Spoken Word Society, a student exhibit at Albright, and First Snow—weather dependent, of course."

First Snow is a sledding party sponsored by the Physics Club. It's on the calendar every weekend starting in November, so it's always a bit of a crapshoot. No one from the Calendar or the *Times* ever covers it, citing unpredictability and failure to realize that snow was falling. Therefore it's constantly on the chopping block. "Didn't we kill this thing last year?" Whitney whined when she saw the proposal a few weeks ago.

"Only a handful of people go, but those who do, like it," Guthrie said.

"Ugh, the Physics Club is always trying to come up with these real-world applications for physics that are supposedly fun," Whitney said. "When will they get a clue that *physics fun* is an oxymoron?"

I happen to agree, but now I'm crossing my fingers for snow, otherwise we'll be stuck applauding bad rap disguised as poetry. The forecast on my phone looks promising but changes almost hourly. The only drawback to choosing this event is that many of the Thatcher guys will already be there, so we won't really add much in terms of attendance numbers.

I pick up the toy bike I bought for Declan at CVS, which has been sitting on my desk since break, and speculate whether I'll actually have the guts to give it to him. I try not to read into the fact that I haven't seen him since school started and wonder if he'll be at First Snow.

The more I think about the weekend, the more I feel that just blowing out one event won't make enough of an impact.

"Then we should refocus on boycotting a big event this weekend. It'll be such a strong statement," Jess says.

"Maybe the dance?" Opal asks.

"'Boycott the Dance' just doesn't have any bite to it," I say. "Especially since there's one every weekend."

"Maybe not, but it is the one that will hit Whitney and Lila the hardest," Opal says.

But even after we start spreading the word, not showing up at the dance feels far too easy, like it won't cost anyone anything. Also, if no one but the quad crew shows, will anyone even care?

As the weekend approaches I become more convinced that it's not going to work. If we want the Calendar's attention, it has to be dramatic. Only a complete, weekend-wide fail will get them to take us seriously.

Opal and I meet with the producers and stage manager of *The Rocky Horror Picture Show*. We tell them that they don't need to change anything about what they're doing but that their attendance might be sparse this weekend.

"Uh, normally this is a cause we'd totally get behind, but the understudy is on this weekend. It's her first chance to play Janet for an audience." The stage manager looks torn, and I truly am sympathetic to what she's saying. Still, there's no other time to do this.

"Is there a way you can guarantee her the next performance?" I know I'm grasping at straws, but being a dream crusher isn't something I want to add to my resume.

They all shake their heads. "The lead is on a college tour this weekend," one of the producers says. "Unless something catastrophic happens for the late winter or spring performances, there's no way she'd miss them."

"Could we talk to the understudy?" Opal asks.

Ugh. Bad idea. I shoot her a warning look, but she doesn't pick up on it. I want to stay as far away from that as possible. But the next thing I know, they're ushering in a cute, innocent-looking girl with big green eyes and long golden waves. I feel like I'm about to rip the head off a doll.

"Hi, we're here to apologize in advance." I look at her wide, blinking eyes and hypnotically long lashes and have trouble continuing. Opal nudges me. "We're going to call for a boycott of all campus events this weekend, and that includes your show. Please know that it's not personal—this is the weekend it has to happen, and we sincerely wish that your big break was next weekend. Or last weekend. Or any other weekend but this one."

"We wanted to come say this in person," Opal says, "so you know that we're not doing this without awareness of the pain and inconvenience we're causing certain individuals. But we believe we're acting for the greater good." Opal's obviously much more eloquent than I am.

"Okay," understudy Janet says in a shaky voice. "I mean, people can still come if they really want to, right?" She looks to the producers. "We're not canceling, are we?"

"No, and I'm sure your closest friends will still come," I say. "Bottom line is, if it doesn't turn out to be standing room only, we wanted you to know why." My confidence in this mission is massively undermined at the moment.

Understudy Janet nods, on the verge of tears. I feel like a monster, but the stage manager motions to us, so we make a quick exit. "Thanks for the open lines of communication," she says as she walks us out. "What you're doing isn't going to be popular, but I give you credit for telling everyone involved to their faces."

Bolstered by that sliver of encouragement, we approach the poets. We get a more lukewarm response than we did from the *Rocky Horror* people, but somehow we stick to our guns and hope that our profuse apologies will buy us enough goodwill that they'll forgive us for derailing their event.

But when I see the artist's name on the announcement for the Albright exhibit, my heart sinks. Declan O'Neill.

CHAPTER THIRTY-SIX

Naturally, I'm the one assigned to talk to Declan. Even Bettina refuses to be the bearer of this news. I pace outside Thatcher one evening after dinner, trying to work up the nerve to text him.

"You looking for D?" I turn as C.J. walks up the path. "It's freezing. Come wait in the common room." He escorts me to a room across from the foot of the stairs, then goes to find Declan. It smells like boy in here. Not quite as eye-wateringly pungent as a locker room or Leo's car when he forgets to clean it out after a few practices, but close.

"Hey, what's up?" Declan says as he plops down next to me, slouching low, his long legs wide. He looks cozy in pj pants and a hoodie.

I jump off the couch. "Oh, nothing," I say. Declan raises his eyebrows. "I mean, I need to talk to you about something." I stay standing and even start pacing again.

"I feel like I'm about to get a lecture," he says, eyeing me warily.

"Why? Have you done something wrong?" I ask.

"No. Not that I'm aware of."

"Then stop being paranoid." I sit back down.

"You're stalling. Is this about what happened at the squash courts? Or more accurately, what didn't happen?"

"No!" I say, standing up again.

"Whatever." Declan says it easily, but stares me down with a mischievous grin. I bite the inside of my lower lip to keep from smiling back. "And yes, even though I haven't been around, we're still friends."

"You might not think that in a minute."

"Uh-oh."

"Yeah. I need to talk to you about the whole Calendar thing. Basically those assholes killed our petition for an election, so we have to use other methods to convince them to change the way they do things."

"Okay. I'm down."

I force myself to continue. "Well, we're organizing a boycott. We want people to focus on going to one thing that's typically on the chopping block. If the weather cooperates, we want to make it the First Snow."

Declan shrugs, not understanding. "So? I like sledding."

I sigh. "Your gallery exhibit opens this weekend, and we're going to ask that people not attend your reception."

As what I'm saying becomes clear, Declan rubs the back of his neck, his mouth tight. "That's . . . not good."

I sit next to him again, sideways so I can face him. "It's not personal, obviously. We just think if the campus feels like a ghost town, it'll make more of a statement." My conviction plummets once again, and my voice shows it. The whole point of this is to make things better for people like Declan and Understudy Janet. At best, the payoff of this stunt is going to be long term, but it might not come at all. "Our first idea was less extreme, but we didn't think the Calendar would get the message."

"No, I understand. And I think it's important." He finally looks at me but returns his gaze to his shoes after a second. "It's not like I thought hundreds of people would show. But my advisor and some of my teachers are going to come. They're going to think it's strange if the place is empty."

"Trust me, they'll know what's going on. The entire campus will. I promise it won't reflect badly on you." I have no idea if I can deliver on that or not, but I know I'll do everything I can to make it happen.

Declan gives a wan smile. "But the saddest part is that I was going to ask you to go with me."

"Oh. Really?" I search his face to see if he's serious. When I see that he most definitely is, I become preoccupied with a thread hanging off the cuff of my sleeve.

After a few long moments of my not coming up with anything else to say, Declan laughs. He reaches for the TV remote. "Yes, really. And yes, I remember what you said."

I sit there, too flustered to respond.

Saturday morning, when I awake to flurries and inches of snow already on the ground, I leap out of bed. I still get overly excited about real winters. I'm also the only one who doesn't own ski pants, so Jess lends me a pair of hers. I don't even care that they're the most hideous shade of orange that I've ever seen.

We trudge up to the top of a giant hill, which is aptly nick-named Heartbreak Hill, after the infamous one in the Boston Marathon. The infirmary resides at the bottom, off to the side in a small brick building. Its proximity does provide some mea-sure of comfort.

The Physics Club is already set up, handing out plastic sleds, old-fashioned wooden sleds on runners, aluminum saucers, and rubber inner tubes. They've even thought to supply thermoses of hot chocolate and paper cups with mini marshmallows. Even though the sky is a foreboding, icy shade of gray, waves of laughter warm the air. I keep my face turned upward for long minutes, letting the fat flakes land, then melt on my skin.

People are already starting to make runs down the hill. In true physics-geek form, there's a girl at the bottom of the hill with a stopwatch and clipboard and a guy midhill with a video camera. Another guy at the top walkie-talkies with the girl in order to get the most accurate run time. They discuss the sledders' height and weight, sledding position, and, of course, vehicle of choice. Amazingly none of this nerdliness detracts from the fun.

There are only about twenty of us here to start, and failure looms as a very large, very real possibility. On the positive side, the smallish group actually makes it more enjoyable.

But by midmorning more people have arrived. Our group has probably at least doubled in size, which is respectable enough that I can completely relax. Howard, the walkie-talkie guy, has started pushing people downhill in order to keep things moving.

When it's my turn, he actually backs us up to get a running

start. "You're too light," he says. "You won't get much momentum on your own."

"Be careful with her," someone says. I look up to see Declan. He grins at me. "Not that she's breakable."

I get off my sled to talk to him. "Hey. Thanks for coming. I still feel terrible about tonight. You sure you don't hate us?"

He looks down, his fists jammed into the pockets of his jacket. "I don't hate. The show is up until break. I just envisioned something different for my first big opening."

"Well, I'm definitely going as soon as the weekend's over, and Jess said she'll write about it for the *Times*."

"Cool." He smiles. "So I guess we should do this." Declan kicks a plastic sled down the hill, then runs and jumps on it, and rides it like it's a snowboard, all the way to the bottom. He's so casual about it, like he was born with a sled attached to his feet, and pumps his fists into the air as he jumps off. Everyone stops to applaud.

Howard comes back to check on me. "You going to stand there and stare?"

I close my mouth and sit down. Howard runs as fast as he possibly can while hunched over, clutching the edge of my saucer. Behind me I hear him grunt as he gives me a final shove before hitting the ground.

So that's how I find myself careening toward the bottom of Heartbreak Hill at full speed, screaming. At the last second I flip my saucer over to avoid hitting a tree, doing a full-frontal face-plant in the snow. "That was your best time yet!" the girl with the clipboard says.

I haul myself to my feet, groaning. I imagine that I look like the Abominable Snowman, with snow packed onto me from my face to my feet. In the middle of the hill, Declan grins as he gives me a thumbs-up.

"What was that?" I ask when I catch up to him.

Declan laughs. "Damn. I should've listened to my mom. She told me I'd regret quitting." He looks at me intently through thick, dark lashes and gives a lopsided smile before taking another run.

The sun edges its way through the clouds as the sledding continues. We don't leave until the last stunt has been attempted, analyzed, and documented and the last drop of hot chocolate drunk. There's not a popular person in sight, yet this is easily one of the best times I've ever had at Winthrop.

Aside from sneaking around to scout events over the rest of the weekend, we stick to the dorms. It's beyond boring. We have Netflix marathons, study, and eat never-ending amounts of delivery food.

Remy and C.J. report that campus is dead and suggest meeting at the Study. "You should come," Raksmey says. "You're getting stir crazy." That's a true statement, but I stay behind, feeling guilty about the havoc we're causing.

I remind myself that this whole idea originated with other students in mind and that we're not doing it to be spiteful. As Opal said, "Coming from a place of negative energy wouldn't be good for anybody."

When it's dark out, I take a brisk walk around the eerily quiet campus. I poke my head into the gym, which emits pulsing music just like it does every other Saturday night. The dance floor is deserted. Only a handful of people lurk along the walls, well out of the spotlights. It's still somewhat early, so this might not mean anything, but if this event and the Deadlies show stay quiet, I'm pretty sure it means we win. What we do next with that win, I have no idea. I'm realistic enough to know that we can't keep asking people to essentially ground themselves until Whitney and Lila stop being so power hungry.

I think about Declan and can't resist texting Opal to see if anyone went to his opening. *Not that I know of,* she texts back.

Going by end-of-the-night reports, we effectively closed down the school's social life. We all agree that the best possible scenario is that Marshall gets skittish and reconsiders our petition. Maybe by now he realizes that Whitney has no intention of letting him back in her life in any real way and that ignoring the entire student body isn't the kind of legacy he wants to leave.

"Even if you don't get to run for Calendar president, they're going to have to change how they handle things," Opal says.

"You would think," I say. It's not just that I'm skeptical about their willingness to change; I've also realized that I was getting into the idea of running the Calendar and seeing what kinds of improvements we could make before we leave Winthrop.

I keep my phone by my side all night long, but Marshall doesn't call or text. No one does.

CHAPTER THIRTY-SEVEN

The Thatcher guys quietly take up our cause. They set up a website to post photos from First Snow, and C.J. and Declan come over to show it off to us.

"That's awesome!" I say. "Can anyone go on it?"

"It's password protected," Declan says from his sprawled-out position on the couch. "But you guys are special. We'll share it with you." He winks at me without smiling, and I think about how I haven't asked him about his show yet or given him the toy bike I bought him over Thanksgiving.

"And there's a full report on our findings!" C.J. says. "With charts and graphs! That's some next-level shit right there!" He takes an eager scan of our polite but definitely uninterested expressions. "But you guys don't care about that. Look, more pictures!"

Remy leans forward to scroll through some of them. "Can't believe I missed it. Are you going to do another one?"

C.J. snorts. "We were lucky to get this one on the schedule."

"Maybe if there's an outcry for more sledding—" Opal says.

"Which, dammit, there should be," I say, reaching out to meet C.J.'s hand for a high five. "You should post video. Wasn't someone wearing one of those forehead cameras? That would be hilarious to see. Also, I'd actually elaborate on the physics-experiment part. Right now all you say is that it's sponsored by the Physics Club, but you don't make it sound at all fun. Talk about the different sleds and how their respective features make each run unique."

"That's what the charts are for," C.J. says, wounded.

"Fine. But say it in words, so nongeeks can understand too. And it wouldn't hurt to mention the hot chocolate." I look up to baffled glances.

"It sounds like you want us to make it more geeky, not less," C.J. says.

"Well, yeah. But in a techy, extreme-sports-enthusiast kind of way," I say, nodding at Declan. "Not just formulas and stuff. I'm serious. If you get another slot, you should let me write your copy."

"You should," Opal says. "She got Yoga Connection off the ground after three years of fruitless attempts."

"And she masterminded Ghouls and Graves without making it cheesy," Bettina adds. "I would never have thought that a high school party could revolve around art." This is the first time she's voiced any enthusiasm for that event, which miraculously I haven't taken personally.

"Hey, can we add pictures from Club Raks onto your site?" I

ask. "It's kind of stale news now, but according to Jess, the *Times* wouldn't touch the story, and I bet some people would want to see what it was all about."

I stand, and Declan looks up. "Where you going?"

"To get my camera. You want to come with?"

He shrugs and follows me up the stairs. When we get to my room, I go straight for my desk to grab my camera, but the sound of the door clicking shut startles me. I turn around to see Declan leaning against it. "Oh, did you not invite me up here to make out?" he asks.

I bite my lip to keep from laughing. For some reason his very direct style of flirting doesn't embarrass me as much as he seems to think it will. "No? Obviously wishful thinking on my part. Awkward," he says.

"No. But I do have a present for you." I scoop up the bike and bring it to him.

"For me?" He steps forward, looking genuinely touched as he takes it from me.

"I saw it and thought of you." I don't know how, but I'm only now realizing that I've just given him a reminder of a part of his life that he's chosen to walk away from. "Sorry if that's weird. I mean, I know that's not what you do anymore." Why doesn't life have a rewind button? I go back to my desk for the camera.

"No, don't apologize. That was nice of you." He holds it like he doesn't quite know what to do with it. I wish I could grab it out of his hand and throw it in the trash for him. Instead, I decide to distract him with an abrupt subject change.

"I still feel terrible about your show," I say. "How did it go?"

He sighs and returns to rest against the door. "It was okay."

I groan. "Sorry."

"I got all dressed up, and we didn't even take pictures because it looked too empty and sad."

Even though I can tell he's teasing, the guilt is crushing, and I hide my face in my hands. "Stop! I already feel terrible."

But Declan chuckles. "I'm kidding. Kind of. Most of my teachers were there, so I filled them in on the boycott. At first they thought it was interesting, then I told them my friend was responsible, and they thought it was hilarious."

"Oh no."

"Yeah. You're lucky I like you."

I raise my face to find him staring at me. "Look, I kind of feel like I owe you more of an explanation," I say.

"I don't need one," Declan says. "Some things cannot be rushed."

Suddenly I don't know where to look. "Why are you so sure there's even a thing to be rushed or not rushed?" I ask.

"I'm not," he finally says, and I'm surprised to feel a pit forming in my stomach. "I just hope that there is."

Those words feel so daring and brave, especially because they have to travel the several feet between us. "Well. Do you want to know what happened?" I ask.

"If you want." His tone is intentionally casual.

So I tell him. I tell him about my parents, my mom's business, my job, how I tried to cover it up, and how it all completely backfired and cost me my friends and my boyfriend.

"What was the point of pretending?" Declan asks. "If you can't be honest, those don't sound like such great relationships."

I sigh. "I'm not even sure what would've happened if I'd told them. Maybe nothing. Maybe I created all this drama by myself." He's still listening. He knows that's not all there is. "I guess working with my mom and that stupid movie were my special things, and I wanted them to keep being true."

"You're not special because your mom made some movie."

"Thanks. But after I got here it took over my identity. And I clung to it because I had nothing else to offer."

"I can't believe you think that about yourself." His voice is low and soft, his expression concerned.

I haven't moved any closer to him. "I don't know. Everyone here is exceptional. And if not actually them, at least their families are."

Declan snorts. "Yeah, well, I hope you know by now that there's a lot of posturing and bullshit when you first get here. But I think it's because they drill it into our heads that we're the best and the brightest and we all secretly feel like we must be the one mistake. The one who doesn't really deserve to be here."

"You feel like that too?"

"Not anymore. But when I got here, I'd just quit the thing that had been my life. Even though I knew those sports weren't for me anymore, I felt bummed at everything, including myself."

"But at least you had art."

He shakes his head. "That was something I discovered here. I wasn't used to having a lot of time on my hands and had to look really hard for ways to fill it."

"Well, you definitely found one you're good at." I can't hide my bitterness. Winthrop students land on their feet, almost effortlessly, it seems.

255

"Unfortunately, my first attempt at finding a new interest wasn't quite as constructive," he admits. "I almost got kicked out sophomore year for partying, which I'm sure you know, since pretty much everyone does. And then I didn't know who my friends were anymore and had to find something new to throw myself into." He watches me for a reaction.

"I remember hearing about it but never knew any details," I say.

"When I lived in Webster, someone brought back all this booze after he went home for the weekend, and we stashed a little bit in everybody's room."

"Where'd you hide it?"

"The usual places. On top of the ceiling tiles, in trunks, behind furniture. I used some emptied-out bottles of Centrum, because they're white and you can't see through them. Oddly enough, I felt less nervous hiding them in plain sight. Until Mr. Guerra came by to talk to me and I was drinking from one of the bottles. If it'd been Chris, I might've been able to talk my way out of it." Declan grimaces, remembering.

"I guess house counselors are pretty much required to ask questions if they see you swigging from a vitamin bottle," I say.

"And I had three others sitting on my dresser. What can I say? I was a sophomore. So anyway, I had my disciplinary-committee hearing, and I got probation for the rest of the year and fall term junior year."

"Is that why you moved to Thatcher?"

"Yeah. Not that I expected anyone else to step up and take the fall with me, but no one even said anything to me. It was like they all wanted to forget it happened as quickly as possible.

Even Remy, who I'm totally cool with now, completely disappeared on me at the time."

I think about Remy's initial reaction to my breakup with Leo. "It takes him a minute to get on the right page, but he gets there eventually."

"That's the perfect way to put it," he says with a rueful grin.

"But you seem like you ended up in a better place."

"Sometimes things have to end to make room for something better. Maybe you haven't found it yet, but you still have plenty of time."

I smile and walk toward the door, hesitant to say what I really want to. "I've missed hanging out with you. That's probably selfish of me, but I just want you to know that."

He takes my hand, and it's somewhere between friendship and something more. "It's cool. I know what you mean, and I can wait until things clear up for you," he says.

"But the year's half over. What if they don't?" I ask. At the moment that still feels like a very real possibility. I'm afraid to hear his answer.

Declan gives my hand a squeeze. "Then I'll still be glad I got to know the brains behind Ghouls and Graves and Club Raks."

Downstairs, I sit next to Declan as he uploads all the photos from my camera onto his laptop. And I stay there, glued to his side, as he clicks through them, choosing which ones to post. He glances at me a couple of times, but I don't move away. He lands on one of us dancing only inches apart with one of his hands on my hip. His face is turned away from the camera, but my eyes are closed and my smile is happy and genuine. My hand covers his, possessive, keeping him close.

CHAPTER THIRTY-EIGHT

By the end of the week, the newly dubbed Winthrop Underground website has gone viral. Everywhere I go someone requests the password. "Okay, but don't tell anyone," I say before giving it out. The more we can build intrigue, the less likely it is that the Calendar will be able to continue ignoring us.

I cross paths with Whitney on the quad. We're the only two on the walkway, but she blows by me like I'm not even there. I can't imagine she's responding well to the pressure. Two major events and one entire weekend have bombed on her watch, and everyone knows that we're at least partly to blame.

It's killing me not to know what's going on, so I ask Guthrie to meet me at Perk Up.

"Thanks for coming," I say when he walks in.

"Hey, Skylar. What's going on?" he asks, sliding into the seat across from me. He takes his hat off but not his coat. Guess this won't be a long conversation.

"That's what I wanted to ask you," I say. "Is the Calendar getting the message?"

"Not really sure," he says, shrugging. "Whitney canceled this week's meeting, so we haven't been able to discuss it."

"Interesting," I say. "It's probably for the best. Whitney tantrums are never fun, and with Lila fueling the fire, it's got to be unbearable."

"Listen, I get what you're trying to do. I wish it wasn't wreaking so much havoc, but I get it. But if Marshall won't come around, I don't see what good you're doing by making everyone sweat it out like this."

"Did you want to order something?" I ask Guthrie when the waiter comes around. "I'll buy, since I asked you to meet." I silently hope he just orders a coffee.

"No thanks. I'm good." He smiles apologetically at the waiter, who nods and walks away. "I just wanted to come by to tell you that I think you made your point but I'm not sure continuing to screw around with everyone's weekends is going to work in your favor."

"A lot of people's weekends already suck," I point out. "At least we distributed the suckage more evenly."

He smirks at that. "What do you think is going to happen? Has Marshall said anything?"

"No, he's avoiding me."

Guthrie rolls his eyes. "That could be about anything. You just need to be aware that the tides could turn."

"Well, it's not like I thought we could boycott indefinitely," I say.

"Do you have any more tricks up your sleeve?"

I duck my head to take a sip of my latte. "Unfortunately, if I did, I don't think I'd be telling you about it."

After Guthrie leaves, I sit a while longer and think about what he said. He'd laughed when I said the part about not telling him. I wonder if he could see that I was bluffing.

"Hey, has anyone actually read this thing?" I'm sprawled on my bed, flipping through a copy of the Calendar bylaws, but my door is open, so I'm assuming other people can hear me.

"Read what?" Samantha calls back.

"The bylaws."

"Yes. Front to back," Jess says, sticking her head in my room.

"Then why don't we know about this clause where we can get faculty sponsors for an ad hoc election if the student petition doesn't come together?" I ask.

Opal comes in carrying her toiletries. "Did you read it carefully? First of all, we have to get five faculty sponsors, and I know from trying to get Yoga Connection started that it's not as simple as merely asking. Some ask for a full written explanation of your request, with supporting documents. Then it involves a whole hearing in front of Student Council, with speeches and questioning and everything."

I sit up. "Yeah? So?" She and Jess exchange wary glances. "Seriously? We've come this far, tortured a bunch of people so we could hopefully make a difference, and we're really going to draw the line here? You guys have to be the laziest activists I've ever met."

"She's right," Jess says with a sigh.

So we stay up until the early hours of the morning crafting our position paper and use screenshots from Winthrop Underground as our support.

"We're barely even two weeks into winter term, and already we're pulling an all-nighter," Opal says, yawning.

"I know, but if we get this done tonight, we have a shot at getting this wrapped before we leave for break," I say.

"Why all the sudden urgency?" Jess asks. She's lying on my bed with her eyes closed, the gallons of coffee she consumed having apparently no effect on her.

"I'm just . . . done. Ready to put this all behind me. I can't go on fighting with Whit forever." Exhaustion from more than just the all-nighter has worn me thin, and tears start welling up in my eyes. I brush them away quickly, but the tremor in my voice outs me.

"I agree," Opal says. "Resolving this one way or the other is the last thing you need to do to cut your energetic cords with her. And probably other parts of your past."

She means Leo. "Exactly," I say with an impatient sniffle.

"I'm just happy that you're not a total idiot," Jess says kindly. "Declan's awesome. You better not screw it up."

"Jess, slow down. She's not ready yet," Opal says.

I have to laugh. "You said the exact same thing to me after Rally Weekend."

"I know," Opal says, "and I meant it, but at least I can see that you're trying, and really, how much more can we ask?"

"Thanks. That's generous of you."

For the rest of the night, we alternate taking forty-minute naps, so that by the time the sun rises, our paper is finished.

CHAPTER THIRTY-NINE

The auditorium stage feels enormous once you're standing on it. After a week and a half of chasing down faculty, presenting, and begging, here we are.

Even though I'm still offstage and Opal's by my side, I feel as though I might pass out.

Due to popular demand, or maybe morbid curiosity, Marshall has made this hearing open to the public. In my shortsightedness I never imagined that the speech and debate portion of my mission would take place in front my ex-boyfriend and half the student population.

I'd asked Declan not to come, and he'd readily agreed. I think he's almost as nervous as I am. He even thought to ask the Thatcher guys not to come, knowing that more people would make me more anxious. The rest of my dorm mates are helping Yasmin get ready for her string quartet's performance, so that takes some pressure off. Opal slaps my hand to stop me from mangling my index cards.

One hour, I think. That's how much time they've allotted.

The Student Council takes up the first three rows. Leo sits off to the left, considerably out of my sight line. Whitney and Lila huddle together in front of the podium.

Looking totally nonplussed, Whitney turns to the microphone with what can only be called a winning smile. "Thank you all for coming and on such short notice. We understand that this unscheduled meeting is a major inconvenience. Anyway, the reason for our being here is that there's a small faction of Winthrop students who've decided that they're unsatisfied with our traditions." She pauses to let that sink in and looks around with a conspiratorial smile. From where I stand I can't see the Student Council's reaction. At least they're not laughing.

"The Social Calendar has been accused of holding Winthrop back, of systematically shutting down the new and adventurous. While that's certainly not true, we all know that Winthrop boasts a long and celebrated history, which sets us apart. Some campus events have been in place for a hundred years and are institutions. A key component of my job as president of the Calendar is to preserve the integrity of those events.

"At the same time, to say that we don't allow room for diversity of interests is a blatant mischaracterization. Every weekend there are events that are decidedly not interesting to many of us." There are some titters at this. Whitney looks around as if to say, Am I right?

I shuffle my index cards, rearranging them so that I open

with my point about these nonmainstream events. But then I decide it's best not to react, and put them back in the original order. I don't want Whitney to dictate the pace and points of my speech.

Whitney nears the end of her allotted fifteen minutes. "But oftentimes, even with the best intentions, the organizers fail to translate their personal passion and enthusiasm into a successful event. Maybe the people challenging our positions would prefer to let people flounder indefinitely, but we see that as unnecessarily cruel. Not everyone possesses the skills to host and entertain."

The audience laughs some more. Whitney leans on the podium with her elbows, as if she's having an intimate chat with a couple hundred of her closest friends. "We have to ask ourselves if any of us is really ready to prioritize the experimental over the established and beloved." She cuts a sideways glance at me before grinning at the audience. Lila starts the applause.

"Your turn," Whit says as she breezes by. Those two small words convey so much. I come close to falling for her mind games but wrestle my nerves under control and lift my chin before stepping out onto the stage.

This is it.

I clear my throat. It doesn't help. I reach for my bottle of water but set it back down on the podium. I fumble with my index cards, noting that the sweat from my hands has actually made some of the ink run. The top card is almost illegible. Opal looks on, alarmed, as I crumple the cards in my fist.

"Thank you all for being here. I just want to say that this was a last resort. We tried working within the limitations of the Calendar but weren't being given fair consideration." I hear myself sounding whiny. *Snap out of it.*

"Anyway. I had a whole speech prepared, but I'd actually like to share some more personal thoughts." Everyone is alert and paying rapt attention. Guthrie gives me a discreet, encouraging nod. I just have to relax.

"This year I've been experiencing a wholly different side of Winthrop, one that I'd never given much thought to before. It wasn't by choice, and I definitely didn't embrace it right away." I smile at Opal, and she grins back, which makes people chuckle. "You know what I'm saying.

"Honestly, it took me a while to see that I'd been missing out. On one hand I agree with Whitney: the traditions of this school are time-honored and make our experiences special. But that's not the only reason we come here. As stellar as Winthrop's faculty, academics, and reputation are, we have something that I'd argue is even more valuable: each other." I take a deep breath. "Getting to know my new dorm mates and learning about their interests and talents exposed me to things that didn't make it onto my radar in three whole years at one of the best high schools in the country."

I make eye contact with Leo, and he appears to be listening so closely that I lose my train of thought. "So, uh, our goal in taking over the Social Calendar is not just about continuing token representation of the different groups here. It's about offering meaningful support to make sure we all get to experience everything that this school has to offer."

Marshall starts clapping, but I'm not done yet. "And yes, I think if we have an event on the Calendar that doesn't live up to expectations right away, we give it a chance. We want the Calendar to be an organization that nurtures ideas. Maybe some event planners are idea people and not great at execution. Why can't the Calendar serve as a resource for them, not just write them off when they don't deliver immediately? Sure, there will be duds, but so what? We have the time and space to let people try. And that's what we're really asking for and where we've found the current leadership to be unyielding and lacking."

While the audience applauds, I glance down at my cards to see if I missed anything. I glossed over entire sections, but I feel I covered what most needed to be said. When I look up, both Leo and Marshall are out of their seats, leading the standing ovation. I smile, unsure of how to react.

Whitney storms the stage and hip-checks me out of the way. "I guess it's debate time," I mutter, taking a bewildered step back.

She ignores me. "Okay, that was touching, but spoken like someone who truly has no idea how hard it is to run the Calendar. This is a tough job that needs someone who can make difficult decisions—like, yes, telling people that their best effort didn't cut it." Her voice sounds simultaneously strangled and shrill. "It may seem harsh, but it's necessary. Winthrop has a brand. We stand for something. It does none of us any good if we dilute that message. Everything from admissions to alumni support to college acceptance to future career networking depends on it!"

I wish for a giant hook to drag her off the stage. Fortunately,

Marshall comes up to take the mic. "Thank you, Whitney and Skylar." He looks at me. "Do you have anything to add?" I shake my head, so he turns back to the microphone. "Great. If you could wait in the lobby with your co-candidates, we'll take our vote."

The four of us walk up the center aisle and out the door in the back of the auditorium.

There's a row of chairs set up across from a banquet table. Opal and I sit, but Whitney and Lila pace the lobby, on the verge of boiling over.

Finally I can't take it anymore. I stand up. "What are you so mad about?" I ask Whitney. "I'm the one who should be furious. I never would've thought you could be so unforgiving. You can blame it on the fact that I lied to you, but I can't help thinking that this was the way it was going to go down no matter what." I cut a narrow-eyed glance at Lila.

Whitney wheels around on me, midpace. "I'm mad because you started making noise about all this bizarre stuff you never gave a shit about before! And if you'd taken my advice and given me a second to process what you did before breathing down my neck, it wouldn't have come to this."

"You mean I was supposed to wait obediently while you were turning all our friends against me until you were ready to include me again? Is that really what you expected?"

"How about go away quietly and ride it out until graduation like any sane person would?"

I snort. "Sorry I didn't turn out to be passive enough for you. *You're* doing a good job falling in line, though."

"Oh, please." Lila rolls her eyes.

Whitney glares at me, disgusted. "Winthrop is an elite school because it's known for turning out a certain kind of student. Maybe those students who don't come from backgrounds like ours should try harder to fit in. Then they might eventually become leaders instead of resigning themselves to being the geeks who get exploited by the leaders. And then we'd actually have a network worth networking with. *That* is what Winthrop's trying to give us."

Right now it seems unfathomable that we were ever best friends. I might have been snobby and exclusive, but I was never so calculating. "I mean, you sound ridiculous."

"You have no idea how the real world works. If you somehow manage to get into a decent college, it'll be because Winthrop is the one nonlame thing you have going for you. As we're all painfully aware, you don't have the movie card to play anymore." Whitney shakes her head like I'm the most lost of all the lost causes.

The door opens, interrupting our argument. We're expecting Marshall, but Leo comes out. "Hey, this is going to take a little bit longer than we thought." He shoots me an apologetic smile.

I stand up. "Is everyone allowed to stay through the deliberation?"

"We're not sure. That's one of the things we're deliberating. We've never had this situation before. I mean, obviously." Leo shoves his fists into his sweatshirt pockets and glances at the ground. "Uh, anyway, I voted, so I can leave. Marshall said he'll text you guys."

"Ugh!" Whitney glares at Leo like it's his fault. "You have got to be kidding me."

Opal grabs her bag. "I'm going to go help Yasmin."

"Hang on, I'll come too," I say.

Whitney and Lila look at each other. "I told you they don't really care about winning," Whitney says.

Leo taps me on the elbow. Opal notices and says, "Just come whenever you're ready." She takes off, leaving me to deal with this awkwardness by myself.

"Can I walk you?" Leo asks in a low voice.

Lila watches us with a scowl while Whitney presses her ear to the auditorium door, trying to hear.

"Sure." I hold the entrance door open.

It's pitch-dark out now. We linger outside, unsure of what to say. Leo sighs. "Can we go somewhere?"

I hesitate, but if anyone would understand my missing her special moment to talk with Leo, it's Yasmin. I realize that I've been a terrible, self-absorbed friend and still haven't seen Declan's exhibit. "Let's go to Albright." It's only up for another week, so I decide to risk bringing Leo. I doubt Declan's hanging around there all the time, and besides, it's not like Leo knows anything about my flirtation with Declan.

"The art gallery?" Leo cocks his head, confused.

"Yeah. We can whisper." We start walking. "So you had to miss intramural soccer for that?" I hate that I still know everything about him.

He laughs. "It was totally worth it." He's quiet for a minute. "Sky." My stomach tightens at hearing his old nickname for me. "What you said in there? That was incredible. It's exactly how I think about Winthrop but have never really tried to articulate."

Rather than bask in the glow of his compliment like I once

would have, I rush to make conversation. "Actually you're a perfect example of what I was talking about. You're friendly to everyone and always open to trying things." I hadn't thought about it before, but it's absolutely true.

"I guess you know how I voted." He nudges me, and I smile without looking at him. We reach Albright and hurry through the glass doors to escape the cold.

When it was rebuilt in the 1990s, Albright caused quite an outrage with its white cinder-block-and-glass exterior. People were scandalized and even compared it to the glass pyramid at the Louvre, which I guess was very controversial back then.

Since the gallery's open to the public, there are people walking around, studying the art. Some sit with sketch pads, others listen to headsets with recorded information about the famous pieces.

I glance over most of it, really only interested in finding Declan's drawings. If Leo notices that I'm not really taking it all in, he doesn't mention it.

"This fall has been so tough," Leo says.

"I have to say, getting moved to Abbot might've been a blessing in disguise. Those girls were so supportive, and they weren't under any obligation to be." That wasn't meant to be a dig, but he looks stung. I don't even consider apologizing.

Leo stops in front of a large painting of a red square on a white canvas. "I'm glad. Not about the way things happened. But that you got to see a different side of Winthrop."

And suddenly my patience and curiosity evaporate. Leo's sincerity feels condescending. "Thanks. I was as surprised as anyone that there's life outside the quad. So are you still dating that girl?"

He meets my gaze. "You mean Miranda?"

I suppress a sigh. "Sure. Whatever."

"That didn't work out."

"Oh. Shame." I study Leo and try to picture us back together. He's still achingly handsome and intelligent; even after everything that's happened, I still think he's one of the kindest people I've ever met.

"Why are you looking at me like that?" He seems uncomfortable, and I realize that I've been staring at him analytically, even critically.

"Sorry. I guess I'm trying to figure out what we're doing. You made it pretty clear at your game that we weren't getting back together."

We step back into the hall and walk to the next room. Leo takes a deep breath. "I know. Are you mad that I wanted to hang out?"

"No, of course not. But I guess I want to know what it means."

"Is it okay if I say I don't know?" I must look either extremely disappointed or severely pissed—or maybe both, since I can't decide which one I am. Because he says, "I'm sorry. That's pretty weak after all this time. I just wanted to talk more after what I heard you say."

"Okay." Am I fine with that? Do I want this to be more than that? I have no idea.

Leo nods. "When you were up there, I realized that I was

wrong in thinking you were someone I don't know. The things I loved most about you are obviously still there." He searches for the right words. "Your loyalty, your optimism . . ."

My eyes are locked on his. I can't think or look away. What am I supposed to say? I worked so hard to let go of him. It's one of the most difficult things I've ever had to do. And yet letting him back in would be so easy and, in many ways, such a relief. "What are you thinking?" he asks.

"Nothing," I whisper.

"Look, I don't know. I just wanted to acknowledge that I've missed you and that I'm happy that you really are the person I thought you were. You know?"

I nod, like I have any idea what he's talking about. "Yeah."

We get to the last room, and without reading any of the tags by the pieces, I know we've found Declan's exhibit.

There are only twelve drawings. All of them are done on white paper with pencil. I turn and look at a rendering of a bowl. "This is nice," Leo says. "We probably have a lot more to talk about, and I totally understand that my reaction hurt you."

I keep nodding as I move ahead of him. When I get to the last piece on the wall, I draw in a sharp, surprised breath.

It's the drawing Declan did of me while I was in the studio. I'd seen it before, but it looks different, finished and displayed on a wall. It's also his only drawing of a person, which makes me feel weirdly vulnerable and exposed.

I turn away, hoping Leo won't see the tears forming in my eyes. But he does and comes closer to me. "Are you okay? You don't even like art." Then he notices the piece. He can't stop staring at it. "Wow," he finally says.

Because anyone looking at it would know the artist had feelings for the subject. I admire Declan for being so brave, but I'm also flustered.

Leo moves to the next wall, not angry but clearly thrown off. "I didn't know that was here," I say, reaching out to touch his arm. "Leo. You were an amazing boyfriend, and if I could go back to the way things were, I probably would." Tears start falling down my cheeks, and I brush them away impatiently. "But you weren't there when I needed you. And you totally underestimated me. You were the person who knew me best, and you didn't think I was capable of the things I've done."

"That's not true," Leo protests.

"Yes it is. I saw how surprised you were on Halloween about Ghouls and Graves being my idea, and I'm getting the same incredulous look from you now. Do you have any idea how shitty that feels? A group of total strangers believed in me more than my best friends and my boyfriend."

The look on his face guts me. He covers my hand with one of his. "Maybe I did screw up, but you left me hanging," I say. Leo looks down. I still hate seeing him hurt. "Trust me, all I wanted was to get you back, and I can't believe I'm saying this, but things have changed, and even though you might be able to see me as the same person, I'm not."

He stands there, arms hanging limply at his sides. "I'm sorry," he finally says.

"Me too."

• • •

I slip into the back of the concert hall just as Yasmin is finishing her solo. And she's killing it. The entire room is enthralled, watching her.

She's in complete control, inhabiting the music, drawing out some notes for effect and then flowing effortlessly over others. She wears a long, pleated steel-blue skirt and a navy short-sleeved cashmere sweater; her face is all concentration and feeling. And I've never seen her look more breathtakingly beautiful.

I see Declan sitting in the middle of the audience. His head is tipped back, eyes closed, feeling the music. I need to thank him for including me in his show, and after that I don't know where to begin.

CHAPTER FORTY

When the concert lets out, I'm the first one to the door. While everyone else is in a state of bliss, I'm wired, buzzing with nerves. Most head back to the main campus to squeeze in a little more hanging out before curfew. I stand next to the entrance, waiting for Declan.

Opal and Remy come out. "Did you see any of it?" Opal asks.

"I saw the end. She was so amazing. I wish I brought her flowers."

"Bettina got her some from all of us." Opal notices the distracted, crazed look on my face and turns to Remy. "Where's Declan?"

Remy shrugs. "He must still be inside."

I run back in, but there's no sign of him. Yasmin's talking with teachers and some of the other musicians at the foot of the stage. I squeeze in to give her a hug. "I caught some of your solo. You did a beautiful job."

"Thank you. Opal said the hearing went great! Tell me all about it tonight."

Barging into a boys' dorm isn't a brilliant idea, but at least I'm mostly sure the Thatcher house counselor won't write me up for it. I pound on Declan's door and, when there's no answer, hurry back outside. I text him. No reply. Curfew is in thirty minutes.

Finally I get a text, but it's from Jess.

I think D saw you going into Albright with Leo.

Oh no.

I sprint toward the quad. It's so cold that snow refuses to fall. Running in this temperature feels like I'm stabbing myself in the lungs with icicles.

The Saturday-night movie is just letting out of the gym. I stop amid the crowd and let people flow around me as I search for Declan. I check my phone again. No text. Opal and Remy are heading toward me. "Now have you seen him?" I ask.

"No, and I have to tell you, desperation is not a good look for you." Remy laughs when I punch his arm. "Opal said you went off with Diaz?"

"Yes, and Declan saw us! I'll fill you in later." Remy looks concerned, but I wave them off so I can focus on trying to find Declan.

"Calm down," Opal says. "Are you walking back now?"

"Not yet."

"Don't miss curfew. Declan will still be here tomorrow," she says.

"I think I can make it back in ten."

"You can't," she says.

"Just don't wait for me. Save yourselves." I'm still hoping that Declan will miraculously materialize. Remy and Opal can see there's no reasoning with me and disappear without saying goodbye.

And then I finally see him. He's one of the last few headed down the path from the Canteen, and he's alone. People whose dorms are close by loiter in front of the gym, so at first he doesn't notice me. I run toward him at a full sprint, almost knocking him down as I collide into him. "Hey," he says, looking down at me with a furrowed brow.

"I have been looking for you all over campus," I say while doubled over and wheezing.

"Yeah?" he asks. His face is void of expression.

"Yeah. Where'd you take off to so fast after Yasmin's concert?"

"I just . . . wanted to get out of there." He shoves his hands into his pockets. "What did you need?"

I reach up, place my hands on his shoulders, and stand on my toes. His expression turns to shock, but I block it out and forge ahead. I close my eyes and kiss him, letting my lips linger on his for a few long seconds. His lips are warm, which feels nice, but they don't move at all in response to my kiss. I'm beginning to fear the worst—that he's changed his mind, that I made a terrible, mortifying mistake. But when I pull away, I see that he looks confused rather than angry.

"I saw you go into Albright with Leo," he says. "Why would you bring him to my show when I asked you to go with me? Didn't you think that something might be up?"

"I know, but I wasn't thinking about it." I scramble to explain. "I wanted to make sure I saw it before break, and he wanted to talk. The two things were not related, it was just horrible timing. You know I feel terrible that I didn't get there sooner."

He gives me a long look. "Okay. And this?" He gestures between us.

"We don't have time to totally go into it, but Leo and I are completely done."

A smile creeps onto Declan's face, and he wraps his arms around my waist. "In that case I'm sorry I didn't kiss you back," he murmurs. "Promise I'll be ready next time."

I collapse against him, thankful that I didn't just humiliate myself in public. "How about now?"

People are staring, but Declan doesn't care. He grins and ducks his head to kiss me again. He buries his hands in my hair, tilting my head back, his lips brushing against mine briefly, tenderly, before kissing me like he means it.

It's like slipping underwater. I can't breathe, and I don't want to. My hands slide under his jacket, feeling the fabric of his shirt drag under my fingertips as I move them down his back. His hands fall to my hips and pull me closer.

When we finally break apart, campus is deserted. Declan laughs. "I'd walk you home—" he begins.

I kiss him one last time. "Make sure your phone stays on." And with that I race toward Abbot, faster than I've ever moved in my life.

I'm only a few minutes late for check-in, but Dr. Murdoch's sitting in a chair in the common room. I'm praying she doesn't know what time it is. No such luck. "Hello, Skylar."

Panting and sweating from my run, I croak out, "Sorry, Dr. Murdoch, I lost track of time."

"Yes, well, I better take a look at you." She walks over to me. I try to stop gulping air and stand up straight so she can inspect me. "Your eyes are very bright, and you look a little manic, to be honest, dear."

But who needs drugs when making out with an amazing boy is more intoxicating than any drug could possibly be? "Must be adrenaline. I think I'm just not used to running that fast. I swear, I have not broken any rules tonight." Except for going into Thatcher without signing in and, oh god, why did I say "tonight"?

Thankfully, Dr. Murdoch gives me a vaguely warning look but doesn't press me. "Congratulations on a successful hearing. I'm rooting for you."

I stop, touched. "Thank you, Dr. Murdoch."

When I'm finally under the covers with my phone silenced, there's already a message from Declan.

Did that just happen?

I smile. Sorry for the ambush.

"Excuse me, are you really going to ignore me? We didn't even talk about the hearing." Opal's reproachful glare cuts through the dark. Still I sneak a glance at my phone.

No problem. I liked it. (Obviously) :) Where'd you go?

I wrench my attention back to Opal, but I'm sure she can hear the distracted smile in my voice. "I know. That was insane.

I haven't even been able to think about it. Why haven't they told us anything?"

Opal sits up. "Poor Marshall's probably dealing with Whitney and hasn't been able to notify us."

"You're that sure we won?"

She shrugs, supremely confident.

I actually manage to put my phone down and focus. "Is it because of Whitney's meltdown? That was such an unflattering moment."

"Definitely didn't help. It made her seem not grounded. Anyway all we can do now is wait. Seems like you'll have no problem keeping busy. I take it you found Declan?"

"I took your advice and kissed him."

"This is so exciting! What did he say? Was he surprised?"

"That's an understatement." I giggle, picturing his expression right before I pulled his face to mine. "We didn't get a chance to say much, because I had to fly back here." My phone vibrates.

Opal lies back down. "Answer the poor boy. He's probably extremely confused."

I read his text:

You there?

Sorry. Was late. Inquisition from Dr. M + Opal.

Ah, got it. So was it awkward going to my show?

Oh my god, I didn't say anything about the drawing.

> Yeah, but I don't care. THANK YOU. The whole thing was incredible.

A minute later he responds.

> Thank you for going, and glad you got to see it. And you're welcome.

> I'm so happy. I finally feel like I have closure.

> You sure?

My response is immediate.

> Yes.

A second passes and then,

> Feel like an early game of squash tomorrow?

I laugh out loud.

> See you there at 8.

The next morning Declan looks sleepy and cute in sweats, a flannel over a T-shirt, and a gray knit cap. We go into the court farthest down the hall and don't turn on the lights. The glow from the hallway illuminates the room just enough. We spread our jackets out and sit on the floor, facing each other.

"You had a very big day yesterday," he says.

I nod. "A lot of things clicked into place. My speech ended

up being so much more personal than what I had planned, and it sort of broke some things open."

"Like what?"

I fill him in on my revelations about what it is that I think I'm going to take with me when I leave Winthrop. About how moving to Abbot gave me something I wouldn't have even known was here for the taking and how close I came to missing out on that. "It scares me to think that I might have graduated and left, still in my oblivious little bubble."

"But you know what they say: ignorance is bliss. You would've been okay."

"I wouldn't have met you."

"True. And that most definitely would not have been okay." He smiles, and I trace his jaw with the back of my hand.

"I know we're not done talking, but all I can think about right now is kissing."

Declan grabs my hand and holds it. "Talk fast."

I smile. "So the Leo thing. He said he was wrong about me not being the same person, and it all sounded so sincere and perfect. Exactly what I've thought I wanted him to say since we broke up." Declan's body tenses. I squeeze his hand. "I didn't know how to get closure with him, but when it finally happened, it was almost automatic, like a switch flipped in my brain and I could see everything clearly."

He nods, and I can tell he's not jealous or threatened.

"But what I want to say most of all is, thank you. For showing me both by example and by being such a good friend that making even a pretty big mistake doesn't mean you're a total screw-up. A lot of people in my life would've had me believe that about myself, but getting to know you and my dorm mates changed all that."

"You're welcome," Declan murmurs. "But you did this all on your own."

I lean in to kiss him, finally done talking, but he stops me. "You were right about taking your time," Declan says. "Waiting for you was totally worth it."

"Sorry about the bike," I murmur, looking at his lips.

Declan leans his head back so he can see me. "What?"

"The stupid toy I gave you. I don't know why I thought that was a good idea."

He brushes my hair off my cheek. "It wasn't stupid. It gave me encouragement, like maybe you wanted to know me better."

"I guess it took my brain a second to catch up with my actions, but I'm glad you understood what was going on."

And then finally we're kissing again, and unbelievably, it's even better than last night. He might have been fine with waiting, but I'm making up for lost time.

CHAPTER FORTY-ONE

Nothing brings me back down to earth like a college counseling meeting, so of course that's the first thing on my schedule for Monday morning. The essay I sent Ms. Randall yesterday was not the one she's expecting. Can't wait to hear what she has to say about that.

But when I walk into her office, the usual feeling of terror is absent. Maybe it's because I'm so spent from the weekend that I don't have the bandwidth to be worried about anything else.

"This is not the topic we've been working on," Ms. Randall says before I even sit down.

"I know. I decided to focus on other strengths I believe I have. While I've learned a lot about the film business and developed certain skills while interning for my mom, I do think I have other interests that I'd like to explore."

"So I read. Your essay focuses on what you believe is your knack for publicity and events promotion?" She waits for an explanation.

I nod. That's what I wrote; no sense in being bashful about it now.

"That is not something that's considered a typical area of excellence for Winthrop students." Ms. Randall sips her coffee and waits. But for once she doesn't look angry or frustrated.

"I agree with you. But that doesn't mean there's no value in it in the real world." Her thoughtful look is veering more toward skeptical. "Ms. Randall. You told me I had to dig deeper. And so I thought long and hard about what it is that I enjoy, about what might come easier to me than it does to others. It's true, as you pointed out, that the clubs and events I helped popularize didn't depend on my talents or abilities. But getting people there to experience them did. And so not only did I discover that there's even more talent at this school than I ever knew, but I feel that we achieved something huge in bringing together students from all different cliques. It was actually very cool and restored my faith in Winthrop."

"How do you propose to use this skill?" She's not shutting me down, and I'm grateful for that minuscule break.

"I'm not sure. Aren't there colleges where I can prepare for a career in publicity or marketing? Maybe I'm not cut out for liberal arts. Maybe my college experience needs to be more grounded in practicalities."

Ms. Randall does something I haven't seen her do in any of our previous meetings. She sits back in her chair and stares at the ceiling, lost in thought. A good five minutes pass. "It's very late in the game to have such a huge shift in direction."

"I know," I say.

"Not many students apply to undergraduate business programs from Winthrop," she says. "Let's schedule a meeting for one week from today and agree that we'll each have a list of six colleges."

I'm shocked. She's not telling me that I'm delusional or useless or wasting space or that she can't help me. "I'll be ready," I promise.

"We'll both need to research, and you'll have to spend most of winter break filing applications. We'll need to keep in touch," she says. I can't believe she's willing to talk to me while she's supposed to be on vacation. Maybe she supports me more than I thought.

"And before I forget, your SAT scores were respectable. I'm pleased that you took my advice and prepared for the test." She looks mystified, like she thinks she might be the victim of a prank.

"Next year, if you have any students who are financially incapable of paying for a private tutor or prep course, Raksmey Tan in Abbot House is a fantastic tutor and has exceptionally reasonable rates." Raksmey's too good to keep a secret.

"I'll keep that in mind," Ms. Randall says. "Thank you for the tip. I have to say, I always suspected that you had more layers. I'm impressed that you met the challenges of this year so beautifully."

This is going too well. I better get out before she has a chance to reconsider.

"And, Ms. Hoffman. Your word for next time?" And here it comes, the last-minute whammy. *"Strive."*

It doesn't escape my notice that it's the first time I haven't felt offended by her word choice.

My phone pings just as I'm about to get up. I sneak a glance at the screen while it's still in my bag. It's a text from Marshall: *Congratulations.*

Ms. Randall greets my grin with a questioning look. "Also, I'm the new president of the Social Calendar," I say.

Late in the afternoon I lie on my bed, talking to Jordana, filling her in on recent developments.

"I can't believe Whitney. She's gone off the deep end," Jordana says.

"I know. It still makes me sad." Anger usually prevails when I think about Whit, but every now and then the loss of her friendship hits me.

"Maybe she'll snap out of it before the end of the year."

"I seriously doubt it. I think I have to assume the worst and be pleasantly surprised if anything like that happens."

"You didn't think Leo would ever come around," Jordana points out.

"And I really never thought I'd be the one to decide against getting back together," I say.

"Declan sounds perfectly dreamy, so it's not that shocking," she says. "There must be an overabundance of dreamy guys in boarding school, which is totally unfair."

"I know. College is going to be a major letdown after this place."

"Well, the good news for me is that things can only get better. So what are you thinking? Any West Coast schools?"

"Bigger schools with active campus-events centers that have business majors. Some schools even have busy performing-arts centers and get major bands and stand-up comics to perform. All of it's run and promoted by students. It's so weird that I'm not applying to a single liberal arts program. It's unheard-of out of this school."

"Well, at least you'll be able to find a job," she says.

"Do you think any of our list will overlap? How many colleges did you end up with?"

"Fifteen. My parents are even telling me to add more. I don't think my college counselor has any idea what he's doing. He's just encouraging me to throw stuff at the wall and hoping that something sticks."

I laugh at that image and feel another twinge of appreciation for Ms. Randall. "I hope we at least get to be closer together," I say.

The Calendar's Executive Committee sits around one big table. Everyone looks around, uncertain, as if they've landed on the moon. Guthrie, who was the first to arrive, gives me a supportive wink. The vote took most of the weekend, with 90 percent of the student body weighing in on who they wanted to be president and vice president of the Calendar for the rest of the year.

Marshall was quick to inform us that it wasn't a landslide victory, but we hardly cared. "Congrats, you guys," he finally said. "Whitney might've actually done you a favor by killing your petition. We got to hear your vision for the first time, and people liked what you had to say."

Now I keep Marshall's words in mind and take a deep breath. "Hey, everyone. Welcome to Lower Left." A nervous giggle bubbles up from the group. "We know this is a big change, but our goal is to not make it too disruptive. Most of you attended the forum, but to recap: the main thing is, we want to be open to all ideas and give people time to work out the kinks in their events. That's it. Thanks for not jumping ship," I add, glancing at Elizabeth, Olivia, and Guthrie.

Surprisingly, only Whitney and Lila opted not to return to the Calendar. After a bit of begging, Raksmey and Yasmin are taking their spots. I told them that we need good juniors to step up and run things next year, pointing out that they're actually very social and that while the events they spearheaded didn't quite get off the ground, they both exhibited natural leadership ability.

The meeting goes smoothly, and I can tell that people want to give us a chance. We just need to get through the rest of this term. Most of the events have already been scheduled; all Opal and I want to do is add one new event each weekend. Then someone brings up the weekly dance.

"Are we going to cut it?" Elizabeth asks. I can hear the tension in her voice.

"I don't know. Is there a way we can keep it but make it more interesting?" I ask.

"Can we make it monthly instead of weekly?" Yasmin asks.

"What about making each one a different theme?" someone offers.

"Or a different DJ for each of the three hours," another girl chimes in.

With a few more suggestions thrown in, we have an actual collaborative session going. It's so refreshing to hear individual voices instead of just echoes of Whit's.

When the meeting breaks, Elizabeth and Olivia stay behind. "We might be too stuck in our ways to really help you," Elizabeth says.

I shake my head. "As long as you're willing to be constructive and try, then I know we could use your experience. The Calendar will definitely be better with senior members in place."

"We'll stick it out for a while at least," Olivia says.

It's not a total vote of confidence, but I nod anyway. "Thanks for being open-minded."

"So we heard about your mom's movie," Elizabeth says.

I wondered how long that would take to get out. I only learned about it earlier in the week, when my mom called. She finally got a script that the studio approved. *Still Over It* is officially green-lit and going into preproduction at last. The entire movie industry is freaking out about it.

"We're completely thrilled," I say. "I'm really glad my mom never gave up." It's funny. This news would once have mattered to me in a completely different way. I'm over-the-moon proud about it, but this time I have a little bit of distance.

"And now we get to see what happens!" Olivia squeals. "Do you know anything about casting?"

I shake my head. "Not yet, but a few fan sites are already up and running. I'm sure they'll post the minute anything happens."

I can tell by their eagerness that they'd love to stay and grill me for more information. But if my old friendships are going to be rekindled—which I'm not ruling out—it's not going to be because of the movie.

Fortunately, Opal waves me over. "I'm going to call that a raging success. You?"

I shrug. "I'll take it. When we get back, it'll feel more like a fresh start anyway." Winter break is hurtling toward us. We all leave next week.

"You actually pulled this off!"

I laugh. "Are you kidding me? This would never have happened without you. Helping you start the Yoga Connection and seeing how many people were willing to try something new? That was a total game changer."

"See? All good things come from yoga." Opal crosses her arms and smiles.

"Maybe you can visit over break," I say. "We can brainstorm the rest of the year."

"I'd love to," Opal and Declan say in unison. He swooped in from nowhere, leaning over my shoulder to kiss me.

"Where'd you come from?" I ask, my hand on his cheek.

"I came to celebrate with you."

I grin. "Now that my parents don't have to sell their house, we'll actually have room for both of you."

Declan and Opal bicker about what they want to see and do

in LA. It's so sweet and funny that I can't help gazing at them with a big smile on my face.

If someone had told me that this is how my senior year would turn out, I would never have believed it. Obviously, there's no way I'd change a thing.

Acknowledgments

I would like to thank my wonderful boys, Jackson and Elliott, for being the best sons I could hope for. I am lucky to be your mom. Thanks for all the hugs and special cheers.

Thank you to my amazing editor, Wendy Loggia, whose insightful feedback and confidence were instrumental in coaxing an actual book out of my original manuscript. You make the process as painless as it can be. Thanks also to the Delacorte Press team, including Krista Vitola, Angela Carlino, and Candy Gianetti, for lending their skill and creativity to this book.

Tremendous thanks to Adriann Ranta, my lovely agent, for superhuman patience and so much thoughtful advice.

I would be lost without my writing community. Thanks to Chandler Baker for daily accountability; to Virginia Boecker, Jennifer Brooks, Kelly Loy Gilbert, Lori Goldstein, Lee Kelly, Michelle Krys, Stacey Lee, Kim Liggett, and Kristin Rae for friendship and support; and to the entire LA writer crew, especially Kerry Kletter, Kathy Kottaras, Michelle Levy, Nicole Maggi, Mary McCoy, Gretchen McNeil, Corrie Shatto, and Nicola Yoon, for perspective and priceless camaraderie.

Extra hugs to Nori Horvitz and Amber Sweeney, two bloggers among so many wonderful ones, who went above and beyond.

Thank you to Caroline Tse of SayFINN Design Agency for all things website and swag related. Our sushi lunches are the best deal in town.

I'm grateful to Laura Pirri for mining high school memories with me, and to Heather Pottle for the fac brat view.

Thanks to my family—to my mom and dad for sending me to private school, to my cousin Nelson Wen for sharing thoughts about boarding at said private school, to Raksmey Tan for letting me use your name and for being awesome, and to Dana and Kevin Breen for entertaining me with tales from your former lives as dorm parents.

Lastly, to my husband, Andrew, thank you for being my rock and my biggest supporter. None of this would be possible without you.

CHARLOTTE HUANG is the author of *For the Record*. She grew up in the Boston area and was a day student at a prestigious boarding school, where she didn't quite hit her stride but made great friends and got good at writing ten-page papers in one night. She lives in Los Angeles with her husband and two sons.

Visit Charlotte online at charlottehuangbooks.com

Follow Charlotte on